CRUISIN' FOR A BRUISIN'
A Claire Gulliver Mystery

Also by Gayle Wigglesworth

GAYLE'S LEGACY,
RECIPES, HINTS AND STORIES CULLED FROM A
LIFELONG RELATIONSHIP WITH FOOD

TEA IS FOR TERROR

WASHINGTON WEIRDOS

INTRIGUE IN ITALICS

CRUISIN' FOR A BRUISIN'
A Claire Gulliver Mystery

by
GAYLE WIGGLESWORTH

Library of Congress Control Number: 2007936849

ISBN: 978-0-9759621-9-0

Koenisha Publications, 3196 – 53rd Street, Hamilton, MI 49419
Telephone or Fax: 269-751-4100
Email: koenisha@macatawa.org
Web site: www.koenisha.com

Acknowledgements

As always happens when writing a book, I am confronted with how little I know about so many things. I then have to find the answers. In this book, besides dragging my good-natured husband off on yet another cruise to Alaska, I also had to seek out some experts. I would like to thank them all for their help, but I would like to specifically thank these people for explaining things to me. Thank you to Charlie Mongeon, M.D., who is a good friend of my dear friends. He shared his experiences in serving as a ship's doctor on a major cruise line for several years after retiring from practice. Thank you to my good, long-time friend, Barry Price, who was willing to answer my questions about some fuzzy aspects of California law. Thank you to my brother, Gib Coates, who helped me with some of the questions I had about the use of deadly drugs. Thank you Martin Lorin, M.D. who caught more than a few mistaken commas, his medical expertise saved me from showing my ignorance to everyone. And I especially want to thank Duane Miller of Juneau Alaska, who didn't panic when I told him I was looking for a spot to *dump* a body. He really got into the spirit of the hunt and willingly shared his knowledge of the area with me.

And again thank you to my daughter Janet Hancock, my sister, Teresa Grill and my husband, Dave, for reading this manuscript in its early stages and being brave enough to critique it for me.

I want to state these people are not responsible if I didn't get it right. I freely admit to taking liberties on occasion, for instance the story of the Princess Sophia is true, whether or not the people in my story were actually onboard is doubtful. Also, there is not, to my knowledge, a cruise line named Call of the Seas, nor a ship named Dreamy Seas, but there are many similar. Additionally, some of these names or people may be similar to people you know, but I assure you they are all figments of my imagination and not meant to portray any actual persons. And lastly, while any mistakes I made have to be laid on my shoulders, I have tried very hard to get it all right.

Dedication

I want to dedicate this book to all those people who have shared the cruising experience with my husband and me during the past several years. Especially, I dedicate this to those who accompanied us on that first cruise to Alaska; my sister Connie and her husband Bob, my niece, Leslie and her friend, Enda, my friend, Sherrill, my friend since eighth grade, Vanya and her husband Jerry, and of course my husband, Dave. I confess I borrowed heavily from that experience.

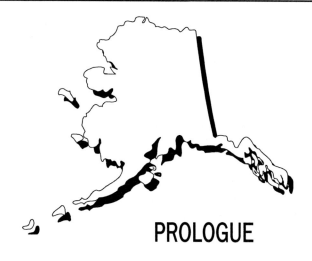

PROLOGUE

"Are you crazy?" His tone was incredulous. He just couldn't believe what he was hearing.

"Now wait a minute Sean." Ian laid on a thick brogue, even knowing his brother was immune to the charm of it. "Don't be hasty. It'll be fun. Like old times. Come on, surely you haven't lost all your sense of adventure. I can't believe you've morphed into a senile lump of a man. And what else will be you doing with your time?"

Sean didn't say anything, so Ian pressed on. "You won't be involved. It's just a trip we're taking. And what could be more innocent? Thousands of people do it every year. Just two doddering old fools off to see the world."

He laughed. "Well, all right, not the world, just Alaska. But everyone wants to see it. Everyone our age has dreamed of going. What would be more natural than us deciding to take a trip to celebrate my retirement? It's perfect."

"Ian, you said you were retiring. And I've been out of it for forty years. I have no intention of getting back in the game, and you know that." Sean's gruff voice was loud as if volume alone could convince his brother.

"Sean, Sean, I would never ask you to get involved. I understand you completely. And if it was me who found the girl of my dreams, then I too, would have given it all up as

2 • Cruisin' for a Bruisin'

you did. I promise you, you won't be implicated. You won't even know what I'm up to. You're just along for the ride and, of course, for cover.

"Sean, truly it will be a grand adventure. This is a wonderful ship, top of the line. We'll meet interesting people, visit historic towns in Alaska and be pampered for twelve days. And I'll be paying for everything. You'll have a vacation for free. What do you say, Sean? Will you join me?"

His voice became husky as he admitted, "I need you, you see. With you, we'd just be two aging brothers getting reacquainted while fulfilling one of our dreams. Without you I would be alone, odd, noticeable."

Sean stirred uncomfortably while he considered his brother's request. And if something did go wrong? How would he explain it to his kids? What would his grandchildren say? No one knew this part of his history.

Ian was smart enough to remain silent while Sean mulled over his proposition. In all their lives Ian had never asked Sean for his help, even though they both knew Sean owed Ian plenty.

"Why do you have to do this one last job? Why press your luck?" Sean wished it would just go away so he wouldn't have to make a decision.

"This is important to me, Sean. I have to do this one. It's a perfect set up and I promise you, nothing will go wrong."

"How do you know?" he asked suspiciously, as if he didn't already know Ian was certain of his facts.

"I have my sources. I've been working on this ever since I decided to retire." His voice was filled with regret as he admitted, "Hell, you know I don't really want to retire, but I've noticed little things. I'm not as strong as I was, or as sure of myself. But for sure I'm smart enough to realize I need to get out while I can. Still, I promised myself this one last job before I retire. And I'm going to do it. All these years I've waited for just the right opportunity, but it never came.

Now suddenly it's here. Now is the time and I need your help, Sean."

Sean was annoyed at his brother for putting him in this position, unwilling to agree, yet unable to refuse. "How can you get it off the ship? What if they search us?"

"Sean, Sean, don't worry about what you don't want to know about. We'll be as distressed and outraged as anyone. I'm prepared. I know you've been out of it, but surely you remember how good we were. How good I am. We were never caught and for good reason. I don't intend to be caught this time either.

"Just pack your dinner jacket and a snow parka and meet me in San Francisco. I'm sending you the information in the mail with the plane tickets. We'll have a great time.

"And Sean...? Thanks. I really appreciate this."

After Sean hung up he realized he hadn't actually agreed to go, but then he shrugged. It didn't matter; he was going. Ian knew him too well. And really, now that he was retired he had plenty of time to dawdle away. It may as well be on a cruise to Alaska.

CHAPTER ONE

Claire was breathless with anxiety as she hurried forward, awkwardly clutching the jackets she had retrieved from their cabins. Growing up in San Francisco she had witnessed countless gleaming ocean liners slipping under the bridge in pursuit of adventure on the high seas. Finally, she was on one and she didn't want to miss a moment of that experience.

She reached a jog in the narrow passage and randomly selected the right path as she continued toward the forward bank of elevators, which would take her to the top of the ship. However, halfway down the corridor a door opened and people crowded out into the corridor, blocking her way. She paused, giving them time to move down the hall in front of her, but they didn't.

A tall, well-dressed man leaned over a bent old lady, his concern apparent on his face. The old lady had a death grip on his arm and was visibly upset about something as she insisted, "I won't. This is just too ridiculous."

The third person, a middle-aged woman, danced with nervousness, her face screwed into a determined grimace. "It's all been arranged. You can't just..."

The younger man murmured in the old lady's ear, but apparently he didn't convince her.

"Change it!" she barked, refusing to be moved.

Claire's "Excuse me," as she tried to get through was completely ignored. They didn't even notice her, and then another person joined the fray. This one a tall man dressed in the white garb of a steward, or perhaps he was the butler.

The ship's horn blared, echoing through the corridor. Claire felt motion as the ship moved into the Bay. The conversation taking place in front of her just seemed to get more heated as all four people vehemently discussed their problem. And while Claire caught an occasional word of the exchange, she wasn't interested in getting involved. She only wanted to get by in order to be on deck when they passed under the bridge. Suddenly she realized there was another way. Time was wasting when she could already be topside.

She turned around and went back to where the passage split around the center of the ship and sped down the left side to the elevator. She shook her head in irritation over the foursome in the corridor. She had no idea what the problem was, but she wondered why that ancient woman was even on board. She was way too old to be traveling.

"There you are. Did you have a problem?" her mother asked with a worried frown. "I thought something happened to you, or you got lost."

Even though Claire was now in her forties, a successful entrepreneur and living her own life, her mother still lived in constant fear for her safety. The least provocation would convince her Claire would be snatched away from her as her husband had been, and her own parents.

Claire explained with careful patience, "Mom, it's a really long way to our cabins and I got caught up in a clog in one of the corridors." She handed out the jackets to her mother, Ruth, her mother's best friend, and Lucy Springer, her travel-writer friend. It didn't take long for them to zip up and head outside.

The wind tore at them, grabbing the door out of Claire's hands and slamming it shut behind them.

Claire set her sunglasses on her nose, hoping they would protect her eyes. While it had been a warm and sunny September day, here on the San Francisco Bay at five o'clock with the late summer fog just waiting to slip over the hills and through the Golden Gate, the wind was cold and fierce. In fact, the wind tugged alarmingly at Claire's glasses and blew her dangling earrings out parallel to her shoulders.

"What?" she shouted to Lucy, unable to hear what she said.

Lucy just shook her head and motioned Claire to follow her further towards the bow.

It was amazing how many of the passengers had elected to ride outside for their departure in spite of the cold and wind. But then they were headed to Alaska, so everyone was prepared for cold on this trip.

The Bay couldn't be more beautiful, touched as it was with the gold of the late afternoon sun. The water was deep grayish green, the sun catching in little flashes on the peaks of waves. The usual crush of Saturday afternoon sailboats were intermingled with the brightly colored sails of the windsurfers, who dared ride their boards far into the Bay to make the most of every gust of wind. They looked like a flock of large butterflies fluttering over the water.

Alcatraz Island seemed close enough to touch as they passed. In fact, she could see tourists lined up for one of the return boats. Angel Island loomed in the background, cutting off her view of the picturesque village of Tiburon, which she knew hid behind it.

At Ruth's nudge she turned around and posed with Lucy and Ruth while her mother snapped a picture, then with Lucy and her mother while Ruth snapped one with her camera, but then she moved away to position herself for their approach to the Golden Gate Bridge.

She couldn't believe how high it was. Somehow she thought the ship was so big she would be much closer to the top when they passed under. She could see the figures up there, just dark dots against the glare of the late sun. Ruth was looking for her neighbors, who had promised to bring their children down to wave good-by to her from the bridge. Claire didn't see how anyone could recognize anyone from this distance. But people around her were waving and she could see the little ant-like figures waving back from their perch high over their heads. And then they were under the bridge, the big ship bucking through the treacherous current where the ocean entered the Bay. She grabbed the rail to steady herself and saw her mother beckoning her, as she and Ruth headed inside. The fog seemed to be loping toward them, the wind pushing it forward while the ship ploughed determinedly through the waves to meet it. She turned and carefully made her way to the door, noting that a few hardy souls were apparently staying until the last glimpse of land was gone.

Inside, protected from the wind, Claire slipped her sunglasses in her pocket and held the rail to the stairway tightly as she fought the lurching of the ship while she ascended to the cocktail lounge at the front, top of the ship. They had checked it out earlier and decided this was definitely the place to have cocktails before dinner. She removed her jacket and ran her fingers through the tangle of her short hair as she made her way across the crowded room, dropping gratefully into the cushioned chair they had saved for her. The waitress approached bearing a tray of drinks.

"We ordered you the special for the day, a Gold Coast Sling, all right?" Ruth asked, reaching for the gin on the rocks which had just been placed in front of her.

"Great." Claire eyed the tall golden colored drink wondering what it contained. Then remembering she was on vacation, she decided she didn't care how potent it was. She could always crawl to her cabin if necessary.

Millie, Claire's mother beamed. "Well everyone, let's toast to a great adventure." She lifted her glass and gently tapped each of the others. "I'm so glad you both decided to join us for this cruise."

Millie, with Claire's encouragement had signed up for a cruise to Alaska with her church group scheduled for last May. But then her bosses at Richman Cadillac had surprised her with a retirement gift of a cooking course in Tuscany. Unfortunately it was scheduled at the same time as the cruise. At first, it didn't matter because Millie flatly refused to go to Tuscany. It was too far away and way too foreign for her tastes. But eventually Claire and Ruth had convinced her she couldn't pass up the opportunity and waste the money the Richman brothers had spent. So Millie talked to her travel agent and found, while she couldn't get a refund for the cruise, she could change the sailing date with no penalty. Ruth, who had agreed to go to Tuscany with her and even attend the cooking class with her to gain her agreement to go, was more than willing to go to Alaska with her in September. Ruth loved to travel and did so whenever she had the chance.

Millie was the complete opposite, which was strange considering her daughter, Claire, owned and operated the popular Gulliver's Travel Bookshop on the San Francisco peninsula. The Alaskan cruise had been intended to be Millie's first foray into the travel world, but of course, that trip to Italy and the Tuscany cooking school really became her first big adventure. And Millie enjoyed it immensely, in spite of the fact it turned out to be more adventurous than she ever imagined. But that was something she never talked about, especially not to her daughter.

So now the Alaskan cruise, scheduled and paid for, was going to be another travel experience and one all four ladies were looking forward to. They expected to be totally pampered while their senses were assaulted with the beautiful scenery of Alaska.

"You know, I'm quite excited about this cruise. This ship is much more luxurious than I expected." Lucy looked around as she sipped her drink. "I think this is going to be totally different than my trips to England. I'm so glad you called me, Claire."

"Oh, oh, I can see the title now," Claire swept her hand across her forehead, "*Gardening Amongst the Glaciers.*"

Lucy wrote travel books about England and specialized in English gardens. Claire had originally met her when she lectured on England at Claire's bookshop and subsequently, they became good friends.

They all chuckled, imagining a new line of books for Lucy, as they sipped their drinks and glanced around the lounge at the other passengers already having a good time.

Millie and Ruth had been excitedly discussing this trip all summer. Then, three weeks ago Millie's travel agent had mentioned the cruise line was offering half fares to fill their remaining openings. Millie, remembering how envious Claire and Lucy had both been about the pending cruise, decided they should all go. When Claire passed the information on to Lucy, Lucy not only agreed it was too good an opportunity to pass up, but she convinced Claire to go too. The cabin they shared was inside on a lower level with no window, but the travel agent assured them they wouldn't even notice. They would have a TV hook up with the camera on the bridge so they could see what every other cabin saw and, she explained, they wouldn't be in their cabins much anyway. Somehow they were persuaded.

"My goodness the fog is thick. I hope the captain can see where he's going." Millie's forehead was deeply creased as she peered out the window at the dense gray.

"Don't be silly, Millie, they use radar just like the airlines do. They don't have to see to see." Ruth spoke a little sharply. She sometimes became impatient with Millie's worries.

"Of course, of course, I know that. I wasn't really worried." Millie straightened up and looked around, lowering her voice. "Except that lifeboat drill kind of spooked me. I mean what a way to start a trip. I just look at those tiny lifeboats and shudder. They sure didn't look big enough to hold everyone."

"Mom, every time you fly they give you a safety demonstration just in case. This is the same." Claire's voice was soothing, as she tried to convince her mother to forget her worries.

"Don't you just love to wonder who all these people are and who's with whom?" Ruth changed the subject.

"You mean who's sleeping with whom?" Lucy responded, eyeing the crowd eagerly. "Before we get back I'm sure we'll know quite a few of them and can probably answer that question with some accuracy."

"Well, at least Mom will be able to," Claire said. "You wait and see, she'll know most of them before the first week is over. When I caught up with her in Florence last May, I swear she knew everyone staying at our hotel, and it was a big hotel."

Ruth laughed, nodding her agreement, while Millie just shrugged.

"I can't help it, people just talk to me. So of course, I have to be polite."

Then she joined them all in a giggle. It was true. She loved people, talking to them, hearing about their lives, even looking at endless pictures of grandchildren. For all those years, while living and working in the same neighborhood in San Francisco, she was always acquiring new friends. She always knew who moved into the neighborhood, who had a baby, who was sick and who died.

"Well, concentrate on finding us some eligible dance partners, will you Millie? It would certainly spice up the trip." Lucy, a very attractive woman in her fifties was checking out the room. "See there? That one. The big guy over there? He looks interesting. And he looks about your age Millie. He could do for you or Ruth, don't you think, Claire?"

Ruth extended both hands, palms out and shook her head. "Oh, no, not me. I'm just here for the fun, no romance for me."

Claire looked at Ruth with surprise and then inquiringly at Millie.

Millie explained, "Ruth has a new beau."

"Ruth! Who? When did this happen?" Lucy and Claire said in unison.

"Why didn't you say something?"

And then, "Who is he? Where did you meet him?"

Ruth waved the waitress to bring another round and shrugged, a little embarrassed by their interest.

Millie tried to help her friend by explaining. "Remember me telling you about Sam Ng. He was the man from San Francisco, who was at our cooking school in Tuscany with his wife? And she got sick at the school and died right after it was over. You remember, Claire? I told you how sad that was." She paused for Claire's nod, then continued. "Well, at the school a group of students always played cards whenever we had spare time. And you know who is the card shark?" She indicated Ruth with her head. "So this summer Sam Ng was having a poker party with some of his friends and he invited Ruth and Randy Jackson, another of our fellow students from down on the peninsula, to join the game. And Ruth has been playing with them ever since."

Ruth nodded. "And that's where I met him. His name is George Chang and he's a prominent local businessman. He's a widower with two grown children. We just hit it off." Ruth actually simpered.

"Ruth, that's wonderful. Is it serious?" Claire eyed her mother's friend with curiosity. She had known Ruth all her life. Ruth was like an aunt in lieu of the siblings neither her mother nor her father had. Ruth was gregarious and fun loving. She was proud of the fact she still wore the same size she did in high school, and while she still wore her hair and make up in the style of her younger years, she wore the current fashions in clothes, no matter whether or not they suited a woman of her years. Ruth had been married four times, two ending in divorces and two in widowhoods. Usually she was interested in any opportunity for romance.

Until now! This avowal she wasn't interested was an entirely new response from Ruth and one that made Claire wonder about George Chang. He must be special.

"Don't be silly, Claire. Of course it's serious. Why else would she be swearing off men for the entire cruise?" Lucy smiled at Ruth. "Good for you, Ruth. There's nothing like a little romance to stir the blood and brighten your life, right?" Then she turned and looked directly at Millie. "I guess we'll have to see if we can catch that good looking fellow for you, Millie."

Millie looked shocked. "Me?" Her voice actually faltered.

"Well of course. Don't worry, I'm watching out for Claire and me, too. I think a tad of romance for each of us is what we need to make this cruise perfect."

Claire laughed. "Well, good luck, Lucy, but that might be a big undertaking. I understand there are way more single women on these cruises than there are men."

"Well, we only need three. That doesn't sound too hard, does it?" Lucy appeared very confident and actually the way she said "only three" didn't sound impossible.

"And we only want a little romance. We're not looking for life commitments."

Claire nodded, although she was dubious about Lucy's plan. It was easier to agree and worry about the details if and when Lucy found them candidates. "Well Lucy, if you're taking orders I like mature, but not old, and still virile. I don't care about the hair, but please find me some one with a sense of humor."

"Hey, this isn't a dating service, you know. Give me a break. I have a limited pool of resources."

Claire looked around at the variety of people in the lounge. The crowd was eclectic and noisy. It was hard to pick individuals out of the group, but one thing was for sure, everyone was ready to have a good time.

Lucy put down her empty glass. "Ladies, I'm going down to the cabin to freshen up before dinner. I'll meet you outside the dining room in a half hour, okay? Claire, do you want me to take your jacket?"

Claire got up. "No, I'll go with you. Mom, do you want me to take your jacket?"

"Would you, dear? And Ruth's too. Here's my room key."

Claire, her arms full of jackets once again, prepared to traverse the length of the ship. "I don't think we have to worry about using the workout room, Lucy. If we make this trek to our cabin a few times a day, it should help counteract all the food we'll consume." She got off the elevator at the sixth level to drop the jackets off at her mother's cabin while Lucy descended to the second level where their cabin was located near the back of the ship.

* * *

"Excuse me, sir?" The tuxedo clad man spoke into Ian's ear.

Ian looked up interrupting his anxious scan of the passengers still straggling into the huge dining room. He recognized the maitre d' he had met with earlier, just after boarding, in fact.

The man glanced around the faces at the half full table and then said discreetly to Ian. "We find we do have a space available for you and your brother in the late seating, as you requested. If you would follow me..." he turned and nodded to the waiter, who stood behind him with fresh place settings to prepare the table for others.

Ian shrugged at Sean as they both stood, laid their napkins down, nodded cordially to the others seated at the table and followed the maitre d' out of the dining room, passing another host leading a group of four to the table they had abandoned.

"What's going on? I thought you wanted the early seating?" Sean whispered.

"I don't know, but I do know I paid plenty to make sure we got seated at the right table, so let's just follow him."

The maitre d' led them to a secluded corner near the front entrance and smiled apologetically. "Thank you for following my lead. There has been a bit of a last minute muddle. The party you requested to be seated with changed to the late seating. I felt obligated to honor my agreement with you, so I did some fast shuffling to get you changed too. I hope you will be satisfied with my efforts."

Ian smiled. "That's perfect. Thanks for taking care of it. I'd much rather be at the later seating and I did so want to surprise my friends by appearing at their table."

Sean didn't say anything, but managed to nod with a small smile.

"Fine. Just present yourself back here at the late seating and you will be seated at the table you requested."

The maitre d' nodded firmly and turned away. The first night of a cruise was always his busiest time with everyone requesting changes, early to late, late to early, big table to small intimate table, and the worst was still to come. Tomorrow he would be trying to satisfy those people who found they didn't like their table companions and so now want to be moved to another table far away.

Ian watched him go back to the cluster of people near the host station and then turned to Sean. "Hey, bro, let's go have a drink."

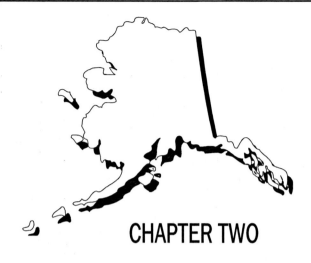

CHAPTER TWO

"Table eighty-four for Springer, Gulliver and Clarkson." Lucy smiled brightly at the incredibly handsome maitre d' as she handed him the engraved card with their dinner seating assignment.

He paused just a moment to smile back at her before consulting his list. "Oh, ladies, we've had a slight change. We have moved you to table seventeen, a most congenial group and in an excellent location. I'm sure you will enjoy it." He turned to one of his assistants and murmured further instructions before stepping back and waving them into the vast and ornate dining room.

Claire and Lucy exchanged questioning looks at the last minute change, but they followed Millie and Ruth through the labyrinth of tables and chairs in the dining room.

"Here you are, table seventeen."

The man gallantly held out Ruth's chair while Millie took the next of the four empty seats on one side of the oval table. Lucy slipped into the next one leaving the end one for Claire.

That last chair was to the right of the chair where sat the very same old lady she had seen in the corridor earlier. There was no getting out of it. All the other seats at the table were filled. She couldn't believe with almost a thousand people at each sitting, she had somehow been placed next to the person, who must be the oldest on the cruise. She just hoped the lady wasn't senile and deaf. Well, she thought, so much for Lucy's plan for finding romance for her. She sat down hoping no one guessed the reason for her hesitation.

Mentally she chastised herself. It's only a meal, after all. How bad could it be? But when the woman's claw-like hand grasped Claire's arm to pull her closer and Claire choked on the scented cloud of Jean Nate bath powder which, in spite of its liberal use, failed to mask the slight odor of decay emanating from the elderly woman, she wondered if she could make it through dinner.

"My dear, I'm Florence Bernbaum. And you?" Her voice quavered with age, but her faded blue eyes had a sharp gleam.

Claire forced a smile, then coughed to clear her throat so she could speak. She was determined to be polite and make the best of the situation. "I'm Claire Gulliver, from Bayside. That's down below San Francisco a bit. Do you know it?"

"Of course, of course, I was born and raised in San Francisco. I'm quite familiar with the area."

Claire heard her name and turned to smile at the others around the table as Ruth introduced each of their party.

"Sean Gallagher, here, and my brother Ian. We're glad to meet you all." Sean still showed the remnants of his Irish good looks, even though his hair was white, his complexion a tad too ruddy and his body, softened by time, had slid down to thicken his waist. His brother was obviously the younger. His hair was still salt and pepper, his large body still looked hard and his handsome face was etched with deep lines around his mouth, eyes and across his forehead, which instead of aging him seemed to add distinction. He smiled his greeting and his eyes lit his face with a bit of devilment.

Claire pulled her leg back from Lucy's kick. She didn't need the sharp jab to notice that fate had dumped two of Lucy's three male targets right in their lap.

"Dr. Richard Walmer," the man sitting across from Claire said pompously, "and this is my dear, great aunt, Florence Bernbaum."

Dr. Walmer looked to be in his forties. He was thin, darkly tanned, wore a small moustache and was impeccably groomed. He was obviously taken with his own importance, but to his credit he appeared to be very fond of his aunt.

"The Meriwetters here, Harold and Pearl," the florid man announced, then added, "from Houston." His lively wife, probably in her mid-to-late thirties, was almost dancing in her chair, she was that excited.

"This is going to be so fun. I've never been on a cruise before." She looked around the table. "I hope you all will make sure we do everything right."

Lucy shook her head. "I think we're with you. This is our first cruise too."

Ian shook his big head. "Sorry, ladies, this is a first for Sean and me, too."

They all looked to Dr. Walmer, who reluctantly shook his head. Mrs. Bernbaum nodded. "Of course I sailed before. On the Luraline. What a wonderful ship. It was so sad they disbanded the company. But things change and that was long ago. I'm not even sure cruising is the same now as it was then. This ship appears to be lovely. It is certainly large."

Millie laughed. "Well, Mrs. Bernbaum, you are our resident expert and we will look to you for guidance on the protocol."

"Good evening, my name is Pedro and I am honored to be your waiter for this trip." His smile was warm as he passed out the menu cards. "Here are the selections our chef has chosen for the first night of our voyage and while you're deciding on your choices perhaps I can bring you a cocktail? Will any of you be having wine tonight?" He nodded at the response. "I will send our sommelier over as soon as you've seen the menu. I think you will find we stock an extraordinary wine cellar."

Pedro was back with the drinks in very quick order, took their meal selections and left them to get acquainted over their drinks, promising the sommelier would soon appear.

"What did you order, Mom?" Claire leaned forward to talk around Lucy.

"Lamb chops. I couldn't resist."

"I decided on the Turbot in parchment. It sounds divine." Lucy smiled in anticipation.

"Ruth ordered the Turbot, too. What did you order, dear?" Millie asked.

"I ordered the Pork Roast in Apricot/Orange Glaze. Doesn't that sound good?" Claire could almost taste it. "I hope the food is at least half as good as it sounds. Wouldn't it be awful to be stuck on a ship that served mediocre food?"

"Oh no, that won't happen, not on this ship. We checked carefully. It's our first cruise, you see. This ship is rated very high in the food categories. That's why we chose it over all the rest."

"Well, one of the reasons," Harold clarified Pearl's comment. "We chose itinerary first, then food, and then we had a whole list of categories we compared before selecting a *Call of the Sea* cruise."

"So, have we selected the best?" Ian asked.

Pearl nodded. "You bet! This ship was voted best in last year's *Conde Nast* Readers' Poll. That's a really big endorsement."

Claire was having a hard time following the conversation at the other end of the table. The noise in the dining room seemed to be increasing in direct proportion to the rounds of drinks served. And, while Mrs. Bernbaum had finally released the grip on her arm in order to examine the menu card, she now was leaning toward her, grabbing at her again. Clearly she had something to say.

Claire fought her inclination to turn to Lucy on her other side and graciously bent her head close to hear the old lady.

Mrs. Bernbaum had probably never been big, but she looked as if she had shrunk as she aged and now she was wizened and wrinkled. Her hair was unfortunately thinning, so her pink scalp showed through the white curls covering her head. Her dark blue dress had been fashionable about thirty years ago, and it had probably fit her then. Now it was too big. She had a large patterned scarf draped over her shoulders and fastened to her dress with a large, garish pin, made up of a large red central stone, slightly irregular in shape, almost heart shaped, surrounded by alternating white stones and lime green stones. The entire pin was outlined in small red stones, their color matching the large central stone. It, like its owner, looked a little shop worn, as if the gold luster was wearing off and the stones were slightly dingy. Claire realized Mrs. Bernbaum had made a valiant attempt to dress for dinner and felt ashamed for being so critical of her. She told herself sternly she should be admiring her spunk for taking this trip at her age instead of being so irritated for getting stuck with her as a dinner partner.

"I'm on a life quest," Mrs. Bernbaum announced firmly. "That's why I'm going to Alaska." She saw the puzzled look on Claire's face. "You know, the hundred things you want to do before you go? I've wanted to go to Alaska. I always meant to go, but with one thing or another I somehow waited until it was too late."

She let go of Claire's arm and sat back in her chair. "At least that's what I thought until Dickie just appeared." She smiled, glancing over at her nephew, who was engrossed in a conversation on his other side. "He made it all possible. He's a genius, you know. He's made my dream come true."

Claire nodded vaguely, not fully understanding what Mrs. Bernbaum was saying.

"Your nephew just appeared?" she asked tentatively.

Mrs. Bernbaum nodded. "Yes, he's the son of my husband's nephew. We never knew about him. I'm afraid his father was not the most responsible person around. Sweet, fun, endearing, but he was totally self-absorbed. We didn't even know he had a son, but Dickie looks just like his father did at his age. I'd know he was his son even if I hadn't seen the birth certificate. Apparently he left Dickie's mother before he even knew Dickie was on the way and so maybe he didn't even know he had a son. Thank goodness Dickie's mother kept track. She told Dickie he had relatives in San Francisco in case he wanted to look us up someday. So after his mother died, he did." Her smile told of her pleasure. "And it was a lucky day for me."

Just then Dickie, Dr. Walmer to Claire, turned. "How are you doing, Auntie?" He gently squeezed her hand setting on the table near him.

"Fine, fine, just telling this young lady how lucky I was you found me."

Dr. Walmer looked at Claire and smiled. "Lucky for both of us. We're the last of our family. Each of us thought we were alone in the world. How lucky we were to find each other."

Mrs. Bernbaum beamed. "Dickie is thinking about setting up a practice in San Francisco so we can be near each other."

Dr. Walmer nodded. "Maybe, Auntie, just maybe." He looked at Claire explaining further, "I recently broke up my partnership in Florida and so it makes sense to settle near Auntie. We'll see what happens after the cruise."

"Are you a medical doctor?" Claire asked, feeling the need to make polite conversation.

Dickie nodded. "I'm a Longevity Specialist. I had quite an extensive practice in Florida. But when one of my partners decided to retire, we needed to regroup so I thought it was time for a break. Maybe I was having a mid-life crisis. Anyway, I decided to check out the relatives in California."

"Longevity Specialist? What is that?"

"Oh my dear, I said he's a genius, and he is. He knows just how to give me a shot of pep so I can do the things I want to do. I can't tell you how grateful I am. It's no wonder his practice was so successful in Florida. And I'm sure it will be even more popular in San Francisco."

"Actually, Auntie, that's only a small part of what I do. I specialize in extending life to the maximum. That includes the patient's ability to remain active and functional beyond previous life expectations. You know, there are new discoveries everyday. I just put those discoveries to use." He smiled at his aunt again, but just then Pedro and his assistant arrived with their appetizers.

Harold and Pearl were right, the food was exquisite. The meal proceeded at a leisurely pace as course after course was delivered and devoured. Wine had been ordered and poured, and more ordered. It was a wonderful beginning to the trip. Everyone had different plans for the trip and had pre-selected different shore excursions for their many stops, so now they realized they would all hear about the excursions they missed from others at the table, who had taken them.

Finally, after refills on the coffee, Ian announced he and Sean were going up to the Starlight Lounge to check out the music. He had heard there was to be dancing tonight. Harold and Pearl were ready; they said they loved to dance.

Ruth was willing and Lucy was eager. Millie was persuaded by Sean's assurance it would be fun. Dr. Walmer demurred, saying he needed to see Auntie to her cabin, but said he might be up later.

Claire shook her head. She had put in a full day's work at her bookshop before even leaving for the ship and it was now her bedtime. "I promise, I'll get all rested and be ready to party tomorrow."

Then as they all pushed away from the table, Claire, in a flash of generosity born from her guilt over her uncharitable attitude toward the old lady, offered, "Mrs. Bernbaum, would you like me to walk you back to your cabin and then Dr. Walmer can go with the others?"

"Oh, dear, that is very thoughtful of you. Yes, Dickie, go with the others. There is no reason to see me to my cabin if Claire is willing to do it. I'm a little tired myself. And Anita is waiting for me. She'll see I get my sleep."

Dr. Walmer looked skeptical, but as his aunt was so certain he gave in and headed toward the forward elevators with the others.

"What's your cabin number, Mrs. Bernbaum?" Claire asked, not even flinching when Mrs. Bernbaum's hand clutched her arm.

"It's eighty, forty-six. I don't have the key, but Anita will be waiting for me."

"Who is Anita?"

"She's my caregiver. She's not feeling well. I guess she's not as enamored with cruising as Dickie and I."

"Oh, that's too bad. Did the doctor give her something for sea sickness?"

"No, Dickie did. But so far it hasn't helped much. I think it's partly mental. She didn't think I should take the cruise and she didn't want to come, so it makes her sick. You know?"

Claire nodded realizing Mrs. Bernbaum was still pretty sharp. "Do you need a caregiver?"

"Well, I suppose not, but she makes my life easier. She takes care of my clothes, fetches and carries for me and sees that I get all my pills at the right time. I'm still capable of taking care of myself, no matter how slow I am at it. However, to hear her you'd think she is all that is keeping me alive." Now her eyes were snapping with irritation. "She thinks this is a foolish venture. She didn't want to come, but she really didn't want me to come without her."

"Has she worked for you a long time?" Claire asked, thinking Anita didn't sound like a very pleasant companion.

"Not long, about four years. And she has her good points. She's very reliable and she is conscientious. I think maybe she's started thinking that I am the child and she's the adult. That attitude causes clashes, because while I may be older than God, I still think I'm in charge." Her laugh was almost a cackle as they arrived at the cabin door.

Claire recognized the stern faced Anita, as the third person in the group blocking her passage earlier. Now, her complexion slightly green, she answered the door with cross words. "Do you realize how late it is? I was getting worried."

Mrs. Bernbaum ignored her. Hanging on to Claire's arm she dragged her into the room. "Claire, this is Anita. Anita, meet Claire. And yes, I know what time it is, and since we just finished dinner I think you can expect this is the time I'll be coming to bed every night."

Anita shook her head muttering low, but Claire could hear the words, "You'll need more than a shot of pep from Dr. Feelgood, if you keep this up."

Claire saw they were in a living room with a small dining area which led out to a good sized enclosed veranda.

"Wow, this is way bigger than my cabin."

Mrs. Bernbaum shrugged. "It's small, but comfortable. We have twin beds in the bedroom so Anita shares with me. This is called a suite. I just couldn't see taking one of those little cabins. Dickie is in one down below and he says it's fine, but I like having a little more space."

After depositing Mrs. Bernbaum in one of the armchairs, Claire headed for the door, eager to get tucked into her own tiny cabin in the bowels of the ship. "Nice meeting you, Anita." And just as she went out the door, "I enjoyed talking to you at dinner Mrs. Bernbaum. Have a nice night." And as she closed the door and headed back to the elevator, she realized with surprise she had enjoyed talking to Mrs. Bernbaum in spite of her initial apprehension.

* * *

He had managed to contain his fury through dinner and even act pleasant when they went to the Starlight Lounge for music and dancing, but now, out on the deserted deck for a spot of fresh air before bed, Sean erupted.

"The *Heart of Persia*. That's your last job? This is your perfect opportunity? Are you crazy, little brother? You don't remember what happened to Pap?" His angry stride moved them away from the protection of the superstructure out near the pool where the biting cold of the wind hit them with a shock.

"Now keep calm, Sean. Of course it is the *Heart*. It had to be the *Heart*. I promised Pap I'd get it back for the family. I didn't tell you before for just this reason."

Ian's righteous attitude only fueled Sean's anger.

"Darned right you didn't tell me. If you had, no way would I be here now. In fact, I'm thinking of disembarking when we get to Victoria."

That alarmed Ian. "Now Sean, don't be hasty. That would really call attention to me. That would jeopardize the whole plan."

Sean looked at Ian, calculating the effect on him. "Would it stop you from stealing it?"

"Of course not. I told you I promised Pap. I always intended to get it, and with my retirement looming, it has to be now. Without you here, it will just be more risky for me, but that won't stop me. I'm going to have it."

Sean sat down at a table behind the protection of the Plexiglas barrier and looked at his brother earnestly. "Ian, don't you remember it was this same crazy quest that caused us all so much trouble. Don't you remember Pap's determination to have it is what caused him to hook up with those Zappas brothers? If it wasn't for the *Heart,* Pap would be alive today. And we would still be the Rourke brothers. We wouldn't have had to change our name to Gallagher to avoid the publicity circus the papers made out of the whole affair."

He shook his head wearily. For a moment in the dim light he looked as if he was about to weep.

Ian laid his hand on Sean's shoulder a moment before sitting in a chair facing him. "Look Sean, Pap made a critical mistake joining up with the Zappas. They were trash, bad through and through. But he didn't know that. He didn't know they would be carrying. He couldn't have envisioned they would turn that heist into a blood bath. You know he didn't approve of violence."

Ian looked off into the darkness, remembering the last time he saw his father, still and gray-faced, tubes attached to him, his hospital room guarded closely by grim faced policemen.

"Maybe it was better he died from those bullets. He would have never been able to stomach the trial and then all those years in prison because of the Zappas."

"Ian, he had the *Heart* in his hand. He was guilty. That wasn't the Zappas."

Ian shook his head. "Of course he stole the jewel, but he didn't kill anyone; he didn't have a gun on him. It was the Zappas, they deserved what they got. Not Pap. Pap just got involved with the wrong people. It was my fault really; if I hadn't been off on spring break with my friends he would have asked me to help him.

"But I wasn't there when he needed help, so he found the Zappas." Ian looked at his brother, the miserly clear on his face.

"You've been blaming yourself all these years? You are crazy! Pap was a grown man, Ian. You were a college kid. If you were gone for a few days he could have waited. No, he decided on what he was going to do and who he was going to use. It had nothing to do with you. You've been blaming yourself for no reason. If you were available he still wouldn't have used you. He said you had to finish college before you could go into the business with him. He meant it."

Sean looked at Ian with pity. "You've wasted a lot of years making this into something it wasn't. He could have used me, did you think of that? I was out of school then. I was even working with him then.

"You know why he didn't? It was because he knew how dangerous it was. He let his emotions rule his logic. He found out the *Heart* had changed owners. He thought it being so close was a sign to him to act. He had to have it and he was willing to take ridiculous risks to get it. He didn't want me to be involved; he wouldn't have even considered you. He chose the Zappas because he didn't care how risky it was for them. He thought that by being daring and bold he could pull it off. He was determined to have it back and he paid dearly for that decision."

Then he muttered, almost under his breath, "We all paid dearly for that decision."

Sean released his breath in a deep sigh. "I'm tired of all this. I'm going down to bed. You coming?"

Ian shook his head. "In a while, I need to think a bit."

Sean headed for the door, walking like an old man; the conversation and the memories taking their toll on him.

* * *

The door opened abruptly before he even finished knocking.

"Well, where in the hell was she? I waited at the buffet for two hours, dawdling over the food, trying to remain inconspicuous and I never even saw her. And I never heard from you." Kim was more than annoyed. She was angry.

He held up his hands in mock surrender. "Sorry, really. It was all a mess and I couldn't contact you. I called your cabin, but you had apparently left, so there was no way to alert you of the change."

She looked at him doubtfully, then sighed, shrugged, turned and led the way into her cabin. "We're going to have to work out a way to send messages. This could get dicey."

He nodded. "The old lady refused to go to the early seating. She said families with small children and doddering old fools ate at the early seating and she was neither. She couldn't be convinced, so everything had to be changed. It cost plenty in tips to the maitre d', but it finally got worked out."

Kim looked alarmed, then sympathetic.

He assured her. "So from now on she'll be eating at the eight-thirty seating and judging by today, we won't be finished until a little after ten. I'm sure Anita will be dining in the buffet during that time."

Kim nodded. "Okay, tomorrow's another day. I'll do my best."

He smiled with relief as he pulled her into his arms. He needed Kim. He wanted her to stay happy and willing.

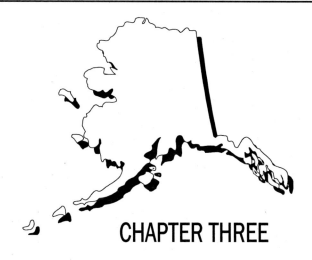

CHAPTER THREE

"Well, good morning, sunshine," Claire said brightly as she dropped into the chair opposite Lucy in the coffee bar.

Millie, who had detoured to the bar to order coffees for them arrived and took another chair. "Lucy, we thought you were going to sleep the morning away."

Lucy shook her head and took another sip of her coffee. "Don't I wish, but there was way too much going on in the corridor to sleep very long. What's with all these morning people?"

She was still a little grumpy. She needed her coffee to get started. "What have you two been doing and where's Ruth? Is she sleeping in too?"

"Hardly! We had breakfast, did the crossword puzzles, checked out the spa, the library and computer room before we lost Ruth to a group in the card room, who needed a fourth for bridge. We're going to the lecture on Victoria before lunch. I thought you'd probably show up for that."

Lucy nodded. "Yes, I plan to attend, but I'm starving." She glanced at her watch. "Oh, well, hopefully my growling stomach won't disrupt the lecture. How was breakfast?"

"It was wonderful. You don't sit at your dinner table, they seat you as you come in and you share the table with whoever else is there," Claire explained, but then Millie jumped in.

"We met this couple, Pat and John, who have cruised many times. In fact, they took this same ship to South America in January so they know just how it works. They told us about the daily crossword puzzles as well as some tips about the shore excursions. They were very nice, weren't they, Claire?"

Claire nodded her agreement, handing her plastic card to the waitress who brought the coffees. "Lucy, do you need another?" She indicated to the waitress to charge her card including another for Lucy. They had each been issued a plastic card on boarding to use in lieu of money as well as an access key to their cabins. It was really a handy system and Pat had explained over breakfast the same cards would be used to swipe through a machine on leaving and returning to the ship at docking so the cruise line could always keep track of who was on board and who was not. It was simple to tuck the card in your pocket, so it wasn't necessary to carry a purse or wallet while on board.

"Well, Lucy, did you have fun last night? I was so out of it I barely knew when you came in."

"It was late. Millie pooped out, then Ruth, so I ended up with some people I met at the dance. We sat at the bar for a while, too long probably. But it was a fun start to our cruise. Oh, and I met the maitre d'. You know, the one who greeted us going into dinner last night?"

Claire's eyebrows rose. "I remember him, of course. And I also remember how good looking he is."

Lucy smirked, nodding. "Isn't he? His name is Antonio Marcelous. He's Italian."

"Didn't Ian, Sean and Dr. Walmer stay to dance?"

"Ian stayed a while. He's a marvelous dancer as your mother could tell you."

Claire looked at her mother curiously. Seeing her slight blush she chided, "I thought you said you left early."

"I did. Well, earlier than Lucy and Ruth, but I danced plenty. My feet were telling me, enough!"

"I saw Dickie enjoying himself with some of the younger people. They all left fairly early. I think Dickie may consider us too old for him, although he's probably older than you, Claire. In fact, I was thinking of him as a candidate for you." She looked pensive. "I don't know if that will work."

Claire shook her head, she didn't think she was Dr. Walmer's type and she really had no interest in testing those waters.

Millie checked her watch and then finished her coffee. "If we're going to that lecture we'd better go get a seat."

Lucy gathered her things, looking around to make sure she had everything in her canvas tote bag. "Where is it?"

"It's in the theatre. I guess they expect a crowd. Come on, it's on the deck above us. I think we can take the stairs faster than using the elevator."

* * *

"Pull." The shotgun barrel came up, followed the clay plate and then blasted it into tiny pieces which fell into the sea in the wake of the ship.

"Pull!" Another target was demolished.

Ian shook his head in admiration at his brother's skill. "Whoa, I guess you must have fed the family well from your hunting trips. Maybe living in that Podunk town in the middle of nowhere was a good experience."

"You bet it was, and not just because of the game I shot. The people are solid, their lives are simple, their values sound. You would have done well to visit more often."

Ian stepped up to the rail, shouldered his shotgun and yelled, "Pull."

Finally, Ian gave up his attempt to best his older brother and they handed the shotguns back to the attendants and headed across the deck toward the door.

The day was overcast, the wind cool, but here the Plexiglas barriers about the rail buffered the wind creating a balmy oasis. They passed the table where they sat talking last night, now peopled by passengers who liked to eat outdoors. A buffet had been set up inside to serve a casual lunch. People could sit outdoors or indoors to eat. Obviously, this was a popular spot and not just for the smokers, who had limited areas on the ship to enjoy their habits.

"Let's check out the buffet." Sean was much more interested in food than his brother was. But Ian followed him inside and helped himself to some of the offerings.

"I can't believe you can eat all that after the breakfast we had."

"Hell, that was five hours ago and then we spent an hour in the gym before skeet shooting. I have to keep my strength up. Eat up, little brother. I'm sure you can work it off before dinner."

Ian smiled. He admitted to being a little over zealous about maintaining his weight. But it was part of his livelihood. He didn't dare let his weight hold him back or slow him down. And he did strength training religiously, not because he liked to show off his muscles, but because he needed those muscles for the work he did.

"So, are you still mad at me? Are you still thinking you want to forget about all this luxury and go home when we reach Victoria?"

Sean took a sip of his coffee and looked at his brother. "I'll stay, if only to make sure you get through this safely. Not that I approve of what you're doing. I think it's a crazy risk, but you're a grown man and capable of making your own life decisions."

He could see the relief in Ian's eyes.

"What did you think of it, after the shock, of course? It's beautiful, isn't it?"

Sean shook his head. "Actually, I thought it looked a little sad. Pap wouldn't have let it get in that shape. He had more respect than that."

"Sean, you ever think what Pap's life would be like if he hadn't lost that hand of poker? What it would have been like for us to grow up if Pap had been the owner of the *Heart of Persia*?"

Sean said truthfully, "I can't even imagine it. I tell my grandchildren, it's not what you have: it's what you do with what you have. Pap spent too much time and energy making up for the loss of the *Heart*. And frankly, I've wondered if that one decision to risk it wasn't what started a whole string of incidents that were destined to end in his disaster. Don't you?

"If he owned the *Heart* would he have continued stealing jewelry? And if he hadn't, would you have stayed with it all these years?" Sean mused, thoughtfully.

"And for sure he wouldn't have gotten involved in that plan to retrieve it, which resulted in his death. If only he had passed on that one, he wouldn't have died of gun shot wounds.

"You know only a couple of years ago there was a story about it on one of those news shows. It's like it will never, ever go away."

He looked at his brother seriously and continued, "Ian, Pap's proclivity for jewels, especially those not belonging to him, has shaped both of our lives and not for the better. Frankly, you've been infected with the same malady he had. The *Heart of Persia* is not yours. Give it up. You've managed to stay free all these years while accumulating a nice bank account. Why risk a comfortable life for the ownership of something Pap wanted? How smart is that?"

Incredulity spread over Ian's face. "Give it up? You're the one who is crazy? Didn't you see the gleam? Didn't it wink at you and promise you the riches Pap wanted us to have. There, except for the turn of the wrong card, is our heritage. It should have been ours. And it will be!"

"Ian, I loved Pap. He was a super guy and a wonderful father, but he was a crook, a jewel thief, Ian. And you're making too much of this *Heart of Persia*.

"And Pap made too much of having it. He had it in his hand. The one precious stone he owned honestly, but he still risked it on a turn of the card. He deserved to lose it. Don't you see that? If he hadn't lost that hand, he would have risked it again, and again, until eventually he would have lost it. He was that kind of a guy, Ian. He loved the risks. And he loved telling the stories and making up 'what ifs' to drive himself crazy. And now you're doing it.

"Think about this. Think about the risk of what you're about to do. And compare it to the rewards. Will owning it give you that much pleasure? You can't ever let anyone see it or know you own it. What fun will that be?

"And of course, that will only be if you succeed. What if you fail? What if you get caught? What then! Years in a cell, thinking about the mistakes you made; the money you have salted away and can't use. Look what happened to Pap, what kind of end to your life is that?"

But Ian wasn't listening. He had made up his mind. Sean's common sense advice was of no use and so finally Sean stopped trying to make his brother reconsider his plans. He turned his attention back to his plate, hoping things would turn out the way his little brother wanted them too.

* * *

"Oh, there you are." Pearl Meriwetter plopped down in the empty chair at their table, her husband hovering behind her. "Oh, I'm so excited. In the shower this morning I finally realized why your name sounded so familiar." She took a big gulp of air and gushed, "You're Lucy Springer, the writer, aren't you?"

Lucy's eyes widened in surprise. Then she nodded and smiled.

"I've got your book, *Daffodils in the Cotswolds,* at home. My friend gave me a copy and I just love it. Imagine her face when I tell her you sat at our table.

"See Harold, I told you I was right. I wish I had your book with me so you could sign it. This is so exciting. Are you going to Butchart Gardens tomorrow? Will you be writing a book on those gardens? Is this a working trip for you? Will you lecture on the cruise?"

Lucy put up her hands as if to ward off Pearl's enthusiasm. "This is just a vacation for me. With my friends." She gestured to Millie and Claire. "I do intend to see the gardens. Who in their right mind would miss them? But no, I don't intend to do a book. I'm afraid it would take a bit more research than a shore visit on a cruise to prepare for a book."

"Oh, of course. What was I thinking?" Pearl giggled. "But I can't wait until tomorrow. I hope we're on the same tour bus."

Lucy shook her head. "I'm afraid not. My friends and I are hiring a car so we can spend as much time as we want at the gardens and still see some of Victoria before having tea at the Empress. But perhaps we'll see you at the gardens and for sure we'll see you at dinner, so we can talk about what we saw in the gardens. They're supposed to be spectacular."

The disappointment on Pearl's face quickly turned to joyful anticipation at the thought of dining with Lucy for the rest of the cruise. Her husband gently reminded her they were on their way to the second lecture on Victoria, due to start any minute, so she reluctantly left.

Lucy laughed. "Just my luck. There's probably only one of my fans on this ship and she's sitting at my table and recognized my name."

"Well, actually, it is good luck. You probably have several fans on board. Really, it's too bad you didn't know about this cruise earlier so you could have arranged to do some lectures on board. I bet they would be very popular. And don't forget you need all the fans you can get, and I hope they all come to Gulliver's to buy your books."

"Ladies, I'm going to the napkin folding demonstration, so I'm going to disappear." Millie stood up. "If Ruth appears, tell her I'll meet her at the races later this afternoon."

"Races? What races?" Lucy hadn't checked her schedule.

"That couple at breakfast told us about them. They said they were a hoot and we should check them out so we plan to do that. They're scheduled at four in the lounge outside the theater. Want to join us?"

"Maybe. I'm thinking of a swim now. You interested?" Lucy asked Claire.

"No, I'm going to do my email. I promised I'd stay in touch with the book shop in case there were any problems. And then I'm going to find a nice comfy corner and read my book about Alaska. See you later."

* * *

"I thought we should rotate our seats. That way we will all get a chance to know each other better," Pearl announced brightly indicating the chair next to her for Lucy.

Lucy sat down and Claire sat next to Lucy. Ian and Sean were on her right side, then her mother at the end, opposite Pearl. Ruth sat on the other side of the table to Millie's right, then Dr. Walmer, Mrs. Bernbaum, who was across from Claire today, and finally Harold.

Claire smiled and nodded to everyone as she noticed how nice everyone looked. It wasn't formal, but it was dress up night and obviously people had come prepared. All the men wore ties and jackets. Dr. Walmer was in a navy pinstripe suit. Harold looked uncomfortable wearing a tie while his jacket pulled a little over his generous stomach. Ian wore a navy blazer with panache and Sean looked smashing in his gray suit. And the ladies had all done their best. Pearl was in a smart looking suit, with a lime green short-sleeved jacket trimmed with navy over a navy skirt. Lucy was wearing a full skirted silk flowered dress that was very attractive. Millie had on one of her favorite knit dresses, two pieces in a dusty gold color that was very flattering. Ruth was wearing one of her fashionable dresses, sleeveless, low cut and very short. Mrs. Bernbaum was wearing a burgundy dress, again the dress was good quality, out of date and swimming on Mrs. Bernbaum's shrunken frame. The large garish pin was displayed prominently on her shoulder as if it was all that was holding the dress on Mrs. Bernbaum. Obviously it was her favorite piece of jewelry. Claire was wearing a dress she had bought last fall for her trip to Washington D.C. It was a soft Jersey-like material which traveled well and was comfortable as well as flattering.

Everyone seemed relaxed after spending the day at sea, which allowed them to pursue the activities arranged for their entertainment or just laze around and relax. Pearl and Lucy were discussing whether or not the show, a Follies-type, would be good and Millie, Sean and Ruth were talking about the next day's visit to Victoria.

"I was just admiring your watch, Claire. It looks like a Cartier. Is it?" Mrs. Bernbaum leaned forward addressing her across the table.

Claire started, glancing at the beautiful watch she wore. "It is. How did you know?"

"I know my jewelry, dear. Cartier has a distinct look. I have a lovely one myself. I will probably wear it on a formal night. It's quite old and very beautiful." Her eyes took on a distant look. "It was a gift from my true love. It's very special."

Claire smiled. Considering Mrs. Bernbaum's fondness for the ugly brooch she wore, she wondered what the watch was like.

"My true love showered me with jewels," she said proudly. Her fingers rested lightly on the brooch. "I was a very fortunate woman."

She looked at Claire sharply, asking abruptly as some elderly people did, "Was your watch a gift from your true love?"

Just as she said it there was a lull in the conversation around the table and her question seemed unnaturally loud. Out of the corner of her eye Claire could almost see her mother's and Ruth's ears pick up, waiting for her answer. Ever since their visit to Venice in the spring, where they met her friend, Jack Rallins, they seemed overly interested in her love life. Sometimes they couldn't keep from actually inquiring as to his health, his whereabouts, or whether or not she had heard from him recently. And the most irritating part was she hadn't heard from him since then. That worried her and annoyed her.

She shook her head slightly, smiling. "Sorry, I don't think so."

"My dear, surely you have met your one true love by now."

"No, I don't think so." Claire shook her head good-naturedly.

"Don't think so? My goodness, you know when you meet the right one! There is no doubt, you would know it."

"It sounds as if you were very happy with Mr. Bernbaum. How lucky for you," Claire murmured, trying to divert her attention.

"Not Mr. Bernbaum. No, not Bernie. Oh, he was a love all right. He coddled me and protected me, but he knew he wasn't my one true love. He knew he could never repair my broken heart. But he was happy to be with me and he made me as happy as I could be after I lost Nate." Her eyes roamed around the table looking for understanding.

Millie nodded, saying in a sympatric tone, "I know how it is. I lost Claire's father way too early. It was like I lost a part of myself."

Pearl reached over and hugged Harold's beefy arm. "I found my true love and I've still got him."

He patted her hand tucked in his arm.

Sean cleared his throat, but the words still came out rough with emotion. "My Maggie was my true love. There can never be a replacement for her."

"But that's not true," Ruth argued. "When you lose someone so special and live without them, you change. You are no longer the same person. I think that's why it's possible to find a second perfect mate. It's not the same as the first, but then you're not the same, either."

Mrs. Bernbaum looked skeptical, but then shrugged. Obviously for her there was no one to replace her Nate.

Just then Pedro appeared with their entrees and the group turned their attention to their selections for the night.

Claire ate her Alaskan Halibut mechanically while she thought about the conversation. Had she met her one true love? Was Jack potentially her perfect mate? How did one know?

Mrs. Bernbaum seemed convinced she would know, but truly, while Claire had had relationships over the years, none had lasted. No one had seemed to be the one. And while sometimes her feelings for Jack had seemed disturbingly intense, so far they couldn't seem to get connected for longer than a week or two at a time. That didn't bode well for developing a lasting relationship.

And of course his work was a real obstacle. While he didn't elaborate on it, she knew it was frequently a life and death situation for him. That's what really worried her when she didn't hear from him. The world had gone crazy and Jack was certain to be right in the middle of it.

"Good evening. I'm Antonio Marcelous, Dreamy Seas' maitre d'. I just wanted to make sure you are pleased with your dinner tonight." The handsome man smiled as his eyes roamed from person to person at their table.

Claire wondered if anyone besides her and Lucy saw how his eyes lingered hungrily on her friend before moving on to Pearl.

"My prime rib was wonderful, just the way I like it," Pearl gushed. Harold nodded his agreement. Everyone else nodded and smiled, murmuring their thanks for his interest.

Lucy dabbed her napkin to her lips, but not before Claire saw her smile and the sparkle in her eyes.

"Pedro and Juan will do their utmost to make sure your every meal is just what you want. And please, I hope you will let me know if I can do anything to make your meals special for you. I am here every night and most late evenings you will find me up in the Starlight Lounge. Feel free to look me up." Now his eyes and smile were directed boldly at Lucy.

"Wasn't that nice," Millie commented as she watched Antonio move through the tables, stopping occasionally to speak to a waiter on his way out.

"Yes, he has a big job running this operation. I wonder why he singled us out. I didn't see him stopping at other tables." Ruth stared after him with a quizzical look on her face.

"Oh, I'm sure he does, that's his job after all. We probably didn't notice," Pearl said.

"Or maybe he just recognizes this table has the special people," Sean added, smiling around the table. "But I think they do a spectacular job. I've eaten in some five star restaurants which couldn't match this dish." He pointed with his fork to the remains of his duck simmered in cherries and cognac.

"I've noticed the whole crew is very attentive. They all smile a lot and go out of their way to respond if you ask them a question or request anything. I know in their brochure they said they pampered us, but I guess I wasn't really expecting it." Millie looked around with a wide smile. "I find I really like it."

Pearl nodded her agreement. "That alone is probably worth the fare."

"I don't think so, Pearl." Harold shook his head emphatically. "But I admit it does make the price more palatable."

Harold tested Pedro's willingness to do anything by ordering two Cherries Jubilees and one chocolate mouse cake when he came to take their desert selections.

"I can't believe you're going to eat all that, Harold." Pearl was slightly embarrassed.

"Hell, Pearl, you heard the man. Anything we want. And they never give you enough in one little serving. I like Cherries Jubilee. I know one wouldn't be enough."

Ian nodded. "I'm with you, Harold. I would have ordered two, but I'm planning to check out the midnight buffet tonight."

Ruth groaned. "I can't think of eating anything more. I'm stuffed."

Claire just spooned some of the cherries and cream into her mouth, rolling it over on her tongue before finally swallowing it. It was the perfect end to a wonderful meal. She was glad she selected the halibut instead of one of the heavier entries like the Prime Rib, duck or veal. She remembered all of her customers' complaints about gaining weight on their cruises. She had made up her mind she would have to make wise selections or spend a good deal of time every day at the gym. And she was pleased to see every meal had low calorie, low fat selections available.

"What are you planning tonight?" she asked Lucy.

"I think I'll go to the show with you all. Then maybe I'll drop in at the Starlight Lounge for a while."

"Why am I not surprised?"

"Why don't you come?" Lucy urged her friend, determined to see she got the most fun out of her investment in the cruise. "Ruth and Millie should come too. You never know who will show up. And they have two dance hosts on board who are very good dancers, so you can dance with no strings attached. That's perfect for Ruth's pledge of no romance."

There was a sudden flurry as people started to get up from the table.

"Claire, if you walk me back to my cabin, I'll show you my Cartier watch." Mrs. Bernbaum's anxious expression belied her casual request.

"Auntie, Claire probably has plans. I'll walk you back and make sure you're settled. No problem." Richard Walmer seemed horrified at the thought his Aunt was going to impose on Claire.

"No problem, Richard. I'd be glad to walk with her. And I'd like to see her watch and compare it to mine." Claire was just glad Dr. Walmer had finally unbent enough at dinner to insist they all call him Richard rather than the formal title or the name his aunt used. "Don't worry, Mom will save me a seat and I'll be there in plenty of time to see the show," she assured him moving to Mrs. Bernbaum's side and letting her clutch her arm.

Mrs. Bernbaum smiled with gratitude and as they walked slowly through the tables she whispered, "Thank you, dear. I don't like to impose on Dickie too much. Escorting an old woman can get rather boring for a young man."

"You? Boring? Never, Mrs. Bernbaum! But I really don't think you need to worry as it's obvious Richard dotes on you and is pleased to be your escort."

Mrs. Bernbaum nodded happily at Claire's words, clutching her arm even tighter as they maneuvered down the slightly swaying corridor to her room. Claire knocked on the door and nodded cordially to Anita, who answered.

Anita's expression was still sour and her face was even a deeper shade of green indicating her discomfort with the sway of the ship had not ceased. She pointedly looked at her watch conveying her disapproval of the late hour.

"Anita, quit being a pill and get my jewelry case out of the safe, will you?"

Anita grudgingly left while Mrs. Bernbaum settled on the couch, patting the seat beside her for Claire to sit. The jewelry case was rather large and when Anita opened it, Claire almost gasped at the glimpse of the glitter inside.

Mrs. Bernbaum quickly retrieved a watch and handed it to Claire.

It was beautiful. It was platinum, the mesh band and the watch itself was crusted with diamonds in an *art nouveau* style. Claire laid it across her wrist just above her own watch.

"Mrs. Bernbaum, it's beautiful. And there is a resemblance. I hadn't realized."

"My Nate gave me many jewels. Unfortunately I had to sell all of them." The shadow in her eyes told Claire how painful that must have been. Then realizing she had confused Claire, she continued, "That's a long story. I'll tell you sometime as it has to do with this cruise to Alaska. But for now, rest assured that dear Bernie managed to find all the pieces and purchase them back for me. He was such a dear sweet man. I was so lucky to be loved by him. I wish I could have loved him the way he deserved. But I did my best and he knew it. It was enough for him." She sighed, handing the box back to Anita.

"You run along now dear, thank you so much for humoring an old lady. Your mother will be holding your seat for you and I believe there will be dancing later.

"When I was younger I would have been out there dancing until dawn every night."

"Instead of eating until midnight," was Anita's dour comment.

"Oh Anita, it's not midnight. This is a very fashionable hour." Mrs. Bernbaum shook her head. "I had to be very firm with Dickie and Anita on the first night. They had scheduled us for the early sitting. But I refused. It caused quite a stir, but I got my way."

Anita's expression only darkened. "You keep up this schedule and I'm telling you even those shots won't keep you going. You know I'm right," she said ominously.

Mrs. Bernbaum shrugged. "Everyone has to go someday. I'm on my way to Skagway and you thought it was impossible. If I listened to you I'd be wrapped in a blanket like a mummy, sipping tea in my bedroom instead of dining with interesting people on the high seas." She shook her head in disgust. "Anita, I'm telling you to lighten up. I'm doing what I want to do. If I get overly tired I'll take to my bed for a while."

She looked at Claire. "You have to excuse Anita. She can't get used to the sway. Dickie has given her some pills, but she hates the motion and it sours her whole attitude."

"People should keep their feet on solid ground where they were meant to be. If God had wanted us to traverse the water he would have given us fins," Anita grumbled as she took the jewelry case back to the safe set in the cabinet which housed the tiny refrigerator.

Claire took the opportunity to leave, heading back to the theatre, leaving Mrs. Bernbaum and Anita to continue to spar about Mrs. Bernbaum's schedule.

* * *

He knocked softly after looking both ways in the corridor and being sure no one was there to see him. "Kim, Kim, are you there? Let me in." His voice was low lest it carry to neighboring cabins.

When the door opened she pulled him quickly into the narrow hall, closing the door with one hand while the other twined around his neck, pulling his head down for a deep kiss.

"It's about time. I'm tired of waiting here in this cramped cabin. I thought you weren't coming."

"I know, you've been very patient, but don't worry you'll get your reward." He leaned down for another kiss and then turned and led her into the interior of the cabin. He sat on the edge of the bed and pulled her onto his lap. "So how did your day go?"

She grinned at him. "I made contact. She was up at the buffet, just like you said. I asked if I could share her table. I think it's going to work.

"She's so sick she could hardly eat anything. She had crackers and tea, but I urged her to eat potato chips. I told her my steward gave them to me when I was feeling out of sorts yesterday and it perked me right up." She laughed wickedly. "We'll see how that adds to her misery."

"Careful, careful you don't want to alienate her." He looked at her doubtfully. With her perfect makeup and stunning figure, Kim was the complete opposite of her target.

"Don't worry. I didn't look like this at dinner. I didn't wear any makeup and I wore that jogging outfit I brought. With my hair in a pony I could have been her sister. And she thinks I'm working, just like she is. I tell you, we bonded."

"What did you tell her you did?"

"I'm an administrative assistant to a businessman who can't leave his work behind," she said proudly. Then she sobered. "Look, are you sure we need to go through with this? I mean isn't there another way?"

"Hey, don't get cold feet now." He nibbled on her neck. "It's not like I want to do this, but we have to get her out of the way, or it just won't work. I can't think of anything else. Can you?"

He paused a moment looking into Kim's eyes. "The real question is will you be able to go through with it? Can you do it?"

Her face took on a hard look, and she nodded. "Don't worry, I'll do my part. I just wanted to make sure this was the only viable solution."

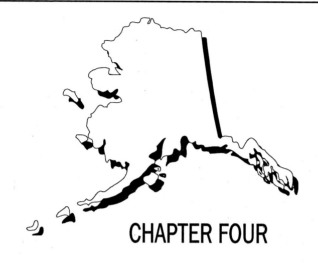

CHAPTER FOUR

Claire gamely followed Lucy through the driving rain, hurrying down the path away from the entry gates of Butchart Gardens. They had left the ship with only one umbrella to share, but found bins of them waiting for visitors to borrow at the gate to the gardens. So now they each had one. That helped keep the rain off, although the little packets containing lightweight rain ponchos they picked up on the ship did a better job of keeping them dry. Claire couldn't help but wish the Gardens had also offered galoshes to their visitors, because it was obvious they would have very wet feet soon.

The path led slightly downhill to the Visitor Center, the Gift Shop and the Coffee Shop. Because they were early, and because of the rain, there weren't many people around yet. Their taxi driver told them they would probably have about an hour before the tour buses arrived carrying passengers from the three cruise ships docked in Victoria today. Lucy was determined to make the most of their time while the gardens were fairly deserted.

"Come on, Claire," she urged. "We can check out the shops later and for sure we'll stop at the Plant Identification Center before we leave." She headed out of the little square past the statue of Tacca, the Butchart

Boar, whose nose had been rubbed copper-penny-shiny by countless visitors who craved a little luck.

Claire was content to let Lucy lead the way. Lucy had been thrilled when she first heard the ship would dock in Victoria, thus allowing her to visit the famous gardens. She refused to be deterred by the dank dark day when they woke this morning, though truthfully, in their windowless cabin in the lower level they really didn't know how dismal the day was until they met Millie and Ruth for breakfast. Still, Lucy would not let the weather interfere with their plans.

Not so for Millie and Ruth, who had both decided to stay on board ship and enjoy the activities scheduled. They couldn't be convinced the gardens would be worth braving the cold rain.

"You two go. We'll meet you at the Empress at three for tea. That's enough adventure for me, thank you very much."

Ruth nodded, for once in full agreement with Millie's caution. "We've lasted this long without seeing the gardens, we can live another few years, I'm sure. And who knows, maybe we'll drive up to Victoria some day and see them."

Since they wouldn't change their minds, it left only Claire and Lucy to negotiate with the taxi driver and set out for the gardens. Somehow the rain, instead of dampening their enthusiasm, only heightened it. Claire had had many special adventures in the rain. She smiled to herself remembering the violent storm she survived with Jack at the Korean War Memorial in Washington D.C. last year. Of course it had been frightening, but it had also been romantic and exciting.

Victoria was a lovely town. Even the rain couldn't disguise its charm. The majestic parliament buildings were impressive. The streets of Victorian houses, bed and breakfasts and little cottages were picturesque. And when the taxi took to the highway, they found it was lined on each side with roses, blooming in every color. The taxi dropped them at the gardens' gate very shortly after it opened, and the driver promised to be waiting there for them when they returned, no matter when that was.

"Oooh," Claire couldn't help exclaiming when they reached the bower filled with hanging baskets spilling over with colorful blooms. "This is gorgeous. What are these flowers? I recognize the fuchsias of course, but these yellow, orange and red ones don't even look real, do they?"

"They're begonias. Tubular begonias and they are spectacular." Lucy had her camera out, her umbrella laid aside while she busily took pictures from every angle, the lattice top of the bower diverting much of the rain.

"You know, Claire, I think I could do something like this at the end of my patio. It would be lovely."

Claire nodded enthusiastically. Lucy had a wonderful backyard and a bower like this would be a great addition. "Would they grow like this in Burlingame?"

"I think so. I'd have to put in a misting system and build a frame like this to give partial shade, but there's a place down off of Highway 92 in Half Moon Bay which specializes in begonias. If they grow there they'll probably do well in my yard." She nodded happily, already planning her begonia bower as she retrieved her umbrella and headed up the steps following the sign pointing toward the sunken garden.

* * *

The heavy downpour made the inside of the ship seem very cozy. Millie stayed far away from all the areas where food was served, in anticipation of the high tea they were going to have later at the Empress Hotel. Ruth had headed to the spa to use the indoor swimming pool, but Millie wanted to find a comfy corner to work on her menu planning. She hoped to finalize her menus for the two weeks after her return and have a menu ready for Mrs. Richman's approval for the dinner party she wanted Millie to cater in October. Ruth scolded her for working on her vacation, but Ruth just didn't understand how much fun Millie was having with this. Claire and Lucy understood probably because they each loved the work they did. She stopped at the coffee bar and ordered a latte and then looked around for a table. Over in the corner near a window was Mrs. Bernbaum, sitting all by herself looking a little lonely.

Millie decided the menus could wait a while and approached saying, "Mrs. Bernbaum, do you want company?"

She looked up surprised and then a pleased expression spread over her face. "Oh, how nice. Yes, please sit down and have coffee with me. I was just looking out at this dreary weather, thinking how glad I am I didn't go on the garden tour."

"Me too. Ruth and I bowed out this morning, but Claire and Lucy went."

"Ah, they're so young they probably don't feel the dampness creeping into their joints." Her laugh was rough, almost a cackle. "Or they're just not wise enough to wait for another time."

The waitress delivered Millie's latte and looked at Mrs. Bernbaum to see if she wanted anything else. When Mrs. Bernbaum shook her head, she left them.

"So where is your nephew today?" Millie inquired politely, knowing how much Mrs. Bernbaum liked to talk about her Dickie.

"He's out in the rain. He's going to the gardens and then to a winery. He says he wants to see it all." She smiled indulgently and then continued. "And Anita, my caregiver is out, determined to have her feet planted on solid ground despite the rain. She is not finding her sea legs and complains all the time. Frankly I'm glad to have her out of my hair for a while.

"Speaking of hair, what do you think of my do? The girls in the salon worked on me this morning and I think they did a nice job."

"Very nice. Isn't it wonderful to have all these services available? I'm really enjoying this cruise. How about you, does it compare favorably to your previous cruising experiences?"

"Oh yes. This ship is so grand and so big. It's like being at a magic resort, isn't it? Every morning we wake up in a different destination."

Millie smiled her agreement, not even minding when Mrs. Bernbaum grabbed her arm pulling her closer to say in a hoarse whisper, "I am so sorry you lost your one true love so long ago. I know how sad that is. And you never found another?"

Millie shook her head, her eyes tearing suddenly, even after so many years sadness enveloped her in a breathless vise.

"My Nate was impossible to replace. Most people don't understand..., but I think you do. Your friend says you change; you become a different person so it is possible to find another perfect mate, different from the first, but still perfect. That didn't happen for me. I don't think it happened for you, either."

"Ruth doesn't understand. She has been married four times. And recently she has found another perfect man. I wanted to find someone else. I wanted Claire to have a father when she was little. It just didn't happen.

"How long had you and Nate been together?" she asked Mrs. Bernbaum gently.

Mrs. Bernbaum stared out the window, as if the rain cascading down the glass would tell her something, then she sighed, released Millie's arm and took a sip of her coffee.

"Not long enough. Not nearly long enough."

She shook her head and looked closely at Millie. "I met him during the war. That was the big war, World War II. I worked for the USO organizing activities for the military personnel going through San Francisco. We held dances four times a week.

"I was a widow. I had lost my first husband shortly after we married. We met in college. That's why young ladies of my generation went to college, you know, to find a husband. So I found a suitable husband just as my parents intended me to do, but he was killed in an automobile accident less than a year later. I was sad, naturally, but I confess I led a frivolous life and I didn't really know grief. As a widow I had the freedom of a married woman during a time when single women had to worry about their reputation. I had no responsibilities, no money worries and as a widow I was free to socialize, to involve myself in charity work and basically frittered my time away.

"Pearl Harbor jolted me out of my easy life. I got involved in the USO. I threw myself into it as if what I was doing would alone make the difference between victory and defeat. Not that maintaining the morale for our troops wasn't important, but now I realize I was just a dilettante. I could have volunteered at the hospital. I could have joined one of the services. But either of those activities would have meant a total commitment. Still I tried to do something, so I poured my energies into the USO."

Her eyes glazed over as she murmured, "It seems like it was only yesterday when I met Nate."

* * *

"Mary, those two girls over there can't be out of high school. Check them out. If they're as young as they look send them home."

"But Flo, we're short girls tonight. Can't we just look the other way? You can see how popular they are with the guys."

Flo watched the two girls; one blond, the other with brown hair, both had shoulder-length curls, which was the style of the day. They wore full skirts, sweaters and bobby socks with their high heeled shoes as many did now that silk stockings were impossible to find. And they were good dancers, which was almost as important to the soldiers and sailors as the fact that they were girls. She was tempted to follow Mary's advice and ignore their age because the girls scheduled for duty tonight couldn't keep up with the number of service men, who chose tonight to attend their dance.

She shook her head. "We don't dare. What if Father Riley finds out? You know how nervous he was about allowing us to use the church hall on Wednesdays. We'd be out on our ear. We promised him no minors. And those girls look like they could be two students from the parish high school."

Then she added, more gently, "I'll call some girls on the back-up list and see if I can get some more dancers here." She headed for the telephone, relying on Mary to sort out the situation with the young girls. She hated being the disciplinarian, but she was in charge and she had worked too hard to set the locations for the four USO dances to lose one because a couple of kids wanted to dance.

Where were their mothers anyway? Didn't they keep track of their kids? Then she smiled wryly to herself, thinking their mothers were probably on the night shift out at the shipyards doing their bit for victory, leaving their kids to fend for themselves.

After twenty minutes of frantic calling she found four women willing to get over to the dance within a half hour.

Two of them said they would bring a friend or two, which would certainly help. Now confident she had solved their crisis she looked around the hall noticing the cluster of uniformed men around the table containing the sandwiches, the coffee and the punch the church's Ladies Altar Guild provided for the dance.

Putting these dances together was a mammoth effort. The location was only one factor. They needed volunteers to provide the food. She had to arrange for the women, who would come and serve the food. She needed girls who loved to dance, making sure they agreed to dance with anyone who asked them, no matter how clumsy or shy the service men were. And of course the music was very important. Sometimes she was able to get a real band, but when she couldn't, Mr. Silva was happy to provide the music. He was a sweetheart. Too old to serve himself, he said he was still good for something. He used two phonograph players and his own extensive collection of records, which included all the popular dance bands. He not only queued up the next record to begin when the previous one ended, but he kept up a lively chatter to encourage mingling.

The music was loud and the dancers enthusiastic. The women who volunteered came to support their men, albeit, everyone's men. They were from all walks of life, some with loved ones of their own overseas. Some just liked to dance. Some only served the refreshments and some just listened to the lonely men talk.

She noticed too many of the men hanging around the punch bowl were wistfully watching the dancers, because there weren't enough women. Her reinforcements wouldn't be arriving for a few minutes so she headed for the ladies room, intending to shoo anyone sneaking a cigarette under the guise of fixing their lipstick back out to the dance floor. This wasn't the right time for primping, she thought.

"Dance?"

She veered around the man blocking her way and then realized he had been talking to her. She looked at him, momentarily stunned by his piercing eyes. He was tall and muscular. Mature, not old and he had a weathered face, the laugh lines framed the blue of his eyes.

She smiled at him. "Thank you, Captain, but I'm not one of the dance hostesses. I'm sure you'll find someone who will be a better dancer over there." She nodded her chin towards the punch table.

He shook his head. "Nope, I've already found someone who suits my tastes. There is no one here who compares with you. Surely you have time for one dance with a lonely flier lad before he's shipped off to fight for you and your country." The smile was lazy but the glint in his eyes was pure devilment.

She laughed, unable to refuse his outrageous flattery and so found herself in his arms and on the dance floor. There, in spite of him being more than a foot taller than her and almost twice her weight, they seemed to float to music as if they were one entity. So of course they danced another one. She was very tempted to follow him for a third song, but fortunately she remembered the rules in time.

"Sorry, Captain, but we're only allowed two dances with the same person before changing partners." She smiled with regret, explaining, "It's so everyone gets a chance to dance, you see."

"But can you dance with me after a break?"

She nodded, suddenly wanting another dance very badly.

He slipped his arm through hers and steered her toward the punch bowl. "Let's have a drink and you can tell me all about yourself."

Flo actually blushed, responding to his charm as she hadn't to anyone else. Later they both admitted they suspected even then they were going to be seriously connected.

* * *

"Oh, that sounds so romantic."

Mrs. Bernbaum nodded. A dreamy smile touched her lips. "It was, but it wasn't easy. There were rules you know. Women in the USO weren't supposed to date men they met at the functions. It was a good rule. It was to keep the activities wholesome, entertaining and not a dating service. Oh, I know, many people ignored the rules. I couldn't, you see, because I was in charge. I had to set an example. But suddenly I found those rules very depressing even though Nate understood."

"But how did you get together?"

"Nate. He took care of it. He found someone who knew someone, who knew someone else and somehow got invited to a charity benefit I was attending the next night. He was introduced to me properly, in front of many witnesses, completely away from any USO activity and the rest was history. He only had five days before shipping out again and we took advantage of every minute. We would have married before he left, but we just didn't have enough time. So we decided as soon as we were together again it would be the first item on our agenda. And he promised me he would return."

Mrs. Bernbaum clasped Millie's wrist tightly, so she couldn't leave before she finished what she wanted to say. She leaned her head forward. "I had been married before, but I didn't know love until I met Nate. I thought I had been happy. I thought I was heartbroken when my first husband died, but it was as if I had been living protected from real life by a gauze screen. When I met Nate everything was so intense. The sun was brighter, the clouds were darker; my love could barely be contained.

"Oh, and I worried so. He was going to England to fly missions over Europe. It was so dangerous. I didn't know how I would live with him gone, but there was no choice. He had to go. I had to be brave for him. We all had to do what we had to do. It was expected in those times.

"We hoped he would get leave again, but he didn't. Thank God, when the war ended he was still alive. But even then he wasn't released immediately. And we waited. He wrote me the most beautiful letters. I still have every one of them. It seemed like our lives were on hold forever.

"Do you remember those years?" she asked peering into Millie's eyes.

Millie shook her head. "I was a toddler. What I remember were the books and movies of that time, but written later, and of course the stories I heard."

Mrs. Bernbaum relaxed, letting go of Millie's arm, and sat back in her chair. "You know, my dear, the worst thing about getting old is finding you can't share your memories with anyone. Suddenly it is as if you were the only person alive who remembers certain times. It's very sad."

Millie felt a shiver, realizing longevity had a price.

"But look at me? I'm starting to get maudlin. I'm sure you have better things to do with your time than listen to me."

"Oh, no Mrs. Bernbaum, I enjoy talking to you and hearing about your life. I hope you'll tell me the rest of the story."

"I will, of course I will. Another day perhaps."

"Ruth and I are going to take a taxi into the city to the Empress Hotel to meet Claire and Lucy for tea. Would you like to join us?"

Mrs. Bernbaum's smile was tremulous. "Me? You're inviting me to join you?"

"Of course, we'd love to have your company. It will only be for a couple of hours and I hear it's very fancy."

"My dear, thank you for asking, but I must decline. I need to take my nap." She smiled ruefully. "The penalty for having the late seating for dinner is an afternoon nap, so I don't doze off during the main course." She struggled to get out of the chair, then stood a moment as if to test her legs before heading for the elevator. "See you at dinner tonight. I'll look forward to hearing all about the tea."

She tottered with determination across the lobby toward the elevators while Millie tried to picture her as she was when she met her Nate.

* * *

"Oh, you didn't wait for us?" Ruth was clearly disappointed.

"Yes, we did. We didn't order anything to eat even though we were tempted. We had to have some tea to warm us up. Don't worry, we'll order it all again."

"Did you both get soaked? I hope you're not going to come down with a cold." Millie took off her jacket and settled in a chair facing her daughter.

"It was cold and damp, but it was wonderful. I think it was even better in the rain. And actually, except for our feet, we stayed pretty dry."

Ruth was busily examining the menu, but Millie took the time to gaze around the elegant room where the Empress Hotel was serving tea.

"Oh my gosh. Look at these prices." Ruth looked up. "Are we sure we want to eat here?"

"Those are Canadian dollars, Ruth," Lucy said. "And besides we deserve to treat ourselves."

"It is very nice here, Ruth." Millie was taken with the ornate Victorian décor, the heavy velvet draperies, the rich carpets on the polished wood floors, while the subtle clink of silver sounded through the room and the crystal stemware gleamed richly in the dim light. The hotel itself was old and elegant, similar to the St. Francis in San Francisco.

"Lucy is right. The price is not the object. This is a treat," Millie told Ruth.

"Well, in that case we'd better do the whole thing and go for the High Tea. It's the most expensive, so it must be the best. What kind of tea should we order?"

"We have Earl Grey and will probably stick with that. So order whatever appeals to you and Mom."

"I like Earl Grey, or perhaps Oolong. Either of those okay with you, Millie?"

The waitress took their order and left them to catch up on the activities of the day.

"Mom, the Rose Garden was outstanding. I took a picture of the most beautiful rose I've ever seen. I hope it comes out because you're going to drool over it. It was crimson, but as the petals unfolded it was white inside with crimson only on the edges of each petal. It was just too perfect!"

"The last of the summer flowers were still in bloom and the fall flowers were just starting to bloom. So we got to see two seasons," Lucy added.

"We bought seeds, oodles of seeds. I got some for you too. I'd show them to you, but they're sealed with an agriculture sticker so we can get them through customs. I thought I might plant some of the wildflowers in that weed patch behind the book shop. And I'm hoping some will take to the planters on my porch at home." Claire always regretted she didn't have the time to do much with her yard, either at home or at the store. And so far she only had a service in to mow the weeds into some semblance of a lawn so her neighbors wouldn't complain. But after seeing these gardens she was convinced she needed to pay attention to the yard behind the store. She could envision a nice patio with flowers and shaded places for customers to sit amongst the flowers to read while deciding which books to buy.

Just then the waitress wheeled out a tea trolley laden with plates and pots. She transferred everything to their table while they sat dazzled by the variety. Lucy said she would pour, so the waitress left them to it.

"No wonder it's so expensive. Who could eat all this?" Ruth muttered.

"I bet we can do a pretty good job of it, I'm starved after all our walking today." Claire used the silver tongs to help herself to a collection of tiny sandwiches and little savories.

"I skipped lunch just so I could do justice to it." Millie heaped her plate.

"Well, I swam, so I'm hungry," admitted Ruth.

"I hope we won't have to ask for more. It would be a little embarrassing," Lucy said and the others laughed. "I know for sure I'm saving room for the sweets."

The four-tiered plate laden with scones, cakes, petite fours and chocolate dipped strawberries looked almost too pretty to disturb, but they knew they would.

"Yummy. Ruth, did you try this? It tastes like that little crab puff your group served as an appetizer in Tuscany," Millie said between bites.

Ruth picked one up and took a bite, then nodded at Millie as she finished it off. "It could easily be the same recipe."

"Did you see any of our table mates at the gardens?"

"No, but I did see a couple of people from the ship. That couple we sat next to at the races and another couple I met in the internet café. Did you see anyone from the table Lucy?"

"No, but maybe they went other places or even wandered around the shops here in town. Isn't this a pretty town with all the flower baskets hanging from the light stanchions? Claire, you should talk to your Merchant's

Association and get them to do that in Bayside. It would really perk up the downtown district."

Claire nodded, then admitted, "They're pretty tight with their dollars. They don't like to spend money on anything, and I can just hear them complaining about how flowers are apt to die."

Lucy grinned, nodding. She knew Bayside was such a pokey little town because the city fathers were loath to spend the money to compete with the fashionable cities of Burlingame and San Mateo which neighbored them.

She changed the subject. "So Millie, what did you do today while Ruth was swimming her laps?"

"I fully intended to work on my menus. But when I went for coffee I found Mrs. Bernbaum sitting up there all alone, so I ended up talking to her until it was time to meet Ruth. She was telling me about how she met her husband, not Mr. Bernbaum, her one true love, you know? She's very interesting."

"Did she grab your arm so you couldn't get away?" Claire wanted to know.

"Yes, as a matter of fact she did, but I didn't mind. You know it must be very hard to want to tell people things when they're all too busy or too disinterested to listen. She told me one of the hardest things about getting old was finding there was no one to share her memories with." Millie shuddered. "I kind of hope I don't live that long."

"How old is she?"

"I don't know, but she was in her thirties when she met her husband in the forties so that would make her ninety something now, wouldn't it?" She looked around to verify her math and seeing them nod she continued. "Really, she's in pretty good shape for her age, wouldn't you say?"

"I guess so!"

"I invited her to join us for tea, but she said she had to nap. She says if she doesn't nap she'll fall asleep in her soup." Millie laughed. "Apparently her caregiver and her nephew scheduled her for the early sitting and she wasn't going to have that."

Claire nodded. "Every time I've seen her caregiver she's made some comment about Mrs. Bernbaum staying up too late. One time she said it would take more than a shot of pep from Dr. Feelgood to keep her going."

"What did she mean by that, dear?"

"Well, Mom, I'm assuming she calls Dr. Walmer that. I got the impression she didn't much like him or the shots he gives Mrs. Bernbaum to give her enough energy for this trip."

"He's giving her shots? What kind of shots? Is that dangerous?" Millie couldn't contain her alarm.

"He specializes in longevity. I've heard of physicians who do that. They use all the newest discoveries to make sure their aging clients get the most out of their life. Believe me, when I start slowing down I'll be getting me a doctor like that." Ruth shook her head as she helped herself to more goodies. "Forget all the doctors who do face lifts, I'd rather be able to do things, to be mobile, to have the energy to do what I want."

"I'm with you on that, Ruth. And Mrs. Bernbaum told me she was on a life quest. She has something she feels she needs to do on this trip to Alaska and Richard made it possible for her to do it, so she's very grateful for his help." Then Claire admitted sheepishly, "I was concerned when I first met her, because she's so old. But really, I do like her. And from the little I know about her I'm sure she's led a very interesting life."

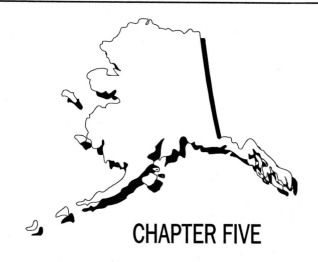

CHAPTER FIVE

The players had all shifted again Claire noticed when she and Lucy approached their table and found that once more they were the last to arrive.

"Lucy, Lucy, sit here beside me." Pearl gushed, indicating the empty chair on her right. "I saved it for you especially."

Claire good-naturedly headed for the only other empty chair, on the other side of the table with her mother on her left and Sean Gallagher on her right.

"I do so want to talk to you about the gardens. We just loved them. And when we returned we had time to explore the city a little and we found a book store. Look what I found." She held up a copy of *An Armchair Traveler's Adventure,* Lucy's most recent book. "I was hoping to find a copy of *Daffodils in the Cotswolds,* but no such luck." Still, Pearl looked very pleased with herself.

"And I was thumbing though it and I found your picture, Claire. I didn't know you had anything to do with this book, but I want both of you to sign it for me, if you will."

Claire met Lucy's eyes a moment and then said to Pearl, "I was a member of a group of people who followed the book's itinerary before it was published. The picture you saw was that group. We didn't really contribute anything to writing the book, we only tested the itinerary. The book is all Lucy's baby." The picture Pearl was referring to was the group picture on the back of the book's dust jacket which they had taken at the San Francisco Airport before leaving on the tour.

Claire felt her heart thump with anxiety as she remembered how naïve and excited they all were when that picture was taken. Then she gave herself a mental shake, it was more than a year ago; it was over. They survived or at least most of them did.

Lucy smiled graciously and took the book from Pearl. Realizing she didn't have a pen she looked around the table until Harold handed her one from his shirt pocket. She smiled her thanks before murmuring as she opened the book to the title page, "Do you want it dedicated to both you and Harold?"

"Oh, both of us please. I can't wait to read it and then if I have any questions, you'll be right here for me to ask you. You don't mind, do you?"

"Of course not. I'd be happy to discuss it and I'm sure Claire wouldn't mind telling you about her trip, would you Claire?" She signed the book and passed it across the table to Claire to sign.

Pedro arrived just then to take their orders and, after the selections were made, attention was diverted from Lucy's book while small conversations broke out around the table.

"Did you go to the gardens?" Sean inquired with interest.

Claire nodded. "In spite of the rain. Lucy and I hired a car and the driver waited for us. It worked out very well and allowed us to spend as much time as we wanted in the gardens and still get back to town to have a sumptuous tea at the Empress Hotel."

"Wasn't that expensive? The car, I mean."

"Well, originally all four of us were going to share, so it would have been much cheaper than taking a shore excursion. However, since Mom and Ruth decided they would melt if they got wet, it was only Lucy and I. So I think it cost about the same as the shore excursion. But," she paused, thinking, "It was still better because we were able to follow our own time line. You know how on the bus you have to be there at a certain time and then wait until everyone else gets there, and there is always someone late, isn't there? So this way we got to the gardens ahead of the buses and when we left we went directly to the Empress Hotel. It was way more convenient."

Sean nodded. "It sounds like it. Maybe Ian and I should think about doing that in Juneau. We're torn between two activities and if we hired a car maybe we could do both?"

He leaned forward to speak around Ruth. "Ian, Claire and Lucy hired a car to go out to the gardens and avoided the time schedules for the shore excursions. If we hired a car in Juneau we could probably have time to take the helicopter and dog sled excursion and still see the glacier."

Ian nodded. "That sounds like a good plan. Tomorrow let's check the times and sign up. Hopefully, they still have space."

"Helicopter ride and dog sledding sounds pretty exciting. What did you do today?"

Sean chuckled. "Pub and Ale tour. You have no idea how many pubs and ale houses they have here in Victoria. I had to have a nap when we returned, but not my brother. He drank me under the table."

"Hey, wait a minute that sounds worse than it was. Sean's just getting a little old, so he couldn't keep up with the rest of us."

Richard offered Sean support from across the table. "I understand completely, Sean. I took the Garden and

Winery Tour. After doing the Gardens in the rain and then tasting all the wines I felt a little like napping too. Fortunately, I was able to snatch a little shut eye on the bus ride back to the ship."

Ian shook his head, his eyes dancing with fun. "Wusses, these guys are wusses." He winked at Ruth beside him. "I bet you could have kept up, couldn't you, Ruth?"

"Probably," Ruth laughed, "But I didn't even try. Millie and I stayed on board until it was time to meet Claire and Lucy for tea. We know enough to stay out of the rain."

"And what about you, Mrs. Bernbaum? How did you spend your day?" Ian asked from the far end of the table.

"I had a very nice time right here on board the ship. I stayed warm and dry, had coffee with Millie and spent some time in the Beauty Salon."

"Ha, I thought you were looking especially charming tonight." He winked at her and her face lit up from the attention. "And tomorrow I see we have dress up night, so we'll all be wanting to look our best."

"I love to dress up, but Harold hates it." Pearl confessed, "So tomorrow I'll be the happy one and he'll probably be grouchy."

"Ah, Pearl, I'm not as bad as that. And besides when would it be that you're not the happy one. I only seem grouchy compared to you." Harold defended himself and everyone laughed, agreeing to the truth in what he said.

"So tomorrow we're going through the inland passage. I can't wait. I understand we'll be very close to shore," Millie said her excitement plain.

"And the sea will be very calm, won't it?" Mrs. Bernbaum asked. "I'll tell Anita she can look forward to a good day."

"Oh, dear, the poor woman is still sick?" Millie looked concerned. "Isn't there anything you can give her to help?" She looked at Richard.

"I've given her the maximum dose. She just doesn't seem to respond. Auntie thinks it's mental, not just physical, so she won't recover until we're all safely back in San Francisco."

"What a shame. Why doesn't she just go back?" Claire suggested, remembering the green look of Anita each time she had seen her. "She could fly back from Juneau, couldn't she?"

"She may as well. Frankly she's so miserable she's ruining my cruise. But since she is also stubborn, I don't suppose she will. However, it's a good suggestion, Claire. I will ask her."

"So we have the whole day tomorrow to lollygag around. I love it. I love looking at that list of activities and planning my day around what I want to do. I think that's what I enjoy the most about cruising," Ruth said with a smile.

"Yeah, and if you plan an activity you can still change your plans. The whole pace of things allows you do as much or as little as you want to do." Lucy grinned, she was enjoying this cruise.

Millie added, "I like how friendly people are. Have you noticed? If you sit anywhere, people sitting near you start talking to you. And everyone is so nice."

"And why wouldn't they be?" Sean said with an arched eyebrow. "The nightly news shows aren't dispensing their load of woe and misery, which alone should make us all the happier. We are all fed and entertained and pampered every minute of the day. Everyone is feeling mellow. It makes for good company."

"Well speaking of good company, will we see you ladies upstairs for the dancing?" Ian asked."

"Of course, do we look like dullards?"

"Not you, dear, never." Ian smiled wickedly at Lucy.

"We're coming for a while, but Ruth wants to play cards so who knows how long we'll be there. What about you, Claire, coming?" Millie looked questioningly at Claire.

"Sure, it's a nice way to end the evening. Mrs. Bernbaum do you need me to escort you back to your room?"

"No, thank you, dear. Dickie is going to take me. But Claire, if you have time, why don't you and your mother come to tea at my cabin tomorrow afternoon? We can see the shore from my balcony while we sip our tea. Bring your friends if you want."

"That would be nice. What time?"

"Come at three if that's convenient."

* * *

"I thought you weren't coming," she complained when he slipped into the chair beside her in the dim piano bar. She waited impatiently, her fingers drumming on the arm of her chair, while he ordered a drink and a refill for her.

"I tried to get away earlier but it was hard. I didn't want to be obvious, so I waited until a couple of others drifted away and then I disappeared. How did the rest of your day go?"

"Just like we planned. I met her for dinner and then we caught the early show. They're not bad, you know. It was a variety show, lots of costumes and dances copied from some of the Broadway shows, but still entertaining. And I mentioned the shrine to her. She's definitely interested in that. I told her I'd see what I could do and let her know tomorrow."

"Well, I've got some good news. The old lady is going to suggest she fly home from Juneau. If she does, the problem will be solved." He grinned, his teeth gleaming in the darkness.

"If she doesn't?"

"Well, too bad for her." His smile was hard.

She nodded. "I called and arranged the car rental from a pay phone on shore, so that's done with no way to trace it to the ship."

"Tomorrow we'll work out the logistics." He finished his drink. "Let's get out of here, I'm feeling lucky tonight. How about a visit to the casino?"

* * *

"Good morning. This is the Captain speaking. The sun has broken through the clouds and it looks like a smooth day sailing up the inside passage. You will see at several points we will be close enough to shore to see wildlife through binoculars, so keep your eyes open. Meanwhile, those of you on the starboard side may enjoy the antics of our escort. We have picked up a school of porpoises. They have been with us for a while and don't mind showing off for you. And no, they are not employed by *Call of the Seas* for your entertainment. Have a nice day and I'll look forward to meeting you at the captain's cocktail party this evening before dinner."

"Which side is starboard?" Millie asked, swiveling her head.

"There, did you see it?" Claire pointed out the window near her. "There they are. Look at them."

"Oh, goodness, how many are there? Let me get my camera, maybe I can get a picture." Millie grabbed her camera from her canvas tote bag and got out of her chair to crowd closer to the window.

Even Ruth twisted around, ignoring her coffee for a moment to see the porpoises gamboling in the sea, keeping pace with the ship.

"Oh, that was fun. I hope we see more and whales too." Millie returned to her breakfast only casting her eyes toward the porpoises occasionally.

"We're taking a whale watching trip out of Ketchikan. They promise we'll see whales and other wildlife too," their table companion, who had introduced herself as Heidi from Phoenix, said.

Her husband, Bob, explained they booked the excursion to be sure they saw whales, not willing to leave the sightings to chance. "I mean what's the first thing everyone will ask us? Did we see any whales? No way we're going to admit we didn't. We're going to see whales and we're going to capture it on tape."

He nodded, clearly pleased with their strategy, while Heidi laughed. "We don't have whales in Phoenix, you know." Her eyes sparkled with merriment. "I noticed you keep your camera with you; that's a good idea. After breakfast I think I'll go back to the cabin and get mine and my binoculars. You never know when whales might appear."

Then finishing their breakfast Heidi and Bob excused themselves. "Don't forget to meet me in the lounge at ten. We're going to be brilliant at Trivia, I just know it," Heidi reminded them as she left.

"They're a fun couple. Can you imagine how hot it must be in Phoenix now? If I lived there I'd probably want to go to Alaska for vacation too," Ruth commented. "So Claire, where is Lucy this morning, another sleep in?"

Claire shrugged. "Actually, I envy her ability to do that. I wake up about seven and no matter how tired I am, I eventually get up. But you know she keeps a different schedule. She doesn't have to get up and get to work at a certain time. When she's writing she does it when she wants. I know she must have come in late last night, but I didn't even hear her."

"Oh, yeah, she was dancing with her friend when Millie and I headed out. She certainly can keep the late hours."

"So I don't expect her to ever make breakfast here in the dining room, but she says she enjoys the buffet up on the top deck."

"Good thing," was Ruth's droll response.

They gathered up their belongings and headed to the library and the daily crossword puzzle. They thought they had time to finish it before the Trivia game. After Trivia they were each heading off to different activities.

"Ruth, do you want to go with us to Mrs. Bernbaum's cabin for tea?" Millie asked.

"I don't know. What's the attraction?"

"Well, I understand from Claire she has a lovely cabin, more like a suite. You might like to see how the other half lives."

"Well, maybe, but I'm thinking I may join the group playing bridge. I'll let you know later, okay?"

* * *

Anita opened the door for them. Claire introduced her to her mother and they went into the sitting room.

"Claire, Millie, welcome. It's so nice of you to come. Where are your friends? Will they be coming?"

"Ruth is playing cards and Lucy is spending some time in the spa. She says she's getting ready for tonight," Claire explained.

Mrs. Bernbaum nodded. "Yes, formal night, I remember." Then addressing Anita, "Anita, dear, after Jorges brings the tea you can go off if you wish. We can pour the tea ourselves. Just be sure you're back by seven to help me get dressed."

The knock on the door arrived as if it were cued. Anita opened the door to a white jacketed room steward whose smile seemed as wide as the tray he carried. He arranged the tea things on the coffee table in front of the sofa with Anita fussing around, making sure it was all just perfect, and then they both left the ladies to their tea and their conversation.

"How is Anita feeling? Any better?" Claire asked with concern.

Mrs. Bernbaum shook her head.

"Is she going to fly home tomorrow, or didn't you suggest it?"

"No and yes. She says she wouldn't think of it. She's here to make sure I survive this cruise. She says she can't trust me to know what's good for me. She insists she'll stay and make sure I make it home." Mrs. Bernbaum made a face. "It sounds noble, but I confess it gets my goat, as if I haven't been taking care of myself long before she was even born. Oh, don't get me wrong. I appreciate her caring about me and her attention to those details I no longer want to take care of. But really, I have Dickie here. I'm perfectly capable of finishing what I started with this voyage."

Millie started pouring the tea, adding milk to Claire's and lemon to Mrs. Bernbaum's when they indicated their preferences. Handing the cup to Mrs. Bernbaum she reminded her, "You were going to tell me why you are taking this trip to Alaska?"

Mrs. Bernbaum sipped her tea, sighed then nodded. "Yes, yes, it's a life quest. You know, one of those things you mean to do before the end of your life? It was a promise I made to Nate.

"I don't think I mentioned he was from Alaska, did I?"

* * *

"Abby, I got the tickets. We need to get to town by Monday to make sure you get on. I booked us in at Ma

Freedom's boarding house. The town is filling up already with everyone wanting to go outside on the last ship."

"Oh, Seth, I don't want to go. Please, let us stay."

His voice gentled. "Now Abby, you know we've decided. You can't have the baby here. And your sister is expecting you in Seattle. She can help you with Rachael when the baby comes. Before you know, it will be spring again and you'll be on your way home to us." He tried to keep his expression positive although he already wondered how they would get through the long dark winter without her and Rachael.

"Nate and I will stay busy up at the mine. We'll just concentrate on working the tailings and hopefully extract enough gold to have a good year."

"But Seth, Nate's so young to be working all winter."

"Abby, Abby, you forget he's nine now. He's a responsible young man. He'll be a real help to me. And I promise everyday he will spend two hours working on the lessons you wrote out for him.

"This is the best way; the only way. Remember we discussed all of this? Really, this is the best way to get through the winter, so don't go changing your mind at the last minute."

Tears spurted from her eyes. Abby threw herself into her husband's arms, sobbing on his shoulder. Finally she straightened, nodding her head she managed, "I know, I know it's the best way. It's just..., it's just I've been having nightmares about it. I feel like something awful is going to happen, and I feel like I have to stay here to make sure you and Nate are safe."

He shook his head, slightly amused despite his distress over her tears. "We'll be careful, real careful," he told her gravely. "You just worry about yourself, the baby and Rachael." He reached out and tenderly wiped a tear from her cheek. "Now why don't you finish your packing and then sit a while and get your feet up. The kids will be coming in soon and there is no sense worrying them with adult problems, now is there?"

She nodded turning toward the wash basin to bathe her face, already mulling over the tasks she had left to complete before they all went to Skagway to await the *Princess Sophia's* arrival.

The days passed faster than they could have believed and too soon they were ensconced in a room in the boarding house in town. Abby felt as excited as the children were at being in town and able to walk down the street looking at the goods in the store windows.

"Oh look, see the pretty baby." Rachael stared with open-mouth admiration at the doll in the window. Where they lived on the mountain near their gold mine, she mostly entertained herself with sticks and stones from the yard, their dog and sometimes the doll her father had carved out of wood for her. Their infrequent visits to town were a source of delight to both children.

Abby and Seth looked at each other, wishing they could spare the money to buy this beautiful doll for their cherished daughter. But they needed to conserve their money. The doll wasn't a necessity and people who lived in Alaska knew how important it was to save their money for the unexpected.

"Here Nate, take your sister in and pick out a candy for each of you." He flipped him a coin, rewarded by the flash of excitement in the children's eyes.

"You go on, Seth. I'll wait here for the kids and then we'll go on to Mrs. Murphy's. We'll see you back at the boarding house before dinner."

Mrs. Murphy, one of the local matrons, was giving her annual pre-winter tea. All the ladies waiting for the last boat to go outside for the winter, as well as all the ladies prepared to hunker down locally for the long months of darkness ahead, would be there. They would dress in their finest, or their traveling clothes, sip tea, renew acquaintances with those coming down river from more remote areas or over the White Pass on the railroad, all converging with one purpose, to flee to civilization before they were trapped by the snow and ice. In previous years Abby had attended this function, but never on the eve of her own departure. Today, besides catching up on the news of her friends in more remote locations, she expected to get more details about the journey she and Rachael were embarking on. Many of these women went outside each year, shuddering at the thought of trying to survive the harsh winter in Alaska.

"Thanks, Abby. You take care to get a little time to put your feet up for a while, will you?" He was worried about his wife. This pregnancy seemed harder on her than the other two. He wondered if it was because she was older, or maybe just that with the other two children plus living on the mountain as they did, life was very hard for her. He was anxious for her to winter outside where doctors were available and where she would have help with Rachael when the new baby came.

He headed first for the harbor to check on the arrival of the Princess Sophia, and then he planned to head for the saloon where the men waiting for transportation outside would be gathered, sharing gossip, making plans and bidding farewell to those who were not planning to return.

The next morning there was a light sprinkling of snow on the ground, but by the time the family finished breakfast the snow was gone and it was raining. Seth and Nate managed to get Abby's trunk down to the wharf where they stood a while watching all the confusion as off-loading passengers and cargo were sorted out from the cargo waiting to be loaded. New passengers were already milling around, too early to board, but anxious to be near the ship lest they be left behind. And, of course, there were the townspeople, already gathering as if this was a circus in town for their entertainment.

Every year everyone, who was able, was at the wharf when the last boat sailed. In Alaska, a huge land with a relatively small population, everyone seemed to know everyone else. They all wanted to wave farewell. Each year the departure of the last ship out signaled the imminent arrival of winter. When it sailed those left behind were trapped until spring. They had no choice but to go about their business of surviving the deprivation in long periods of darkness, their activities curtailed due to snow or ice and bouts of loneliness so desperate that some went mad.

After the family had their noon dinner at the boarding house it was time to leave. Seth and Nate escorted Abby and Rachael to the dock, struggling through the ever expanding crowd to the boarding ramp, then watched from the dock as their women disappeared on board.

"There they are." Nate pointed excitedly. "See, there."

He and his father waved enthusiastically until Abby and Rachael spotted them in the crowd and waved back.

"When they come back, Ma will have the new baby with her, won't she Dad?"

Seth nodded. "It will be good when we see them back, lad."

"What's the new baby to be; a boy or a girl?"

"I don't know. What do you think?"

"I think a boy would be handy, you know, to help with the chores. And I could teach him things like fishing, and setting a rabbit snare." Then he thought a minute. "But girls are kind of nice. And a girl could help Ma and Rachael with the chores, don't you think?"

"Yes, very sensible, but I think it might be a while before the baby is much help with the chores whether it's a girl or a boy. But, I have to say I'm looking forward to bouncing a sweet baby on my knee. Do you remember how cute Rachael was? And while you don't remember, I can assure you that you were a charming little fellow, yourself. Yes, we could use another baby to add a little joy to our lives."

The gangway was taken up, the cables released and, too soon, the ship was sliding away from the dock. The noise was deafening as the crowd on the dock whistled and shouted, their gaiety not quite covering their anxiety or their sadness at separation or loss of the friends who were never intending to come back.

Seth felt a moment of panic. He wanted to change his mind. He admitted right then he didn't want Abby and Rachael to go. But he stiffened his resolve. He didn't dare risk Abby having the baby in the dead of winter in Skagway. There would be no doctors to help. Too many things might go wrong. It would be too dangerous. They had discussed it and made the only decision that was prudent.

The crowd stayed on the dock until the ship was no longer visible to the naked eye and then melted away as the watchers went back to their daily business. Seth and Nate trudged back to the boardinghouse. They planned to be up and out early in the morning.

The weather turned bad as they made their way home. Seth felt satisfaction in knowing he got Abby and Rachael out before winter closed them in, but he and Nate still had a lot to do to get ready for their winter's work. They had mountains of tailings they dug from the mine this summer, waiting to be processed in order to extract the gold. They had a huge stack of wood piled around the shack where it would insulate the walls and still be handy to fuel the fire. They already moved their supplies and the bare necessities for living from their cabin, to the shack built around the entrance to the mine, so they were prepared to be snowed in for periods of time.

"Halloo, the cabin."

Seth and Nate looked at each other, surprised to hear a voice. Seth cautiously opened the door to see old Winslow, crusted with ice, stagger up to the door.

"Winslow, what are you doing out here, man?" Seth reached out to help him over the threshold and into the warm interior of the shack.

"Had to come." His teeth were chattering, so it was hard to understand him. "Knew you had to know."

Seth quickly filled a cup with the strong brew from the coffee pot sitting on the stove and thrust it into Winslow's hands. "Know what? What couldn't wait until the storm abated?"

"The Princess Sophia's gone aground."

Nate would never forget the sight of his strong father turning white, his mouth opening and closing, his whole body shaking, as he leaned urgently over the old man, "My God, tell me man, were they rescued?" The strangled words could barely be understood even though the wide-eyed Nate understood every word.

"They're aground on Vanderbilt Reef. They've sent rescue ships, but the storm's too fierce to get the passengers off. I know the missus just left. I knew you'd have to know."

Already Seth was moving around the room making ready to leave. Instructing Nate, while donning his own heavy garments.

"We have to get down there. Finish your coffee, Winslow. Turn off the lamp when you leave. We have to get there now. Come on Nate. We gotta save your ma and sister."

The trip through the snow, down the mountain to Skagway on snowshoes was hellish. There were times they weren't sure they could make it. The whole way Seth cursed himself for insisting Abby go. Then he cursed the Alaskan weather. He made promises to God, anything; he would promise anything to save his family. But when they finally

*pushed their way into the grim crowd jammed in the Harbor
Master's office in Skagway, it was too late. After setting atop
Vanderbilt Reef for two days while rescue boats hovered
about waiting for a break in the weather in order to make
their rescues, the storm worsened. Sometime after 5:20 p.m.
on Friday, October 25, 1918, the Princess Sophia slipped
into the sea taking all three hundred and fifty-three
passengers and hands with it to an icy grave.*

* * *

"Oh my God, how tragic." Claire was stunned,
completely caught up in Mrs. Bernbaum's story.

Mrs. Bernbaum nodded. "It was awful. It had a
devastating effect on Skagway, really much of Alaska.
Remember that was just at the end of World War I. They
had lost many men in the war and there was a major flu
outbreak throughout the world. This was just one more
tragedy to the world, but it was a huge one for Alaska.
Additionally, it was a major environmental disaster. The
fuel from the Princess Sophia spread through the Canal. It
coated all the victims they eventually retrieved as well as
choking off plant and wildlife in the area.

"But, of course, it nearly destroyed Nate and Seth's
lives. Seth couldn't cope with the disaster, blaming himself,
becoming a little more strange and a little more of a recluse
as each year passed."

"Oh dear, how dreadful it must have been for Nate.
You wonder how he survived in that hostile environment
and with a father not functioning right." Millie was very
distressed.

"He said it was the defining event of his life. His life
before he met me. He always had nightmares of his little
sister calling to him to save her, and of course he couldn't.
He could never get over the nightmares. Despite the horror

of the war, it was his little sister who haunted him right up to the day he died.

"Nate was kind of adopted by the whole town. It's not a very big town, you know. You'll see when we get there. I understand it hasn't changed much or even grown much over the years.

"Various families took turns housing him with them over the winters so he could attend school. Some of the merchants gave him little jobs so he could earn pocket money. But he spent summers with his dad working their mine. They did extract some gold. It was brutally hard work, but they managed to get enough to survive on. When Nate was in high school he attached himself to the man who ran the airport and learned everything anyone was willing to teach him. He became a fearless pilot and skilled mechanic. That's how he ended up a fighter pilot in the war.

"He was in his thirties when we met and he had never been married. He said he could never become committed to anyone. He was never able to develop a relationship until we met. Then it was like a lightning bolt struck the two of us. Everything changed for both of us."

Millie filled their tea cups again and they all sipped while they thought about Nate's story.

"And after the war, didn't he go back to Alaska? Didn't he want to show you where he grew up?" Claire asked.

"Of course he did. He went back several times and I was going to go with him, but each time other things came up. And we felt no urgency about it. We thought we had forever, you see..." Her face was so sad it was heartbreaking.

Claire realizing Mrs. Bernbaum was exhausted, surreptitiously glanced at her watch. "Mom, don't you have a hair appointment? I think you're going to be late."

"Goodness, yes. I hate to leave, Mrs. Bernbaum. You've intrigued me so with Nate's story, but I'm afraid I have to run. We'll see you at the Captain's Reception tonight, won't we?"

Mrs. Bernbaum nodded her head and Claire began to gather the tea things to put on the tray on the table. "I'm afraid we've tired you out, Mrs. Bernbaum. Perhaps you need to take a nap before getting ready."

"Thank you dear. Yes I'll probably have a short lay down. Just leave those, Anita or Jorges will get them later. It was so nice of you to come. I enjoyed the company. I hope I didn't bore you with my stories, but it does me good to remember."

"Not at all, it was so interesting. It certainly gives me a whole new perspective on life in Alaska. I'll probably have to search out some books about the Princess Sophia." She paused at the door. "See you later, Mrs. Bernbaum. And thanks again for the tea and the story."

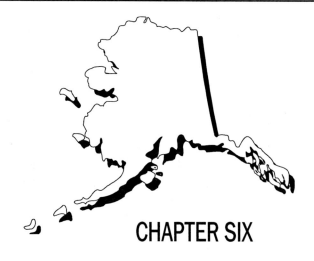

CHAPTER SIX

"You look very nice, dear. Is that dress new?"

"No, I got it for the gala I attended in Washington last fall. It's nice, isn't it? I found it at Loehman's, if you'd believe?" Her dress was a rich blue jersey material. The long A-line skirt clung nicely to her hips, the bottom of the full skirt revealing only glimpses of red toenails in her strappy sandals. The bodice had armholes slanted toward her neck, leaving her shoulders bare. The plain neckline was set off by the heavy gold and lapis lazuli Egyptian style necklace she bought to go with it. The matching earrings dangled almost to her shoulders, swaying every time she moved her head and making her feel sexy.

"It suits you. I feel a little dowdy beside you."

"I don't know why, your dress is stunning. I didn't know you had it."

"It's from one of the Richman Brothers' Christmas bashes. I have a closet full. I never get rid of them and every year in spite of my resolve not to, I end up buying something new to wear." She laughed at her foolishness. "At least it gave me several to choose from for this trip."

"Well, seeing as we both look so spiffy what do you think about having our picture taken together? If it's good we can buy copies, and if we don't like it we'll just leave it."

"Oh, what a good idea. Let's do it."

Claire and Millie went to stand in the short line for the photographer while Ruth and Lucy milled about with the other passengers, sipping champagne and talking to people they had met during the cruise. Even though this reception was for only half of the passengers, the ones who had the late dinner seating, there was still a crush of bodies in the lounge. Waiters moved through the crowd with trays of canapés and glasses of champagne and never got very far before having to return to the kitchen to replenish their trays.

Finished with the photographer, Millie determinedly pushed her way through the crowd in search of Ruth and Lucy. Claire was right behind her carrying a champagne glass. "There you are. Did you meet the Captain?"

"Yes, he's charming. And he looks just how you would imagine the captain to look, tall, handsome, competent and in control. If you want to meet him you'd better hurry because it's almost time for dinner."

"No, I don't need to meet him. At this point I doubt he can distinguish one person from another. Did you want to meet him, Claire?"

She shook her head. "Let's head toward the dining room. I'm hungry."

The dining room looked very festive. It took a moment for Claire to realize it wasn't the room which was festive, it was the people in it. Men clad in tuxedos, white dinner jackets and dark suits escorted their ladies, who wore spangles and beads, silks and satins, as well as sparkling jewels in their hair, around their necks and dripping from their arms. And the sound swelled with giggles, muted laughter and voices a little louder than usual, probably as a result of the champagne consumed before dinner. Accompanying the noise were the soft strains of music provided by a quartet of musicians located at the top of the graceful staircase rising from the center of the dining room to the balcony.

Claire looked around at her table mates. All the men wore black tuxedos except Ian who wore a white dinner jacket. Harold, sitting across from her, wore his with a silver cummerbund and despite his warning of yesterday about not liking to dress for dinner, appeared to be in fine spirits. Pearl wore a beautiful dress in a shimmery silver material which clung in all the right places and had a non-existent back. Ruth wore a deep red crepe dress, long and slinky. Lucy's dress was black, with an off-the-shoulder neck and a short full skirt. Even Mrs. Bernbaum looked exceptionally nice tonight in her light grey dress, which sported the puffy sleeves so popular in the 80's. However, it was obviously expensively cut and her red pin winked proudly from the shoulder of the dress.

The menu choices were in keeping with the special occasion including selections of filet mignon, lobster, crown rib lamb chops or Cornish game hens. Pedro took their choices with much good natured joshing and then left them to the drinks they had ordered.

"Good evening. I hope you are having a wonderful cruise." Antonio, the maitre d', circled their table, beaming with bonhomie. "It is my pleasure tonight to offer you a special appetizer which my good friend, the chef, has prepared only for your table." He signaled to Pedro. "So tonight you will have a little lobster soufflé to start; it will make your meal even more special."

Pedro and his assistant carried out plates holding tiny ramekins filled with a perfect soufflé and set one in front of each person. Murmurs of surprise and pleasure spread around the table as they each eyed the golden soufflés puffed up twice the height of the ramekin and topped with a small piece of lobster and a bit of green herb.

"Thank you."

"How nice."

"Oh, delicious."

Antonio bowed stiffly from the waist, smiling at each, but he winked at Lucy and left them to their dinner.

"Well, can you beat that? Why do you suppose we're getting such special treatment? I don't see any other tables being served this dish," Pearl said in amazement.

"Well, it might have something to do with his late night dance partner," Sean said soberly, nodding his head in Lucy's direction.

"Lucy, is this for your benefit?"

Lucy looking somewhat like the cat, who had swallowed the canary, merely shrugged in response to Pearl's question.

"Well, it's heavenly. I'm impressed the chef was willing to make soufflés when the meal they're serving is going to require a lot of effort by itself." Millie's voice reflected her admiration. She knew how tricky soufflés could be. Delivering ten of them while they were still perfect was almost a miracle.

"I think we shouldn't look a gift horse in the mouth. Lucy, if it's because of you, just keep doing what you're doing," was Ian's advice.

Later when they had finished the appetizers and were waiting for their next course, Claire said to Mrs. Bernbaum, who was sitting beside her, "You're looking very nice tonight. You must have had your nap."

"I did and then Dickie came and gave me a shot of pep."

"What exactly is that, a shot of pep?"

"Well, it's a shot of vitamins he's put together to give me a little energy boost. He calls it a 'vitamin cocktail.' I love it. It makes me feel young again." She smiled at Claire. "Well, maybe not young, but younger."

"Well, whatever it is, it seems to work. And I saw you and Richard at the photographer's booth before dinner having your picture taken. What a good idea."

"He insisted. He said we needed to have one together, while we were dressed up." She smiled as she glanced his way briefly. "He really is the sweetest boy. We loved his father, of course, but Dickie is just so thoughtful and considerate, and I have to admit his father never was."

"Mrs. Bernbaum, that brooch must be your favorite piece of jewelry because you wear it often. But tonight it looks like a whole new piece on that dress. Did Nate give it to you?"

She fingered the pin, looking down on it. "I asked Anita to clean it. Sometimes I don't notice when it has gotten a little grimy. Yes, it was a gift from Nate, and it was a gift from Bernie, too."

Claire's eyebrows rose in surprise.

"We were so happy when Nate came back from the war safely. We both knew how lucky we were he survived all those bombing missions. So many didn't, you know.

"But he didn't come home immediately, you see. While he was waiting to be shipped home he won this in a poker game.

"He loved to play poker. The men in Skagway thought it their duty to teach him certain basics of life and there was a lot of card playing going on during those long winter months. So he was very good at cards. He told me he got into this big game, seven card stud. Do you play poker, Claire?" Then seeing her nod she went on with her story. "Well, this time there was a huge pot. One guy, who considered himself a card shark, obviously thought he had the winning hand, so he added this brooch to the pot to help entice additional bets. He did have a good hand, full house, queens over sevens, I believe. But Nate took the pot with four threes.

"He said he knew he was lucky when he met me. Then he won that pot, which included a lot of money in addition to this piece. He said it was meant for me. He said it represented the luck I brought him."

"What is it? A garnet?"

"Oh no, dear. This is the *Heart of Persia*."

"Wow, it has a name? That sounds expensive."

"I suppose it is, although I haven't thought about its value for many years. The ruby was found in Persia in the seventeenth century. It's a Burmese Ruby, so how it got there is a mystery. It is quite without flaws and very rare. Someone in the French court had it made into this piece. The stone is irregular shaped, somewhat like a heart, hence its name and the other stones are rubies, peridots and diamonds. See, it's a pin and it also has a clasp so it can be worn on a chain as a pendant. Somehow during the French Revolution, it was liberated from its owner and so the record of ownership is somewhat sketchy. The man, who so foolishly added it to the pot, said he got it from a Russian refugee. How it got to Russia, I don't know."

"No wonder you wear it so much. But you said your second husband also gave it to you, how could that be?"

Mrs. Bernbaum's gnarled hand grabbed her arm, pulling her close as she lowered her voice, although truthfully everyone else at the table seemed to be occupied with other conversations.

"Nate's luck ran out and he needed money badly. I sold everything, the house, the jewelry, cars, everything; to raise the money he needed. His reputation was at stake, you see. And it saved him, but the stress, the anguish got him. He had a massive heart attack and died. He was only forty-two years old." The sadness in her eyes took Claire's breath away.

"Later, after I married Bernie, he tracked down and repurchased every piece of jewelry I had sold. It took him many years to finally recover the *Heart,* but he wouldn't give up. He said Nate meant for me to have it. He was convinced Nate wouldn't rest easy if he knew I had sold my jewelry for him. Bernie was such a kind man."

She let go of Claire's arm and reached up to fondle the brooch. "So you can see how special it is to me. That's why I wear it all the time."

"But Mrs. Bernbaum, aren't you nervous wearing it. It must be very valuable. What if someone steals it?"

"Dear, no one thinks it's real. It's so big, you see. Everyone just assumes it's costume jewelry and I never say any different."

"You told me..." Claire was uneasy. Truthfully, she had thought it was costume jewelry and very ugly costume jewelry at that.

"Yes, but I know you're safe, my dear. I know that much about people. I can tell who is a thief and who is not."

Just then Ruth asked across the table, "Are you going on shore in Juneau, Mrs. Bernbaum?"

When Claire looked up she saw Ian staring, and at first she thought he was staring at her and felt a little color creeping up her cheeks. But then she saw he was really looking at Mrs. Bernbaum. His gaze was so intense, she looked herself and saw his eyes were locked on the *Heart of Persia* pinned to Mrs. Bernbaum's shoulder. She flinched with unease. *Did Ian know about the jewel?*

Her brief moment of unease disappeared as the whole table joined the discussion about the myriad of choices they had for the next day. This would be their first port in Alaska and everyone was anxious to see everything, do everything.

And when they finally started pushing their chairs back from the table, Mrs. Bernbaum surprised them all by deciding to join them in the Starlight Lounge for a little dancing to help settle her food.

"It's been such a wonderful meal I just hate to end it. And I feel very good tonight." She took Dickie's arm and proceeded to the elevator.

Pearl and Harold had reached the lounge first and claimed two tables close to the dance floor and pulled up enough chairs to accommodate them. The music tonight was a selection of softer dance numbers from the fifties, sixties and seventies. The floor was crowded, but a few couples stood out. These were people who were "dancers" and used elaborate steps to show off their skill. Some may have been professional dancers at one time, some may have taken lessons and some just loved to dance, so had practiced and practiced. One woman, Millie and Claire had watched since the first night, danced with her partner whenever the opportunity arose. She was always wearing some beret or pillbox hat to match her outfit. Tonight's hat was a beaded red pillbox perched on top of her short curls which matched her red beaded dress. She wore professional dancing shoes. Her husband, who wore a beaded red bow tie and cummerbund with his tuxedo, saw to it she put the dancing shoes to good use.

Her smile was always wide, as was her partner's. They were both enjoying themselves.

Claire told her mother, "Those people are really perfect for cruising. Every night they have dancing and music available before and after dinner. I bet she doesn't have to worry about gaining weight on a cruise."

"She's certainly good. If I could dance like that I'd probably be cruising more often."

Claire just looked at her. "Like I'd believe that after it took so long for us to convince you to sign on for this one?"

Millie giggled. "I do thank you for that, dear. I really am glad you and Ruth talked me into it. I know I'm very reluctant to do these things, but I am enjoying myself. And

I did love the trip to Italy. So who says you can't change as you get older?

"Look at Mrs. Bernbaum dancing with Ian. How old is she? Ninety something? Well whatever, that woman still has moves." Claire watched Ian and Mrs. Bernbaum on the dance floor. Mrs. Bernbaum, tiny in comparison to Ian, still adroitly followed his every step without hesitation.

When the music ended Ian escorted Mrs. Bernbaum back to the table, then took Millie out to the floor. Richard brought Pearl back and took Ruth out. Sean claimed Lucy and Harold had a chance with his wife.

"Don't you want to dance?" Mrs. Bernbaum inquired. "Don't feel you have to stay here with me."

"No, of course not. I'll dance, don't worry. The evening is still young and I'll be here for a while."

"Well, when Dickie comes back I'm going to my cabin. No sense in inviting the wrath of Anita by staying out too long. And I need to be sensible. Tomorrow will come soon and I'm looking forward to my city tour. Nate talked about Juneau a lot. I'm anxious to see it."

The next time the dancers returned Claire danced with Sean. Of the two brothers she felt most comfortable with him. He was a genial man, good natured without that slight gleam of mischief she frequently saw in his brother's eye, which somehow made her uneasy. However, later dancing with Ian, she admitted they were both excellent dancers. The evening wore on, Harold and Pearl left, Richard had never returned from delivering his aunt to her cabin and Antonio joined them, as did Pat and John, an English couple they met at breakfast one morning.

Antonio danced as if he was a professional and took each of the women for a turn on the dance floor, but it was obvious who he was interested in. Claire wasn't surprised to find Lucy and Antonio had slipped away to pursue their own agenda.

"Mom, I'm turning in. It's been fun, but it's my bedtime."

The others cajoled her to stay a while longer, but she shook her head. "It's time." So she left promising to call her mother in the morning when she was ready for breakfast.

* * *

Ian and Sean stood on the dock waiting for the other people scheduled on the helicopter tour and dogsled adventure to arrive. Sean glanced around to make sure no one was close enough to overhear. "Ian, I don't see how you're going to do it. She wears it every day. How can you possibly get it away from her without the ship's security people getting on it like a flash."

Ian smiled. "Did you see it winking last night, Sean? Did you feel the pull?"

Sean was annoyed. He opened his mouth to protest, but then, surprising them both, he nodded. "I have to say it did grab me. It looked beautiful last night. I remember Pap describing it and the look he would get on his face while he talked about it." Then he straightened, gave himself a little shake. "But Ian, I still think it is too risky. Give it up man. Let it go. It was only an old man's dream."

Just then they were interrupted by their guide arriving with the couple who would be joining them for this excursion. They were herded into a van and took off for the heliport, all the time the guide was explaining what they could expect from this excursion.

* * *

The tram rose effortlessly up the cable giving them an unhindered view of the dock, their ship and three other ships lined up along the quay. Claire eagerly snapped pictures hoping to capture the view. And while she looked through the lens she blocked out, somewhat, the fact that she was sailing through thin air, with no support but the cable they clung to. Heights always made her nervous.

"This is amazing. Look, there are four ships docked. I guess tourists are a large part of their summer income. That must be close to 10,000 people arriving for the day," Lucy pointed out.

"No wonder it seemed so crowded when we got off the ship."

It was a clear day, but cold. Very quickly it seemed, the cable car reached the top and everyone assembled for their guided nature walk. The trail leisurely led them through the forest and meadows; frequently they stopped for detailed descriptions of what they were seeing and to snap pictures. Their guide pointed out an eagles' nest high on top of a dead tree. And while they stood there listening to him, the eagle returned, claiming it for his own. The guide was knowledgeable and gave an entertaining, educational overview of Alaska, and Juneau in particular, but eventually, the trail brought them to the Mt. Roberts Nature Center.

"Oh goody, a gift shop." Millie loved to shop.

"And food. I'm a little peckish. What about you all? Do you have time for a bite of something?" And Ruth was always interested in having something to eat.

Claire and Lucy checked their watches and agreed they did have time. "We'll need sustenance to prepare us for our hike this afternoon."

"Oh dear, I hope it won't be too strenuous. I mean it sounded like it's for serious hikers, Claire. Do you think you're up to it?" The frown lines appeared between Millie's eyes.

"Mother, relax. I'm sure I'm up to it. I'm in pretty good shape. All that lifting and shelving cartons of books keeps me strong. I'm sure I'll enjoy it and it's a good way to see some of Alaska, the real Alaska."

Lucy nodded her agreement. She wasn't worried about keeping up with the others as she belonged to a hiking group which went out once a week. The range of mountains on the San Francisco peninsula, which separated the Pacific Ocean from the bayside communities, provided many opportunities for hikers and Lucy's group took advantage of their proximity.

"But I do want to pick up some bottled water and some snack food. You never know when you might need them when you're in the wilderness. It's best to be prepared." Then she laughed at Millie's alarmed look. "Relax Millie, we always take supplies when we hike. It's only sensible. I've never gotten lost or met a bear."

"Well you've never been in Alaska before," was Millie's terse reply.

* * *

The sun was blinding, the crowd confusing, as people lined up to get on the right bus for their shore excursion. Others wandered about looking for friends and a few people negotiated with taxi drivers. Anita glanced at her watch as she drifted toward the street, trying to avoid being caught up in a group destined for one of the buses. *Dreamy Seas* was docked right behind a mammoth Holland American liner, so the crowd was a combination of passengers from both ships.

She still didn't see her friend. She wondered if she would show. She sighed. She was looking forward to visiting St. Terese's Shrine, but if Kim didn't show up, she didn't intend to go back on board for a while. She would just wander around town and enjoy being on solid ground.

Where was Kim? She turned around scanning the crowd, pulling her coat tight around her because of the sharply cold wind.

Honk, honk!

She looked at the jerk sounding his horn, did a double take and then hurried to the street. "I was looking for you in the crowd," she said, pulling open the door to the battered old Jeep Cherokee. She climbed into the passenger seat and fastened her seat belt. "Where did this come from?"

"Rent-a-wreck, just what we need, huh? Did you think I was standing you up?"

Anita nodded, a sour expression passed over her face. "I thought maybe your boss wanted you to do something for him. But I'm glad we're going. I need to talk to St. Terese about a miracle."

"Oh, something wrong?"

"I swear Mrs. Bernbaum is losing it. She was up until all hours last night. She even went dancing after dinner, mind you. Dancing! She's more than ninety; she should act her age. It's all because of this nephew of hers. He is really a bad influence on her. He gives her these shots of vitamins, at least he says they're vitamins and she feels she can do anything." She paused a moment before she predicted with gloom, "She's going to dance herself right into the grave."

"Well, at least it won't be an early grave." Kim giggled.

Anita frowned at her. "That's not funny. She's usually very sensible, but now she's acting like a flighty teenager. Staying up late, having the ladies over for tea parties, going dancing, and now, today, she's going on a tour of Juneau with her precious Dickie. They're planning on taking the tram." She nodded her head at it as they passed the tram station. "This is not going to last. Mark my words. If she doesn't slow down, she'll wear out. Kaput! And that's just what I told her this morning."

Kim looked impressed. "So what did she say?"

"She just waved me off. She told me to go ashore and have a nice day." Anita looked straight ahead her face settled in a grim expression. "It's just not natural. She's an old woman; she should act like one."

Kim had managed to turn the Jeep about so they were now headed down the street in the opposite direction. "Well, let's do that, let's have a nice day. I got some maps and I talked to the people at the Tourist Information booth so I know just where we're going. And if we go too far we'll just run out of road and have to turn around and come back.

"Did you know that Juneau's road only goes forty miles and then ends? You can't get in or out of this town by car. So every person, every car or truck and everything they sell has come in here by boat or plane. It's like being on an island."

Anita interrupted excitedly. "Oh, look, there's the Red Dog Saloon. They talked about it in the lecture about Juneau. I saw it last night on the TV."

Kim swerved to the left with the road, following the flat land along the water's edge instead of going straight, which would have taken them up the hills where the town climbed up toward the mountains.

"Maybe when we come back we can go in there for a sandwich. I'd like to see it. I understand it was built during the Gold Rush and inside is like stepping back in time to those days."

"Sure, why not?" Kim was amenable. She knew they wouldn't be visiting the Red Dog, but didn't see any reason Anita should know that, too.

CHAPTER SEVEN

The hikers were strewn along the boulder-edged path enjoying a well-deserved break. They had been hiking for a while and the last half hour had been uphill. Claire had taken off two of the multiple layers under her windbreaker, one sweater she stuffed in her backpack and the other, the heavier one she had tied around her waist. She wasn't panting, but she definitely felt a little winded. She fished out her bottle of water and took a long drink. Lucy was next to her and looked as fresh as she was when they started.

"Whew, you don't even look as if you need a break."

Lucy smiled. "Maybe not, but I love the chance to sit and look around. You never know what you'll see."

That was true. After they startled some deer and what someone said looked like a bobcat, and in spite of her reassurance to her mother that they weren't likely to find bear, she had been warily eyeing the forest. If they did come across bear, she'd rather see him before he saw her.

But their guide assured them they would be safe and he had a rifle slung across his back which he said was mostly to reassure them, but held powerful enough tranquilizer darts to stop a dozen bears. Actually, he was full of information which he passed on to them at the beginning of the hike, while they were still occasionally meeting other hikers on the trail.

"Don't be wandering off," he told them. "A few years ago a young man from one of the cruise ships, who fancied himself an experienced outdoorsman, took off into the mountains on a hike. When it came time for the ship to sail, it left without him. His family stayed to help search for him, but even with tracking dogs the search teams had no luck. He just disappeared. The following summer he was found, at least his remains were found." He shook his head, a sober expression on his face. "Alaska has its own Bermuda Triangle. It starts in Juneau and goes north and west. We actually lose the equivalent of one person per month here. Sometimes a plane goes down, never to be found; sometimes a boat disappears and many times someone just walks away. 'Gone Missing' is what they say." He shook his head. "Alaska is beautiful, but it's a wild land; don't ever believe it isn't extremely dangerous."

He meant to impress them with the importance of taking prudent precautions before entering the wilderness. He made his point. Take water, food, maps of the trails, tell someone where you're going, or better yet, take others with you. If you get separated or lost, stay where you are, blow the whistle he gave each of them and wait for someone to find you.

It had been a sobering start to their trek through the wilderness. And as they had moved further into a remote area where they no longer met up with other hikers, they were careful to stay within sight of the others in their party.

"I'm so glad we signed up for this hike. You can just imagine we're following a game trail and there are no people anywhere around," Lucy murmured as she lay back against the rock, her eyes dreamy, listening to the music of nature, silence.

The others seemed to be of the same mind, content to sit quietly and absorb the air, the smells, the sounds of Alaska. After a while there was a general stirring as people made ready to continue their hike. This time the guide set a slower pace as they strolled through the forest heading for the waterfall he promised to deliver for the next break. Now the path was very dim, really only a game trail, certainly not like the trail prepared by the Forestry Service which they started on. When they were in the shade they could feel the bite of the cold, the promise of the winter soon to come, but in the clearings and the meadows the sun made itself felt. It was easy to understand how the Alaskans grew such splendid vegetables and flowers in their short growing period, the sun apparently tried to make up for its short appearance with intensity.

They heard the waterfall before they saw it, even if initially they didn't know what they were hearing. The soft roar, first only background noise, kept getting louder as they approached and when they emerged from the trail on the outcropping of granite, there it was. A deep gorge with steep granite sides was in front of them. To the right of where they stood the water fell from above; cascading, foaming, crashing against rocks and slamming into the wall of the gorge on the way down. The spray caught the sun beams, flashing rainbows in all directions, while the water roared its way to the bottom of the gorge.

The guide gathered them around and shouted so they could hear him. They would spend some time here and then head back to the van. If anyone wanted to go down the gorge a bit there was a trail, he pointed over the side of the gorge, but reminded them every step down would mean a triple effort coming up. He instructed everyone to assemble in a half hour at a spot they had passed a little way back.

Claire loved the falls and spent most of her time trying to capture the rainbows on her digital camera. Lucy wandered off with a couple of the other hikers to check out the source of the water. A couple of people investigated the trail down the side of the cliff, but it wasn't surprising to see them decide against going down the deep gorge. It would be a very steep ascent.

Eventually Claire joined the others assembling at the meeting spot. She fished her water bottle and an energy bar out of her backpack and settled herself in for a snack while she was waiting.

"How you doing?"

She stretched out her legs, wiggled her toes in the sturdy walking shoes she brought at Lucy's insistence and smiled. "Great. I might have some soreness in my calves tomorrow, but right now my blood is tingling through my body."

Lucy nodded. "I don't know what I like best about hiking, what it makes my body feel like, or how it affects my soul. You know when you live in cities and are surrounded by people you just need a little solitude and a commune with nature once in a while."

Claire agreed, thinking she should make more of an effort to join Lucy's hiking group from time to time. Then she gathered up her trash, stuffed it with the water bottle in her pack and got to her feet, ready for the final stage of the hike.

This last stage was actually the more difficult. She realized her concern about aching calves was nothing compared to her new concern about the muscles in her shins and at the tops of her knees, which were feeling the strain of the downhill trek. She decided she would rub some ointment on them before she went to bed and maybe tomorrow would be a good day to try out the Jacuzzi.

She was glad when they reached the wider trail near the end. Now the hikers spread out, walking two and three abreast, talking quietly amongst themselves.

"Well, we're at day five, have you found romance yet?" Lucy inquired with an arched eyebrow.

"Me find it? I thought you were in charge of that?"

"Well, I managed to secure three eligible candidates at our own dinner table. I think I more than delivered."

Claire couldn't contain her spurt of laughter. "You? You secured the table mates? Good try, but I think fate was responsible for that, or maybe your friend, the maitre d'."

"Whatever. Do any of them interest you? And what about your mother? Is she interested in either the charming Ian or the sweet Sean?"

"Actually, she hasn't said, but I'm sure she's been enjoying their company, especially on the dance floor. It's nice to have a variety of partners willing and available so we don't have to vie for the attention of the hosts in order to dance. But as far as I'm concerned, they're all either too old or too full of themselves."

"You mean Dickie or Richard as we know him? He's something, isn't he? Oh well, Mrs. Bernbaum is charmed by him and he treats her well, so that's all that counts. I guess I'll have to look around for a different sort for you. Maybe Antonio knows someone who would do."

"Well, speaking of Antonio, Lucy, what's up with you two?"

Lucy laughed. "Those Italians are so charming, aren't they?"

"How would I know?"

"Well, you were in Italy not long ago. You should know how they are. He's no more interested in a serious relationship than I am. But he loves to flirt and I'm fortunate enough to have attracted his attention. He's says on the very first evening he knew he wanted to get to know me. And believe me, with all the unattached women on this cruise, I'm flattered."

Claire watched her friend closely. Seeing how pleased she appeared, she only issued one caution. "Well, just don't lose your heart. It's only a shipboard romance, certainly not worth a broken heart."

"Don't worry about me, Claire. I'm not intending to ever lose my heart again. I've been there, done that, more than once. I know what I want, and it does not include a serious relationship. I just shudder when I hear Mrs. Bernbaum talking about her one true love. I don't believe it."

They fell silent, each occupied with the thought of true love. Claire didn't know if she believed in true love or not. Her mother apparently did, but then the little cynical part of her wondered whether it was her mother's love for her deceased husband or her fear of the unknown which prevented her from finding, or even looking for another love. Mrs. Bernbaum was convinced her Nate was her soul mate even though she had been married once before and once after Nate. And truthfully, her last husband sounded like a true winner. Even so, he was cheated out of her full love by Mrs. Bernbaum's preoccupation with Nate. It sounded like *Gone with the Wind*, with Scarlett O'Hara ignoring the sexy Rhett because of her infatuation with the wimpy Ashley. What a terrible waste that was, Claire thought.

And there was Jack. There was definitely something about the combination of her and Jack which was attention getting. She thought how much more fun the cruise would be with him on board, but then she reminded herself sternly, he wasn't. However, she realized that maybe one of the reasons she wasn't looking for a romantic interest on board was she was always comparing other men to Jack and they fell a little short. Not that he was a paragon. No, in fact, sometimes he was very annoying. But he did make her blood tingle, he did make her laugh and when they were in danger, somehow being with him made her feel safe.

Enough of these useless thoughts about Jack, she told herself as they reached the van. But, she said a silent prayer that he was safe wherever he was.

Everyone was subdued on the ride back to the dock, tired from their hike, and in awe of the country they had seen. Back at the dock, Lucy glanced at her watch and said, "What say we have a beer at the Red Dog Saloon?" She nodded toward the picturesque saloon sitting down the road where it forked to follow the waterfront.

Claire agreed, secretly pleased to have the chance to see the historic saloon. "I just have to get on board with enough time to clean up and change before dinner. Even though tonight is a casual night, I don't think they mean this casual."

The saloon could have come straight from an old western movie. Its double swinging doors faced the street corner. Its brash honky-tonk music spilled out on the sidewalk. It was jammed with cruise ship passengers, who apparently all had the same idea. Undaunted, they squeezed themselves into the crowd and looked around for a place to sit.

"There, see? That's Heidi and Bob. We had breakfast with them one morning and they played on our Trivia team. Come on, she's waving us over. We can share their table."

Bob stood up and secured an unused chair from another table to add to the three they had. Claire and Lucy gratefully joined them and Claire introduced Lucy.

"What do you think? Isn't this something? It's probably just like it was in the heydays of the Gold Rush." Bob sipped from the large glass of beer in front of him.

Heidi was drinking iced tea and picking at the plate in front of her. "Just to tide us over until dinner," was her explanation of the half eaten portion of smoked salmon, diced onions and crackers. "We took a helicopter ride over the glacier. It was amazing, wasn't it Bob?"

When the harried waitress arrived they ordered the same beer as Bob was drinking and then looked around at the interior of the saloon. It was dark, smoky, grimy and full of character.

"Not only has it been here since the Gold Rush Days, but they still have all the dust to prove it," Lucy commented. No one appeared to mind the grunge, people were eating and drinking, while they stared at the stuffed animals and the bric-a-brac stuck to the walls. And the beer was good and cold, what more could you ask?

* * *

For a while Kim concentrated on the traffic moving through the town while Anita seemed content to look at the scenery, but then they were past the congestion and heading north.

"Is the Shrine very far?"

"I think it's about an hour, but allowing for finding our way it might take a little while longer. I think this is our turn-off coming up." She put on her blinker and got into the left lane.

"It says Douglas Island. Is that where it is?" Anita sat up looking around as Kim crossed over the bridge and then, instead of turning left as everyone else was doing, she turned right going north on a road winding around the edge of the island.

It wasn't long before they left all signs of civilization behind. Except for the paved road they followed, they could have been in the wilderness.

"Are you sure this is the right way?" Anita was worried. "I haven't seen any signs."

"I haven't either, but this is the way the lady told me. Maybe they don't use signs for religious shrines. Let's go a little further. It hasn't been an hour quite yet. I sure hope we find it soon 'cause I need to pee."

They continued down the deserted road only passing another car once. It was beautiful country, quiet, peaceful and very green. Sometimes they caught glimpses of the water through the trees on the right, while on the left the vegetation climbed the hills which made up the island.

Suddenly Kim pulled over and stopped the car.

"What? Are we there? What are you doing?" Anita sat forward looking around for a sign.

"I have to pee. I just decided I'm not going to wait. I'm going down behind a tree. I'll just be a minute." And she climbed out of the car and disappeared into the trees.

Anita rolled down her window and breathed in the chilly air. It was very quiet after the motor stopped pinging, only the sound of the breeze stirring the leaves and occasionally the call of a bird.

"Anita, Anita, come here and see this," Kim's voice called.

"What do you want?" Anita yelled back, reluctant to get out of the car, even more reluctant to go into the brush.

"Come on down here, you have to see this." Kim's voice was excited, even though muted by the vegetation.

Her curiosity piqued, Anita reluctantly rolled up her window and got out of the Jeep. She looked for a way through the trees, carefully selecting where she placed her foot for each step, lest she slip and fall. She made her way down the bank toward Kim's voice, muttering to herself. "This better be good, Kim, 'cause I don't like this."

She moved through the trees, peering carefully around to be sure she didn't come across a snake or any other thing repellent to her.

She saw Kim, standing in heavy brush near the edge of the water, her arm out, pointing to a spot out of sight. "Look there, can you see it?" Her voice was excited, trembling.

Anita edged carefully toward Kim until she was right beside her and she still didn't see what she was pointing at. She leaned forward trying to see.

The only and last thing she saw was a brilliant flash of white and then, total blackness.

* * *

Kim held the large rock tightly clutched in her hand, her arm stiff, the vibration of the blow still quivered through her body. Finally, she looked down at the crumpled form at her feet, while she fought to keep the contents of her stomach in place. She had no doubt Anita was dead. Her eyes stared at nothing and blood oozed from the back of her head. Suddenly she turned and heaved the rock as hard as she could into the water. Then she wrapped her arms around her body as a shiver of revulsion shook her.

Kim didn't know how long she stood there staring at Anita's body, but eventually she realized there was danger in leaving her car on the road long enough to attract attention. She made herself feel for a pulse in Anita's throat. She didn't want to touch the body, but she had to do it. He insisted she make sure Anita was dead.

She picked up Anita's purse, thinking how like her to carry her purse with her into the woods, opened it and removed the money, slipping it into her own pocket before removing Anita's ship identification card and pocketing it so she could use it later. She left everything else in the purse and took it down to the water's edge. She filled it with small rocks, closed and fastened it before throwing it as far out in the water as she could. She stood watching while it sank.

She looked again at the body. Anita was wearing rings, a watch and earrings. Heavy gold, not to her taste, but nice. No, she decided, none of it was worth the risk of having something which would tie her to Anita. She left the jewelry, and the body, and headed back to the car.

She breathed a sigh of relief. It was over. Now she realized her determination to overcome her horror at doing the deed must have caused her to over-compensate so she had swung the rock with such force it had shattered Anita's skull with one blow.

But she had done it!

She felt a shiver of excitement run up her spine. It hadn't been nearly as bad as she feared. Now that is was done she felt empowered. Now she felt she could do anything.

* * *

"There you are dear, sit next to me." Her mother indicated the empty chair beside her. "Did you have a nice day?"

"Yes, and no bear." She smiled. "But you were kind of right. Our guide told us they see a lot of them. He was actually carrying a weapon in case we did run into one who was aggressive."

"Yes, he says they don't lose many of their tourists, but sometimes the locals, who think they're more experienced, get tangled up with a crotchety one." Lucy grinned evilly, deliberately baiting Millie. But when she saw Millie's eyes widen with alarm she said contritely, "I'm teasing you, Millie. There are bears; sometimes they can be ornery so they take precautions to make sure no one is hurt. It is really very safe. And it was wonderful, wasn't it Claire?"

Just then Sean and Ian appeared, accepting a menu card from Pedro as they sat down. It was obvious they had been in the sun from the pink glow on their faces and the white around their eyes where their sunglasses sat.

"How was dog sledding?"

"Mush, Haw," Ian reached his arm out as if he was cracking a whip. "We're both experienced now. Next year we'll probably be entering the Iditarod."

"Entering it, hell, we're going to win it. The dogs do all the work. We just ride along and try not to fall off our sleds." Everyone laughed at Sean's assessment of the famous dogsled race, then busied themselves with the menu while drinks were ordered.

"Where are Pearl and Harold tonight?"

"I think she said they were going to one of those Salmon Bakes and wouldn't be back until late," Mrs. Bernbaum told them. "I'm sure we'll hear about it tomorrow."

"And how was your day Mrs. Bernbaum?"

"Oh, my dear, I had a lovely day. Dickie is so good to me." She patted his arm and he smiled at her. "We went on the City Tour and then to the top of the mountain on the cable car. What a view. Then we watched a most interesting video show up there. Did anyone else see it?" She peered around the table and seeing no one did she continued. "It was very interesting, it's a shame you missed it. Anyway, it was a lovely day and even though it was chilly, the air was so crisp it was quite invigorating."

Claire noticed she did have a sparkle in her eye tonight. "Did your caregiver go with you or is she going home?"

The smile on Mrs. Bernbaum's face faltered. "Oh, dear. That Anita, she refuses to go back. She insists she will stay to the end." She shook her head. "She wasn't back from shore when I came to dinner. I hope when she gets here, she'll be in a better frame of mind after spending the entire day with her feet planted on the ground."

"But enough of her. I see by the schedule we will be visiting the glacier tomorrow and I thought if you wanted to sit on my balcony and have tea with me, we would have a ringside seat. My steward said we need to be outdoors when we see it because when the glacier calves, that's when big pieces fall off, it makes all kinds of noise which will be exciting."

"That's very nice of you, Mrs. Bernbaum. I'd love to come," Millie agreed, and Claire and Lucy nodded.

"Are we invited too?" Sean inquired.

"Of course, we'll have a tea party. Everybody come. It will be fun. You'll come, won't you Dickie? I know you're not that fond of tea but..., I know, I'll order some wine too."

Soon, it evolved from a tea party to a tea party with cocktails.

"Oh, Pearl and Harold must be invited. If anyone sees them, please tell them. When the ship arrives at the Hubbard Glacier the naturalist will talk over the speakers, just come to my cabin then. Oh, what fun it will be."

The dinner seemed to pass swiftly. Everyone was talking about their activities in Juneau and what to expect on seeing Hubbard Glacier the next day.

The blare of the ship's horn sounded through the ship.

"We're off. It must be ten o'clock. I'll say this for the Captain, he casts off and docks right on schedule." Lucy glanced at her watch, then looked up as one of the passengers, already on their way out of the dining room, lurched against her chair, the motion of the ship taking him by surprise. She smiled at his embarrassed apology. "No problem, don't worry."

"Ladies, they're having line dancing and the Texas Two Step tonight, are you all going to join us?" Ian's invitation sounded intriguing.

"I don't know how to do the Texas Two Step. Besides, don't you have to wear cowboy boots or something?" Millie wanted to know.

"If you can walk you can do the Two Step. Trust me on this. But I confess I don't know about the boots." Sean shook his head.

"Is it anything like Texas Hold'em? I'm good at that," Ruth offered.

Claire laughed. Ruth did love her cards. "I'm sure we don't need boots. I saw the line dancing lesson they were giving the other day in the lounge when I walked through, and it looked fun."

Lucy nodded. "I'm game."

"What about you, Mrs. Bernbaum? Feel like dancing tonight?"

"Oh, my no, Sean. I'm going to be very happy to go to bed right after dinner."

"Do you want me to walk you back to your room?" Claire was quick to offer.

"No, no, I'll deliver Auntie tonight. Thanks for the offer, Claire. But I might just join you all later to see this Texas dancing."

Ian and Sean pushed back their chairs. "We'll grab a table upstairs. Join us when you can."

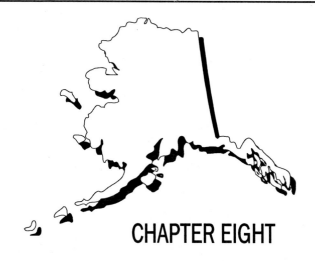

CHAPTER EIGHT

They could hear the phone ringing from the corridor, so Dickie hurriedly inserted his aunt's key card in the door and rushed to pick up the phone. "Hello, hello? Yes, this is Mrs. Bernbaum's cabin. Who? Who is this? I see, yes, I see. All right!" He hung up the receiver and looked at Mrs. Bernbaum with a puzzled look.

"That was security. They say Anita didn't board."

Mrs. Bernbaum looked around the cabin as if Anita might be lurking in the shadows. "Anita didn't board? That's not possible. Where would she be?"

"Are you sure she wasn't going to go home from here? Could she have changed her mind?"

"No, no she would have told me." Mrs. Bernbaum shook her head emphatically. "Besides, she would have wanted me to pay for the ticket, I'm sure." She sat down in the chair heavily, as if overwhelmed by the situation. "Where could she be?"

The sharp knock at the door signaled the arrival of the ship's security men. There were two of them, wearing their discrete blazers with little insignias. Their ramrod stiff posture reeked of a military background.

"Larry Smithston, madam. Sorry to bother you this evening." The one obviously in charge, took charge. "We show Anita Fernandez, assigned to this cabin, left the ship today at ten, thirty-nine hundred. She did not board again before we sailed." His expression was so grim that Mrs. Bernbaum felt a shiver of fright.

"I can't believe it. What could have happened to her?"

"Are you Florence Bernbaum?" At Mrs. Bernbaum's nod, he turned to Dickie. "And you, sir?"

"I'm Mrs. Bernbaum's nephew, Dr. Richard Walmer. I'm also her physician. I'm in cabin sixty, seventy-two."

The Security Officer nodded. His companion made a note on the pad he carried.

"Are you sure she's not on board somewhere?" Mrs. Bernbaum couldn't believe Anita would stay ashore without telling her.

"She did not board the ship madam. We're positive of that. Is she a relative?"

"She's my caregiver. She's been with me for four years now, and she is not a flighty or careless person. I know that. Something must have happened to her. We need to find her? Dickie, Dickie, do something..." Mrs. Bernbaum was agitated. The seriousness of the situation was dawning on her.

"Now, now Auntie, it's probably just a minor thing. Don't get all excited." Dickie's voice was calm as he tried to reassure his aunt. "Officer, what procedures do you use in these situations? It must happen from time to time."

"We've already notified our agent in Juneau and he will begin a search if you don't know where she is."

"I just can't imagine..." Mrs. Bernbaum looked at Dickie with concern as she explained. "Dickie, I'm afraid I was rather cavalier with Anita this morning. She was upset and full of dire warnings about my behavior and I just brushed her off. Do you think I made her so mad she just left?" She looked at the security officers. "She is really a help to me, but she can be a dampening influence. She didn't think I should come on this cruise and she keeps telling me I'm foolishly overdoing it. I'm afraid I've become rather impatient with her. I suggested she fly home from here, but she refused to consider it. She said she didn't dare, as there was no telling what I'd do without her to keep watch over me."

"Could she have changed her mind about going home? Did you check to see if she took any of her belongings?"

Mrs. Bernbaum shook her head slowly. She hadn't even thought of that. Slowly she got out of her chair, the lateness of the day and now this worry made her years weigh heavily on her. She went into the bedroom. Right away she could see some of Anita's things were gone.

She returned to the living room saying, "I'm so mad at her! Her toothbrush, hair brush and a small bag are gone. And it looks like some of her clothes are missing too. Oh, I'm really annoyed with her. This is so unlike her. Did she just want to worry me?"

Dickie hurried to his aunt, slipped his arm around her and guided her back to the chair she had left. "Now, now, I'm sure she didn't mean to worry you. Maybe she was just mad and decided to leave. I'll bet if we call her home tomorrow or the next day, she'll answer the phone."

"She's isn't a hiker? You don't think she would have tried to go off into the woods on her own, do you?"

"Anita? Oh no, she's very much a city person. I don't think you could have dragged her out into the woods." She stopped. "Unless, someone did drag her off." There was a look of horror on her face. "Oooh, could it be the work of a serial killer?" She was getting upset again.

"No, no, it sounds like your caregiver just took off. Maybe she was mad, but if her things are missing we can assume she planned to leave. And she is an adult, so of course she has the right to leave if she wishes. Do you want us to pursue a search of Juneau?"

They all looked at Mrs. Bernbaum while she considered the situation. She looked at Dickie who suggested, "Why don't we wait until we try to call her in San Francisco. If we can't reach her by phone by the day after tomorrow, we'd better take steps to search for her. And if she just missed the boat, she'll probably catch up with us at our next port, right?"

"Yes, our agent frequently works with passengers to help them arrange transportation to catch up with the ship they missed. If that is what's happened to Ms. Fernandez , you'll be seeing her in Sitka. If we hear anything from our agent we'll let you know. Likewise, if you hear from her or contact her, please tell us."

Dickie nodded solemnly. "I think that since some of her things are missing, she must have decided to leave. As soon as we find out for sure, we'll let you know. Thank you for your help."

When Dickie let the men out he returned to his aunt and said, "Now don't you go getting yourself all upset about this. It was very inconsiderate of Anita to act so irresponsibly, but we'll straighten it all out when we get home. Meanwhile, remember this is your life quest. It's something you've wanted to do and you're doing it. Don't let Anita's peevish behavior ruin it for you." He looked at her carefully, trying to interpret her expression. At her nod, he smiled. "Okay, will you need some help getting to bed?"

"I'm not senile yet, Dickie." She realized her reply was a little sharp so she patted his arm and said softly, "I'll be fine, don't worry. I'm tired from our day out so I'm sure I'll sleep in spite of my worry about Anita.

"I can give you something?"

"No, I don't like those pills. They make me stupid the next day. No, if I don't sleep, I'll just sit here and watch the waves. Don't worry, go on and meet up with the others for the dancing or whatever it is you young people do at this time of the night." She waved him away so he left, somewhat reluctantly. She sat back and thought about her conversation with Anita this morning. She still couldn't believe Anita had gotten mad enough to abandon her after years of putting up with her demands. And she was ashamed to admit she didn't tell Anita often enough how she appreciated her care and her attention to all the details, even though she paid Anita generously to do them. Admittedly, sometimes Anita was too bossy, but right now she didn't care about that. She just wanted to know where she was, and that she was all right.

*   *   *

She walked crisply across the marble lobby, bathed in the love shining from Nate's eyes as he stood beside the table waiting for her. She was glad she wore her new Channel suit with the silver fox fur piece draped over her shoulders. She knew she looked smart. She took pride that her tiny hat was tipped charmingly over her forehead, the attached veil slightly masking her eyes. And she knew others, not just Nate, were admiring her. She smiled at him as she slipped into the chair he held. Mariso arrived just then with the drink Nate had ordered for her.

"Good evening, Mrs. Witherspoon. Here's your Martini, just as you like it."

She smiled at him, removing her gloves and carefully laying them on the little cocktail table before taking a sip, then sighing with approval. "Perfect, perfect as usual Mariso, thank you."

Then turning to her husband she asked, "Been waiting long darling? I promise I did hurry."

Nate's smile was indulgent. "No problem, I needed a little time to think; and to unwind with a couple of those."

"What about?" Seeing his puzzled look she repeated, "What were you thinking about?"

"How lucky I am, of course." His tone was light, but his eyes were serious. He scanned her face. *"I still can't believe how lucky I am. I found you. I went to war and came back in one piece. We've been married for five years and, impossible as it sounds, I find I love you more each day. Tell me, how can that be?"*

She reached out and clasped his hand, tears springing to her own eyes. *"Love, I'm the lucky one. You make me so happy."*

"Oops, I guess I should take this back then." He kept his face serious, but his eyes were dancing with mischief.

"What's that? A present? Did you get me another present?" She couldn't help herself, she loved presents; especially she loved the ones Nate picked out for her.

"I thought it would match your brooch."

Unconsciously one hand went to finger the Heart of Persia pinned to her suit lapel at the same time her other hand darted out to retrieve the box he held. She opened it to reveal a bracelet of baguette diamonds and peridots, interspersed with round cut rubies. It was wonderful. She looked at him with shining eyes and then held out her wrist for him to fasten the bracelet.

"How did you ever find something so perfect? It just matches. Nate, you spoil me so." She couldn't stop admiring her wrist, twisting her arm so the dim lights caught in the stones of the bracelet. *"I'll treasure it."*

He watched her closely and deciding she really did love it, he relaxed and sipped his drink. *"Drink up, little lady. We have reservations at Ernie's. We're meeting the Amersans there. Business tonight, but if all goes well we'll stop at Bimbo's 365 for a little dancing before going home, all right?"*

She laughed. Their life was like that, business meetings in posh restaurants, dining with the elite of the city, dancing and clubbing with the trendy group and stunning gifts for no reason at all. And she never took one minute of it for granted. Always, every minute she was thankful for finding Nate. She knew enough to enjoy every moment. But later that night she would wonder if she always suspected it would end suddenly.

It was during coffee and liqueurs, after she and Irene Amersan had returned from freshening their make-up, it happened. The two uniformed police officers pulled Nate's chair back, grabbing him by the arms and pulling him to his feet before slapping cuffs on him.

"Nathaniel Witherspoon, you're under arrest."

"What, what are you saying?" Nate's face turned white, then suffused with the red of either embarrassment or anger.

"Nate, Nate, what's happening?" She was confused, frightened by the policemen's belligerence.

"Flo, call Clarke. Tell him to meet me down at the station..." Nate had control of himself now. Even as the policemen were hustling him out of the crowded restaurant, he called over his shoulder to the Amersans, "Don't worry Buddy, just a misunderstanding. My lawyer will get it all straightened out. I'll call you and tell you all about it." Then with a last smile at his wife, he was gone.

It seemed an eternity, but actually it was probably only a few moments until all the other diners turned their attention back to their dinners, although it was apparent they were still discussing the vulgar interruption.

Flo shook herself out of her shocked trance and smiled apologetically at the Amersans. "I'm so sorry our dinner was interrupted." She signaled the waiter for the check.

"Let me get that." Buddy reached for it, but Flo snatched it from the waiter.

"No, Nate is paying for this." Her voice was shrill with panic as she took bills from her purse and laid them on the tray. Then she smiled tightly, attempting to make the situation seem normal. "I'm sure it is all just a misunderstanding, but Clarke will get it all settled and Nate *will give you a call to explain everything. Meanwhile, I know you will excuse me, I find I have some business to attend to." She got up, collected her purse and gloves, and then strolled through the elite restaurant, chin high, not even glancing at the other diners.*

She took a cab to their apartment building, high on top of Russian Hill overlooking the Bay, where she went directly to the phone and attempted to reach Clyde Clarke. It wasn't easy finding him, but she was determined. Already Nate had been gone far too long. Then as Clyde instructed, she settled in to wait for his call, or her husband's return.

She paced their living room alternating between bubbling rage at the police for treating Nate so poorly and her worry about the cause of the problem. She just couldn't imagine what trouble Nate could be in.

They had married as soon as Nate returned from war, then set about establishing themselves as one of the new hot couples on the San Francisco social scene. Nate had an idea about reopening the gold mine outside of Skagway his father had left him. He spent a lot of time in Alaska investigating the feasibility, working with an old friend, Smithy, who agreed to be his man on site. When the assay reports came in, their excitement couldn't be contained. Nate's father had always claimed the mine was worth millions and now it looked as if it was true.

Nate was in his glory. He oozed optimism. Money poured in, everyone wanted to invest. Everyone wanted to be part of the dream. Everyone wanted to own a gold mine, specifically the Lucky Jewel Gold Mine.

They lived well, and why not? People were shoving money at him. When the mine started producing it was going to be just that, a gold mine, a money well, an infinite source of money. Nate bought them a beautiful apartment; they had a car to use on the weekends if they went to the country; he couldn't buy enough jewelry and furs for his wife, and he invested in the newest, most modern equipment available to free the gold in the mine.

It was a fairy tale. Ever the realist, Florence was aware there were some problems. While Nate didn't tell her what was troubling him she could tell he was worried about something. In fact, he was planning to go north next week, he said, to help work out the kinks in production. But he was confident he would soon have it all under control. After all, he explained patiently, it was a new operation. Smithy, his general manager, was still working out the bugs.

Still, Florence couldn't see how Nate's arrest tonight could have any thing to do with the mine. After all the gold mine was in Alaska, how could that effect them clear down here in San Francisco?

Maria interrupted her pacing when she brought in a tray of coffee and toast. "Is everything all right, Mrs. Witherspoon?"

"Yes, yes thank you, Maria. I didn't even hear you come in." She realized it was morning already and she still hadn't heard from Clyde.

She had only taken a sip of coffee before Maria returned, this time followed by four policemen. Maria was so distressed she was twisting her hands in her apron, "I had to let them in. They have a paper..."

"What is it you want?" she coldly asked the one in charge.

"I'm sorry, madam. We have a search warrant." He handed her the paper in his hand and motioned his men to their tasks.

Flo looked at the paper blankly, then told Maria to go back to the kitchen while she went to the phone and tried to get through to Clyde Clarke. She couldn't reach him and when she hung up the phone rang shrilly. She grabbed it believing it to be Clarke only to find it was Josie, her husband's secretary.

"Mrs. Witherspoon, is Mr. Witherspoon there?"

"No, I'm sorry he isn't, Josie. Is something wrong?"

"Oh, Mrs. Witherspoon, there are policemen all over the place, going through my files, taking papers and records. They say they have a court order. They say they have the right to take anything or everything. I just don't know what to do?"

Flo took a deep calming breath before trying to say anything. "Josie, take the paper from them and then let them take whatever they want. After they leave, do your best to straighten up. I'll get back to you later and let you know what Nate wants you to do. And Josie, thanks for calling."

When she hung up, the phone rang again and it still wasn't Clyde. This time it was one of Nate's investors. He read the story in the morning's Chronicle and wanted to talk to Nate. He got a little nasty with Flo demanding his money back. He said he was withdrawing his investment in the Lucky Jewel and threatened, "Nate had better, by God, get my money back to me."

The next call was from another investor, equally as belligerent. The next was from a newspaper reporter, and then Maria came in saying there were three reporters at the door who wanted to talk to her. That's when she took the phone off the hook and told Maria not to answer the door.

Flo was overwhelmed. She wandered through her apartment, watching the policemen paw through Nate's desk, pushing papers of no interest to the floor, not concerned about the mess they were making. Her bedroom seemed vandalized. Not just Nate's bureau and closet, but her things were searched and discarded in heaps. The bed had been torn apart, the mattress half off the bed, the pillows thrown in the corner. She returned to the living room and sank down on a chair near the window. She didn't know what to do; she didn't know what was happening.

* * *

Mrs. Bernbaum came awake slowly. The heaviness in her heart made it hard to breathe. She lay still, wondering if she was having a heart attack, but then she began to recognize the heaviness as the same pain she felt when they arrested Nate. It was as if it had happened yesterday, instead of more than fifty years ago. She breathed deeply trying to relax, and she remembered. That was the beginning of the end for her and Nate. Events were spiraling out of her control, certainly out of his control. Smithy, his trusted manager shouldn't have been trusted. While he had been an important figure in Nate's past, Nate had failed to notice or remember Smithy's idiosyncrasies. Leopards and men don't really ever change their spots. And Smithy's spots revolved around his penchant for working cons. In the early days he would have been labeled a flimflam man, a con artist, a crook. And no matter that he was Nate's friend, he probably couldn't help himself. When the opportunity presented itself, he went with the con. And that he would so cunningly deceive his friend was the biggest blow of all to Nate.

Nate couldn't believe it, even when confronted with the evidence. The mine had been salted. Oh, there was gold, but the quantity and quality never would have justified the cost of getting it out. Nate grew up on his father's stories. His friend Smithy fed him more and provided the "proof" of the value. Nate believed because he wanted to believe. And Nate's enthusiasm is what convinced everyone of the value of the mine. No wonder he had investors lining up to give him money. No wonder he could afford to live like a prince.

But it couldn't last. The mine needed to start delivering profits and the gold just wasn't there. Nor, was Smithy! He had disappeared shortly after Nate's visit last April, just before they expected the rich ore to start being produced.

Of course no one believed Nate had been bamboozled just as his investors had. And why would they? He was living high off of their investments while Smithy had simply disappeared and with him the entire working capital for the Lucky Jewel.

The whole scheme was going to fall apart, but was hastened when one of his investors went to Alaska on a fishing trip and decided to fly into Skagway to see the mine. That visit to the mine, with the boxes of equipment sitting there, not even opened, was shocking. What was even more upsetting was the fact that the people in nearby Skagway regarded the Lucky Jewel Gold Mine as another of Smithy's stories. They all knew about Smithy and during the long bleak winter they might enjoy listening to his tales, but none of them would have invested a dime in any enterprise he promoted. And they couldn't believe anyone else had.

Nate sat in jail while his investors raged. He told Flo he had to get out to get the money to pay his investors off. That was the only way he could have his freedom and his honor. He was not a cheat. He did not intentionally bilk these people. In fact, he really had only intended to share the wealth.

Clyde Clarke was no help. Flo fired him and hired a street smart guy, who wasn't afraid to do whatever was necessary to free Nate.

Then she began to do what she needed to do to get the money for his lawyer and to reimburse the investors. She started with the most saleable items, her jewelry, the car, the furnishings, then her furs, the apartment, and the furnishings in the office downtown on Sansome Street. Even that wasn't enough. She borrowed from her family, she liquidated all of her own investments and finally, reluctantly she went to Bernie Bernbaum, Nate's favorite jeweler, and offered him the *Heart of Persia*.

Bernie didn't haggle with her. He offered her a price, not as much as it was worth, but more than she feared she would get. It would be enough. She accepted the money, appreciated the sympathy in his eyes and she left her last treasure in his hands.

Mrs. Bernbaum felt the gentle rocking of the ship and it soothed her. The room was a soft grey now; the sun was coming up, early as it did here in the north. It was too early to get up and, she admitted, she was too tired. She closed her eyes and tried to think about Anita, anything to stop her thoughts from dwelling on that time so long ago, that painful time in the fifties when her world fell apart.

* * *

As soon as Kim opened the door he quickly crowded into the passageway, forcing her to retreat ahead of him into her cabin. He sat on the edge of her bed while he studied her carefully, anxious to hear the details.

While outwardly she appeared calm, there was an air of suppressed excitement about her, as if she could explode any minute.

She stood proudly in front of him, a triumphant smile spread over her face, as she bragged. "Everything went just right, just like we planned. All that worry was for nothing."

"No one saw you together?"

"Probably about 4,000 people saw her get into the car, but will anyone remember?" She shook her head grinning. "We went over the bridge to Douglas Island because the woman at the Tourist Information booth warned me of delays on the highway up north because of road work. She said the upper part of Douglas Island was very remote, only a few hardy souls live out that way.

"So after driving for a while I just pulled over to the side of the road and told her I was going to go pee." She laughed, delighted with her own subterfuge. "She didn't suspect a thing. When I saw it was a good location, I found a spot, located a rock and called her to come down."

"Just like that?" He looked nonplused at her casualness.

She nodded. "She thought we were on our way to the shrine, so she wasn't concerned about the delay. Maybe a little annoyed about traipsing through the brush, but curious enough about what I wanted her to see, to do it. She wasn't scared and she died never knowing what was coming. Really, it was a very humane way to go and not even very messy."

Now as if seeing it all again in her mind she couldn't seem to contain her excitement. She paced around the tiny cabin. "You know I really had to psych myself up for this. I mean I knew we had to do it or the whole plan would collapse, but truthfully, I didn't want to do it.

"I know…, I know you couldn't; it had to be me, but still, it was hard. And then it turned out to be so easy. Actually it was kind of exciting, do you know what I mean?"

He looked at her strangely, as if her excitement and enthusiasm were just a little worrying to him. "What did you do with her things?"

Kim pulled open a door of the closet and gestured to a small bag sitting on a shelf. "I sweated that one. The cabin steward hung around and hung around, finally he went away and I got in. I really had to hurry, but I think I got most of it. I should have waited until the old lady went to dinner, then I could have taken my time and made sure I did it right."

"No, no it was better you came right back and removed the stuff before the old lady returned from shore. Who knows what she might have noticed if you waited until she went to dinner." He nodded, obviously pleased. "Apparently they had words earlier in the day. She mentioned it at dinner. So now with Anita's things missing it looks as if Anita left in a huff. It's just what we want her to think."

He reached out and pulled Kim to him, suddenly feeling excited himself. Success had a way of rousing his lust. "You did it, babe. It's going to work."

"And you want to know the best thing?" she murmured between his kisses, "I don't have to hide out in this cabin anymore and I don't have to wear all those dowdy clothes. I can enjoy the rest of the cruise." She wrapped her arms around his neck. "What a team we make!"

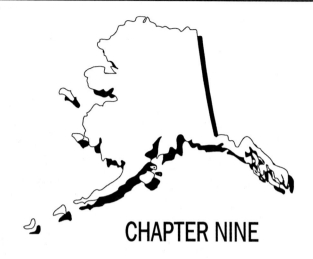

CHAPTER NINE

People were still drifting into the cocktail lounge outside the theatre, gathering for today's Trivia contest. Claire and Ruth sat with Heidi and Bob when Ruth spotted Pearl.

"Pearl, Pearl over here." She waved enthusiastically. "We need you and Harold on our team."

Pearl headed for them, pulling Harold by the hand behind her as they threaded through the tables. "Hi, we'd love to join you." Then turning to Heidi and Bob, "We're the Merriwetters, Pearl and Harold, from Houston. Where are you all from?"

Just then the emcee announced the first question.

"The world's largest office building? I think it's the Kremlin. Isn't it the Kremlin, Bob?" Heidi asked.

"I don't know, maybe something in Asia. I think there is a new building in Singapore that might be it."

"No, no, I know this one. It's the Pentagon," Claire said with authority of knowledge developed in all those years as a librarian.

"Are you sure, Claire?" Ruth was still doubtful.

"Trust me on this one. I know it's the Pentagon."

Heidi, who was recording their answers, looked to the others for conformation and seeing their nods, wrote it down.

"What is the name of the Palace housing the Hermitage in St. Petersburg? Is it called the Winter Palace, the Summer Palace, the Spring Palace or the Fall Palace?"

They looked at each other blankly. These questions were hard.

"I know that one. We've been there, haven't we, Bob? It's the Winter Palace." Heidi started writing it down.

"Wait, are you sure, Heidi? It seems Summer Palace sounds right?" Ruth asked tentatively.

"No, it's the Winter Palace. I tell you we've been there. We know its name."

"Okay," Ruth agreed, looking around to see what the other tables were doing.

"What are the four most popular flavors of syrup at the IHOP restaurants?"

"Now how are we going to know that?" Ruth was worried.

"Think, we can figure it out. Who goes to IHOP?" Claire looked around at the faces of their team.

"We do. Harold, you must know these," Pearl told her husband.

"Maple for sure, they always bring it hot to the table. Butter pecan, I like that one. And what about blueberry?"

"Not blueberry, but maybe blackberry? What do you think?" Pearl looked at her husband.

Harold nodded.

"Come on, guys. We need one more."

"It's got to be strawberry. Everybody likes strawberry."

Pearl nodded. "Yes, there is always strawberry syrup on the table. All right, maple, butter pecan, blackberry and strawberry, I think that's it."

Heidi was writing furiously.

The questions were coming faster now. One of the tables protested. They were falling behind, so the emcee paused for a moment.

Claire took this opportunity to tell Pearl about Mrs. Bernbaum's invitation to view the Glacier from her private balcony.

"Ooh, that'll be fun. I'd like to see one of those big cabins anyway, wouldn't you, Harold?" Harold nodded. He was willing to do anything his wife wanted to do.

Then the questions started again and they argued amongst themselves as they tried to sort out the right answer. Finally they were done and now they all waited eagerly to see how smart they were. There was much cheering and jeering between the tables of contestants when the answers were given. The rivalry was more intense than the prizes warranted.

"Well, we did good, even if we didn't win. Sixteen out of twenty is pretty impressive," Pearl insisted, still feeling miffed because the correct answer was blueberry syrup, not blackberry, in the top four syrups at IHOP.

"Oh look, Pat and John were on the winning team. We'll have to stop and congratulate them, Ruth." Claire waved to the couple they had met at breakfast on one of the first days of the cruise.

"Don't worry, every time we play we get better. Maybe the next time we'll win." Ruth was very competitive. "This is a good team. We've got someone who knows a little bit about everything. Let's try it again, shall we?"

"Okay, next time it's on the schedule, we meet here." Heidi handed the paper and pencil to the crew member who was collecting them and headed out of the lounge with her husband.

Claire rose from her chair to head over to chat with Pat. "See you later at Mrs. Bernbaum's, Pearl. Thanks for joining us; we needed you."

After a few minutes with Pat and John, Ruth reminded her of her lesson. "Enough of these games of skill and knowledge, I'm going to introduce you to a game of pure luck. If you win it will be purely by chance." She led Claire into the casino which, because they were at sea, was operating full force. She wandered around, peering at one machine then another before stopping in front of Slotto. "Here, this is the one."

"But Ruth, this one takes quarters. Isn't that a little rich?"

"Don't be a wussy, Claire. It takes money to win money. And it's not like it's a dollar machine or a five dollar machine. Did you bring your money?"

Claire really wasn't enthused about Ruth's plan, but she dutifully pulled a twenty dollar bill out of her pocket. Ruth showed her how to slip the bill in the slot and then work the machine. "When these three symbols appear, you get Slotto. Then the balls with different numbers on them blow around in the chamber until one drops in the tube. The machine pays you as many coins as the number on the ball that dropped."

So Claire played the slot machine with Ruth at her elbow with every pull. She had to admit the sound effects made it seem exciting. She got Slotto twice, one time she hit twenty-five coins, and one time she hit fifty. Meanwhile her twenty melted away and she added, on Ruth's insistence, another twenty. When she was down to the last of that twenty she objected to adding another.

"Claire, sometimes you have to invest both time and money to hit the jackpot. What's another twenty? This is a life lesson. You need to go for it."

When Ruth was so determined, Claire had learned it was easier to let her have her way. So she inserted another twenty into the machine and on the second pull she hit the Slotto one more time.

"See, I told you." Ruth was smug. "Come on baby, cough up the big one." She talked to the machine as if it could hear her. Or maybe it could. Neither of them could believe their eyes when the ball with one thousand written on it dropped in the tube.

Ruth was as excited as if she had won. A crowd quickly gathered, wanting to see what Claire won. The casino attendant showed up and paid Claire two hundred and fifty dollars for a little more than a sixty dollar investment. But Claire was firm when Ruth advised her to play the rest of the money off. She had her lesson; she invested her money, now she intended to take her winnings and run.

"But Ruth, I'd be happy to buy you a drink for your help."

"Okay, but let's make it a coffee. A quick one, because I have an appointment in the spa in a half hour. I'm getting the works plus a full body massage."

"Aren't you going to Mrs. Bernbaum's?"

"If I get done in time, otherwise I'll see the glacier from the chair while my nails are drying. I feel like I need to pamper myself today and since tonight is another formal night it seems to be a perfect time to do it.

"What are you going to do now, Claire? Lunch?"

"No, I'm skipping lunch today. We had that big breakfast and I'm sure Mrs. Bernbaum will have goodies with tea. And if she doesn't, it won't hurt me to wait for dinner. It would be very embarrassing if I couldn't get into my dress."

"Hah, it would never happen. I don't think I've ever seen you gain weight." Ruth eyed her. "A lot of people would be glad to know your secret."

"No secret. If I feel I've been eating too much, I just cut back or do without a meal or two. I know everyone has an exercise plan, but I get my workout heaving those books around."

"Well whatever, I wish I had your figure, or Lucy's. Now she doesn't heave books around and look at her."

"No, Lucy just looks wonderful. I don't know how she manages."

* * *

"I'll get it." Claire hurried to open the door for Harold and Pearl. "Hi. everyone's on the balcony, but it's really cold. Put on your jackets."

It felt frosty on the balcony, the air sharp, and the smell of snow waffed on the breeze. Many of the outside cabins had tiny balconies, but Mrs. Bernbaum's was quite large, stretching the width of her double wide cabin. It had several chairs and a small table and was enclosed at each end by solid panels allowing some privacy from the balconies on either side. The space was crowded with all Mrs. Bernbaum's guests. They needed to be outside, not only to see clearly, but so they could hear the sounds of the ice breaking off. The ship was parallel to the edge of the glacier and while it was at least a quarter of a mile away it seemed very close, perhaps too close, for comfort. The calm, still, silvery water of the bay was filled with chunks of ice, some big and blue, some small and gray.

The mega movie, *Titanic*, was recent enough to make the passengers all too aware of the danger of floating icebergs. They appreciated the captain's amazing skill in guiding the ship carefully and slowly through the water as he circled the bay in front of the Hubbard Glacier. And continuously, the glacier gave up more of itself, calving into the bay. Large chunks of ice with rumbles and sharp cracks, almost like thunder, shivered then slid, gathering momentum, before crashing into the water displacing big waves of water rushing away from the shore. Some waves were large enough to gently rock the ship. Other than the noise of the glacier calving there was complete silence. It was so eerie that the people on Mrs. Bernbaum's balcony and the balconies on either side of her, found themselves whispering as if in church.

The glacier, itself, was breathtakingly beautiful. When the ship first moved into the bay and the glacier was sighted, it was magnificent, but that was nothing to compare to this closer view. It stretched miles on either side of the ship and it was many stories high, looming over them. And it was blue. Everyone said it was blue; pictures of it showed it blue, but somehow that still didn't prepare one to see it. The color was everywhere, and the huge crevices revealed the blue went deep into the ice. It wasn't just a reflection of the sky in the ice, it was blue ice.

Claire couldn't get enough pictures, until she finally realized the grandeur couldn't be captured in a small picture, so she stopped with what she had. She would have to burn the image in her brain and then the pictures could remind her of the beauty, the immensity and the silence.

Mrs. Bernbaum was the first to go back into her cabin, and slowly the others trailed behind her as the ship shifted and they gradually lost sight of the glacier. When the icy rain started to fall from the clouds, which had been moving in behind them, Claire finally gave up. She closed the sliding glass door behind her, blowing on her hands in an attempt to warm them. "Where is everyone?" she asked her mother and Mrs. Bernbaum.

"They all left. Harold and Pearl were going on top to the other side of the ship so they could see more. I don't know where Lucy went, but she left with Sean and Ian."

"Dickie said he was going to the gym," Mrs. Bernbaum offered. "Here, dear, have some tea. It will warm you up."

Claire accepted the cup and sat down, sipping the hot tea, then seeing some little sandwiches she helped herself. "I can't stay long, I have to go to the computer room and do my e-mails." Then she looked around. "Where's Anita, Mrs. Bernbaum? Did you give her the afternoon off?"

Mrs. Bernbaum's face sort of crumpled. "That girl, really, I just don't know what to do." She was clearly upset.

"What's wrong? Did Anita say something again?"

"No, she didn't say anything. I guess that's part of the problem. She didn't say anything; and she didn't come back from shore yesterday."

Claire's mouth fell open and Millie gasped. "She didn't come back on board? Did she decide to fly home after all?"

"I don't know. Dickie says she must have." Mrs. Bernbaum looked pinched and for a moment Claire thought she was going to cry.

"She took her hair brush and some of her things. Her toothbrush is gone, so she must have decided she was not coming back on board." But before Claire could respond, Mrs. Bernbaum continued, "But I just can't believe she did that.

"I know Anita. She has this strict sense of what is right. And I'm sure she would have thought I should pay for the return fare and she wouldn't have been shy about asking me to do it. I just find it hard to believe she took off and spent her own money."

"She just didn't come back on board?" Claire was amazed. She didn't really know the woman, but she hadn't seemed to be that flighty.

Mrs. Bernbaum nodded. "The security officers came by last night after I returned from dinner. They knew she hadn't come on board, because she hadn't swiped her card. I guess they check all that before they sail."

"What are they going to do? What are you going to do?" Millie was aghast. She couldn't believe Mrs. Bernbaum's caregiver could be so cavalier about her responsibility to the old lady after caring for her so long.

"Well, of course they sailed. They said if their agent heard from her they would help her connect with the ship at our next port. But Dickie says she went home. When we get to Sitka tomorrow he's going to call and find out if she's there.

"But I don't know. If she's as mad as she appears to be, she may not even answer her phone. I just don't know what got into her."

Millie shook her head, making sympathetic clicking noises with her tongue.

"Did they check at the airport to see if she made reservations? Or what about car rentals?"

"Claire, Juneau is landlocked, remember? She could only get out by plane or boat," Millie reminded her daughter.

Mrs. Bernbaum shook her head. "They said she was an adult and she could leave if she wanted. It didn't appear to be foul play since she took things with her indicating she was planning to leave. But they said if Dickie couldn't reach her in San Francisco, they would ask their agent in Juneau to talk to the police."

They all looked at each other. Claire gave a little shiver. It sounded ominous.

"Mrs. Bernbaum, Mom and I have a good friend in the San Francisco police department. If you give me Anita's address and phone number I'll e-mail him today and see if someone can check at her house."

"Oh, would you Claire? I confess I'm worried. I'd feel so much better if I knew someone actually spoke to her. Let me get it for you." She pulled herself up from her chair and moved to the desk where she pulled out a leather bound address book. It took only a minute for her to copy the information on a piece of ship's stationery for Claire.

"Now, I don't think we'll get an answer today," Claire cautioned. "So your nephew might talk to her first. If so, let me know, so I can e-mail Sean and tell him not to bother. Otherwise, as soon as I hear from him I'll let you know."

"Mrs. Bernbaum, are you okay with Anita gone. I mean how are you getting by? Do you need us to help you in some way?" Millie was concerned about the old lady.

"No, no dear, I'm fine. Jorges, my cabin steward, is available if I need something, and Dickie is going to come by to take me in to dinner and he'll check to make sure I get my medicines. I'm sure I'll manage, but thank you so much for asking." She got up to accompany them to the door. "Now don't worry about me. I'm going to take a long nap and I'll see you at dinner. Formal tonight, right?"

As the ladies moved down the corridor, Millie asked with a worried frown, "Claire, do you think you should ask Sean Dixon for this favor? I mean he's a pretty important person now. I don't know if we should impose on him."

"He says he owes me, so here's a chance for him to pay me back. Don't worry. It'll be okay, Mom. He'll probably send one of his officers out to check. And it will relieve Mrs. Bernbaum's mind. You know she's a pretty peppy old lady and despite my initial impression, she's very interesting. I really like her."

"Yes, she's led an eventful life, hasn't she? But maybe a lot of people have if we just took the time to listen to their stories. After all when a person lives almost a hundred years they've seen lots of history happen. It's much more interesting hearing it from someone who's lived through it than it is reading it in history books.

"You know, she asked me to call her Florence. She said that one of the worst things about outliving your colleagues and family is no one talks to you as an equal. No one calls you by your first name and no one can share your memories and stories. That's sad, isn't it? It really made me think. And she's right. Look at our table. We call everyone by their first name, but her. Everyone calls her Mrs.

Bernbaum except her nephew, and he calls her Auntie." Millie shook her head, her sympathy for Mrs. Bernbaum clear on her face.

"Oh, I think I'm going to take these stairs down to my cabin and drop off my jacket. I'll see you later at the horse races, all right?" Millie waved to her daughter and disappeared down the stairs.

Claire took the elevator down several decks to her own cabin and got rid of her jacket, then headed up to the computer room.

She hadn't checked her e-mails yesterday and so paid for that omission by the number which had accumulated. Some notices and spam she quickly deleted leaving only the messages she needed to respond to. Mrs. B, her assistant at the shop, had some questions and needed decisions. She had two messages from the Travel Book Store Association she belonged to and a notice of an upcoming event she wanted to participate in. There were messages from the Bayside Chamber of Commerce and the Bayside Merchants' Association. She read and answered the three messages from friends before she was free to send her message to Captain Sean Dixon at the SF Police Department.

Sean was a buddy of her father's. He had stayed in touch with them all these years, feeling an obligation to see his friend's family was all right. Meanwhile he had advanced through the police force ranks to the level of Captain. But to her he was still Uncle Sean.

Several years ago she had agreed to stop in to care for Ruth's cat and woke up to find herself lying in a deserted warehouse. She had managed to get out of the building before it exploded into flames. While the investigating officers had seemed suspicious of her being in that part of town, even hinting she might have been there to make a drug buy, Sean Dixon had told them in no uncertain words what he thought of their theory. And when the police couldn't find answers to why she was there or to the subsequent attempt on her life, he was embarrassed and grateful when she found the answer herself. He was as proud of her help in nabbing the drug lord, who as it turned out, was meeting in the house next door to Ruth's, as he would have been if she were his own daughter. She didn't think this little favor was too much to ask him. He would consider checking on Anita to be a small price to pay for hearing from her. And Mrs. Bernbaum would rest easier knowing Anita had arrived home safely.

She finished just in time to head for the cocktail lounge for the scheduled races. She wanted to make sure she had time to place a bet. She was hoping her good luck at the Slotto was still with her. She grinned, realizing she had forgotten to tell her mother about her good fortune. Her mother just wouldn't believe it.

Millie waved frantically to her. She, Ruth and Lucy were already seated in the second row of tables, with what looked like the special drink of the day in front of each of them, while they waited for the races to start. It was really a silly game, but judging by the attendance, a popular one. The emcee threw two dice into a box and cruise staff moved each of the stick horses, stuck in buckets of cement, numbered two through twelve, forward each time their number came up on the dice. The emcee was talented and managed to call the race, making it sound just as it did at the real race tracks. The crowd responded enthusiastically, cheering nosily, rising to their feet when their horse took the lead across the path of marked spaces on the cloth spread on the stage. When each race finished the winners crowded in to collect their winnings while the others pushed forward to place bets on their choice for the next race.

It was fun. Claire managed a win in the third race, her mother won the first and fifth. Ruth didn't win and complained loudly about it. Lucy won the third and fifth.

"I quite like this. We should go to the races some day. It's only over at Hillsdale."

Claire nodded. "It might be fun, but I wonder how real horses compare to these."

"Well, in the real races you have to know a little about horses to win," Ruth said sourly, still smarting from her losses. "What are you going to do now?" she asked.

Millie looked at her schedule. "I think I have time to see the movie. I didn't get a chance to see it when it was in town. Do you want to go, Ruth?"

"What is it?"

"*Tea with Mussolini*, with Maggie Smith."

"Sure, sounds good. Claire, are you coming?"

"No, you go on. I'm going to find a nice corner and read my book and maybe look for whales."

"Lucy, want to come?"

"No, I saw it. Actually it was good. But I think I'm going down for a nap. I seem to be dragging a bit today. I need to be bright for tonight."

Claire had wondered how Lucy was going to keep up with all the late nights she was having. A nap sounded like a sensible plan to her.

"I'll see you down at the cabin in time to get dressed for dinner, Lucy. And Mom, shall we meet you both for cocktails before dinner as usual?" she asked her mother as she was moving off.

"All right dear, see you then."

Claire made her way to the Starlight Lounge at the top front of the ship. There, almost deserted except for pockets of passengers here and there, she found a table with comfortable chairs where she settled to look at her book. A waiter stopped by and took her order for the drink of the day, which was her second, but she decided she wasn't counting, and then buried her nose in the book again. A little later she noticed a small commotion and found several more people had settled in and one group two tables to her left were pointing excitedly to the ocean on that side.

Pat, the Englishwoman she had met at breakfast one day, said with excitement, "See the fume. She's coming up. Watch." As if on cue, the whale breached, lifting right out of the water before settling back with a gigantic splash.

There was a chorus of oohs and ahhs. Claire was already fishing in her tote bag for her camera. There were a series of splashes, some fins showing briefly and a few tantalizing glimpses of tail fins, but none of the others chose to show themselves so completely to the floating peanut gallery which was watching their every move.

Finally, it was apparent the show for the day was over and people settled back with their drinks and their conversations. Pat came over and joined Claire for a minute. "Did you get a picture, Pat?" Claire wished she had been more alert and had had her camera ready.

"No, that would almost be a miracle, wouldn't it? They seldom cooperate and breach when we're watching and they never give us enough time to get a picture. But it was exciting, wasn't it?"

Claire nodded. "I'm sorry my mother didn't see this. We're taking the Whale Watching Excursion tomorrow out of Sitka. Hopefully we'll see whales then. Actually, they guarantee we'll see them or our money back."

Pat nodded. "Sounds good. Where is your mum? Playing bingo?"

"No, she and Ruth went to the movies. I decided I needed some quiet time, so it was reading my book or napping. Reading sounded more appealing. There are so many activities available I'm tempted to try to do them all.

But I tell myself, I'm a working girl, this is my vacation, remember to sit and vegetate."

Pat laughed. "Right, having fun can be wearing. Well, I'd better go back to John or he'll doze off. He combines the nap with his reading. But I try to keep him awake so he won't snore and disturb the other passengers."

* * *

"Here, stand behind Mrs. Bernbaum, Ian."

"Can you scoot your chair in closer, Claire?"

"Everyone smile." The flash was blinding, but before they could move away, the photographer called them to wait. "Just one more to make sure we got everyone smiling. Okay, smile." The second flash went off totally blinding them once more.

There was a great deal of shuffling and rearranging chairs as everyone found their place at the table once more and the photographer moved on to the next table.

"Thank you so much for having us in to see the glacier, Mrs. Bernbaum. Harold and I went up to the top to see it from the other side, but it wasn't nearly as nice a view," Pearl told Mrs. Bernbaum with a smile.

"And of course, the company wasn't as congenial," Harold added, winking.

"And the rain started. It was really icy. We only stayed a few minutes before finding some shelter."

Just then Pedro started delivering their appetizers and the diners turned their attention to the food.

Claire noticed how nice everyone looked. It seemed like a pain to dress for dinner, but now she realized it really made it seem like an occasion. The men wore the same clothes they had at the first formal dinner. However, Harold was wearing a red cummerbund and tie to match Pearl's long, strapless red gown. Mrs. Bernbaum was wearing black tonight, which didn't showcase her pin as well as her grey dress did. Millie was also wearing black, a short beaded dress which was very flattering. Claire assumed it was another one from the annual Richman Brothers Christmas party. Lucy was wearing dark blue crepe. The blouse was a deep neck surrounded by soft ruffles, with ruffles around the wrist, worn with wide legged crepe pants of the same color. And the necklace and earrings could have been rhinestones, but knowing Lucy, Claire assumed they were diamonds. Lucy liked nice things and didn't shirk at treating herself. Ruth was also in pants tonight, black velvet with a vividly colored beaded top. It looked very festive. Claire felt a little subdued in her maize colored sleeveless long gown, but she knew the color was good on her.

She hoped the picture was good as she'd like to display it on the bulletin board at the store. She smiled at her friends around the table before asking, "Did any of you see the whale show this afternoon?"

They shook their heads.

So she explained, "It was after the horse races. I was up in the Starlight Lounge reading when this pod put on a show." She shook her head regretfully. "I didn't get a picture. It was just too fast. But one of the whales breached. It was incredible. She came clear out of the water, right there in front of us."

"Oh, I'm so sorry I didn't see it. I hope we see lots of them tomorrow." Millie was wistful. That started a whole conversation about what was happening the next day. It turned out that Ruth, Lucy and Sean were all going deep sea fishing out of Sitka.

"Oh, maybe we'll have fresh salmon for dinner tomorrow," Pearl said excitedly.

"I'm afraid not, Pearl. I was told the chef couldn't allow any local food in the kitchen for fear it might contaminate the other food," Sean explained. "If we catch something the charter company will arrange to have it packed, flash frozen and shipped to us."

Lucy nodded. "Antonio told me it was because of this sickness, that stomach virus, that has been happening on the ships. They've had to take extreme measures to make sure it doesn't occur here."

Pearl shuddered. "Oh, can you imagine how awful that would be. There was an article in the paper about a ship out of Miami, and I guess it was seven days of hell."

"Let's talk about something more pleasant," Millie asked purposely changing the subject. "Ian, what are you going to do while Sean is fishing?"

Ian was taking a kayaking trip, which Sean felt was too strenuous for him. Pearl and Harold were touring the city and visiting the Totem Pole Park.

"And what are you doing, Mrs. Bernbaum? Any big plans?"

"Oh, no, I'll probably stay on board. The next day is going to be a big day for me and I'll rest up for it. But Dickie's taking an excursion, aren't you, Dickie?"

He nodded. "I'm taking a seaplane out to a fishing cabin on a lake for some fly fishing. It sounds fun and I'll get to see the interior."

Sean and Lucy were very interested in Richard's excursion, and they talked about fly fishing versus deep sea fishing for a while.

Millie leaned forward and said to Mrs. Bernbaum, "So is Skagway it? Is that where your life quest is?"

"Yes, dear. I decided that I was going to reunite Nate with his family. He wanted to be buried in Skagway, but I just couldn't do it. All these years I have selfishly kept him with me. But, you know, it's time for me to let him go. I want to make sure he's settled before I pass."

"You have him with you?" Millie couldn't help the surprise she felt.

"Well, his ashes. I have a small box containing his ashes. I've spoken to the funeral home in Skagway and they will make arrangements to bury the box next to his father, mother and sister. I know he will like that."

"But what about you? Don't you want to be next to him? Will you be buried in Skagway too?"

Mrs. Bernbaum shook her head. "No dear. When I purchased a plot for Bernie, I purchased a double plot. I'll rest beside him. He was such a dear man and he did so much for me. It's only right that I be with him at the end." She reached over and patted Millie's hand. "Thank you so much for asking, Millie. You're a very nice person."

A little later Millie asked Mrs. Bernbaum, "Would you like Claire and me to be with you when you lay Nate to rest? We would be happy to do that."

This time there were tears in the old lady's eyes. "Oh, would you, my dear? It would mean a lot to me. I suspect it might be harder for me than Dickie thinks. I don't think it will take long, but if you could come, and Claire, I would really appreciate it."

This time Millie patted her hand. "Don't even think about how long it takes. We'll be there. Plan on it."

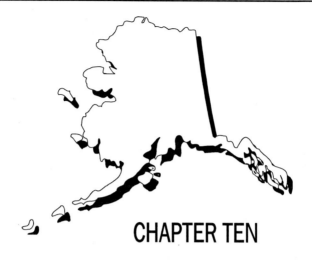

CHAPTER TEN

"Whoops, hang on dear." Millie slung her arm across the front of Claire to protect her, as she had when Claire was a child sitting in the car beside her.

The little boat climbed to the top of the swell and then slid quickly down the other side.

"Three o'clock. Whale at three o'clock!"

Claire swung her binoculars that way, but the next swell was already pointing the nose of the boat into the air so she saw nothing but sky.

"Did you see it?" Millie asked trying to remain seated as the boat lurched down into the trough between the waves.

"There, eleven o'clock. Watch, it's going to... It breached. Eleven o'clock," their guide called excitedly. "We're having a great day today. There, again at twelve o'clock. Did everyone see it?"

The passengers nodded, calling out they saw it, but Claire shook her head glumly at Millie.

"I didn't either, but next time he calls out I'm going to say I saw it. Otherwise he's going to stay out here until we do, and I don't know how much longer I can hold on," Millie muttered out of the side of her mouth.

Claire realized her mother was right. This excursion guaranteed, money back, they would see a whale and as much as they wanted to see one, the sea was so rough and the little boat was bouncing so precariously, Claire was willing to forego the guarantee if they could move closer to shore where the water would surely be calmer.

"Whale at two o'clock."

"Look, there Mom." She pointed in the two o'clock direction with one hand, holding the binoculars with the other and bracing her feet on the floor, hoping to stay in her seat. "I see it!" What she really saw was a wall of water rising in front of her eyes.

"Oh, there it is. I see it. Oh, how exciting!" Millie was working on an Oscar nomination.

Their guide looked around at the thirty passengers hanging on for dear life as the little boat heaved through the water. To him it was a little rough. They felt as if they were in hurricane waters.

"Okay folks, everyone has seen a whale up close and personal. We've had a good day. Now we'll head inland and look for other forms of Alaskan wildlife. Keep a sharp look out as we expect to see sea lions, sea otters, eagles, osprey and perhaps deer, moose or even bear. I'll use the same system to direct your attention to the location whenever we sight something, but everyone should keep their eyes open. No telling what we'll see."

And finally they did enter the calm waters of the inlet and soon they were heading for some rocks near the entrance, which were covered with barking sea lions. Claire and Millie weren't much interested in the sea lions as they saw plenty in San Francisco, but they knew many of the other passengers were thrilled because they were standing up, contorting their bodies for balance while they snapped pictures.

Then as they headed further inland, the ride was so smooth one of the other passengers even dared make their way back to the bathroom on board. The sun came out, bouncing off the water, casting deep shadows amongst the trees along the banks.

The boat stopped moving, the pilot idled, using only enough power to keep the boat in place against the current, so they could see the dark blobs floating in front of them were really a colony of otters. The animals floated peacefully on their backs, their heads and feet sticking up out of the water.

"Mom, look at that one with a baby on her stomach. Isn't that sweet?"

The otters were bigger than Claire expected. She thought they were bigger than the ones she had seen at the Monterey Bay Aquarium, but they had the same cute, wizened faces and sleek fur bodies.

The guide explained they were required to keep the boat a certain distance from the animals. "But laws can't control the animals' curiosity," he said, "so one might swim close enough to get a good picture.

"Please notice how they keep their feet out of the water. Otters live mostly in the water, but they don't like to get their feet wet. Actually, that's because they don't have insulation on their feet, so if they kept their feet in the water they would lose too much body heat through their feet and they could die. Otters spend most of their time eating and grooming their fur. The fur is what protects them from the icy water. The females and children stay together, camouflaged by rocks and seaweed for protection from predators.

"This is a group of females with their young. Can you see how they carry their babies on their stomachs? They teach them to groom themselves and feed them bits of the shell fish they bring up from the bottom. Otters are intelligent enough to devise tools to help them survive. You might see one remove a stone they're carrying from under their front arm to use in breaking open the shell fish. They only intermingle with the males for mating. I think we'll see a colony of males a little further on. The males lead a more frivolous life. They don't have to worry about feeding another mouth, so they like to cavort and play as well as eat and groom themselves. Not a bad life.

"We're going to move on now to watch the males. I don't like to spend too much time near the females as it upsets the mamas to have us so close to their babies." Their guide turned his attention forward, looking for the male colony.

"Did you get a picture of the mom and baby?" Millie asked Claire as she sat back down while the boat headed for their next encounter.

"I think I got a good one, but I'll know when I see it on the computer screen." She craned her neck, trying to see the next group.

The male otters were not far away. The pilot lingered there a while so they could enjoy the otters' antics. Claire was able to zoom in close enough to get some pictures and the people with video cameras were ecstatic. But eventually they moved further inland. Here the lush forest lined the shore and there were no signs of humans. They saw several eagles' nests built at the top of dead trees. These huge piles of twigs were built at the top, their guide explained, as the eagles liked to be at the highest point in order to survey the surrounding terrain. And they saw two eagles, one soaring over their heads and one sitting on a branch near its nest.

And further yet, passing a stream which fed into the inlet or bay they were traversing, there was a bear. He was fishing in the water near the shore and was disturbed by the noise of the boat. With a disgusted expression on his face he turned his back to the intruders and ambled off into the woods. Only one of the passengers was quick enough to get him on camera, but they were all excited at the encounter and very pleased they were on the boat out of his reach.

On the way back to the dock, one of the passengers said he saw a moose, but no one else saw it so it might have been a shadow. They landed back at Sitka after only a short passage through the rough water. The generous tips handed off to their guide indicated the passengers' pleasure with the excursion. They had seen some of the magnificent wilderness Alaska is known for, felt some of the solitude Alaska boasted of and captured pictures of some of the unique wildlife. And if some of the passengers claimed they saw a whale in order to escape the ordeal of the rough water, who cared? Everyone was satisfied.

"Whoa, I'm glad to have my feet on solid ground again. I suddenly have a little more empathy for Anita's sea sickness," Millie said as they walked up the street into town. "I wonder how Ruth and Lucy are doing fishing out on that rough water?"

"Oh, I didn't even think of that. Well, maybe the water isn't as turbulent further out where they were going. I'm hoping they get fish so we can share in the spoils."

"We'll hear soon enough. Let's stop in here for a little lunch, then I'd like to see some of the town and maybe look at the shops. I understand they have a lot of Russian goods here. I wouldn't mind picking up a piece of amber jewelry."

Later, over a cup of clam chowder and a shared crab salad sandwich, Millie told Claire about Mrs. Bernbaum's life quest.

"She's been carrying his ashes around with her all these years?" Claire was shocked.

Millie nodded. "Isn't that touching. But now she says it's time to let go."

"I guess. Fifty years and another husband, and she still hasn't buried him? I'm not sure I think that's touching, Mom. I think it might be a little spooky."

"No, dear. You don't understand how difficult it is to give up your loved one. You know, I slept in your Dad's old flannel shirt for several years before it finally disintegrated in the washer leaving me no choice."

Claire looked at her with amazement. She never knew this about her mother; suddenly she realized how hard it must have been. Her mother had been a young woman. With her husband's untimely death, Millie had suddenly been alone in the world to cope with raising a young daughter. She had to be strong for her daughter when she probably would have preferred to fall apart. Claire reached over and grasped her mother's hand. That reminded her how Mrs. Bernbaum always grabbed her listener's arm to hang on when she was telling a story. Here she was, less than half Mrs. Bernbaum's age, already acting just like her.

Millie patted her hand and then told her, "I told Mrs. Bernbaum we would come to the cemetery tomorrow. I thought she could use some support. Even after all this time it will still be a wrenching experience for her. I know that. You don't mind, do you?"

Claire nodded agreeing. "What time and where?"

"I don't know. I'll check with her tonight. I'm sure we can fit it in around the excursion we booked. I'll ask Ruth and Lucy if they want to come, but they may not want to. They don't really understand Mrs. Bernbaum's feelings for Nate."

"No, they've had different experiences with the men in their lives," Claire agreed thoughtfully.

The women settled their bill and walked down the street towards the Russian Orthodox Church which sat right in front of them requiring the street to branch around either side of it. The little town was a unique blend of Russian frontier architecture and fishing village.

"I just love this town. I read Louis L'Amour's, novel, *Sitka*, when I was young and was taken with the romance of that time. I think they made a movie out of it, too. Anyway, I feel like I'm there. I'm in that Sitka he talked about," Millie said in a dreamy tone.

"I saw that movie. What's interesting about that time is that it wasn't so long ago. Actually, Mrs. Bernbaum's Nate lived here not long after the Gold Rush. When you can talk to someone who knew it first hand it makes it all seem like it was only yesterday. It's exciting, isn't it?

"Here let's check out this shop." Millie's attention was now riveted on shopping.

Claire, good-naturedly, followed her Mother into the shop. They weren't in a hurry, so if Millie wanted to pick up souvenirs, this store seemed to have a nice selection.

* * *

"Whoa, grab that glass."

Sean captured the wine glass just as it teetered on its edge.

Pearl wiped her mouth with her napkin, her face a strange greenish color. "Harold, I have to go. Please excuse..." and she was gone, moving quickly through the tables, heading for the door.

Harold put down his fork and excused himself before following his wife to make sure she made it to their cabin safely.

"Well, everyone else okay?" Lucy asked looking around the table.

"I guess we're going to have a fun night, huh?" Ian didn't look like the rough sea was going to bother him.

"This is nothing. It was really rough out there on the fishing boat, wasn't it girls?" Sean asked Ruth and Lucy.

"Yeah, but not so much so that I let go of my fish." Ruth was proud of the picture she had passed around of her holding a seventy pound halibut. Actually, it was seventy-six pounds and measured fifty-three inches long, as she had told everyone several times.

"For sure, that was a beauty. I'm wishing I was sending home the fillets from a seventy-pounder. Mine seemed a little puny in comparison."

"Your mistake, Sean, was not catching three, like I did. Mine might not have been as big as Ruth's, but the smaller ones are easier to bring in and I ended up with as much fish as she did." Lucy's smile indicated how pleased she was, as if she could control which fish took which hook.

"All I can say is I'm looking forward to cooking it. We'll have a wonderful meal. Actually, with that much fish, we'll be eating it all year," Millie said with enthusiasm before asking, "Mrs. Bernbaum, perhaps you and your nephew would like to join us for dinner one night? Ruth is going to supply the fish and I'm cooking it. Ian, Sean, are you sure you can't stay in San Francisco for a few days? I assure you this will be a meal you won't want to miss."

The ship rolled sharply and Claire grabbed the table as her chair started to slide out from under her. Ian grabbed it and held it steady.

"When will your fish arrive, Ruth?" Claire asked, giving up on her soup. The lurching of the ship was making it too difficult to get the spoon to her mouth with anything on it.

"They said next week. They fillet it, flash freeze it and then overnight it with dry ice. They said I could expect about fifty pounds net weight. It's going to be the most expensive fish you ever served, Millie. But it's going to be delicious. Wait and see."

Pedro and Juan started clearing the table. They didn't seem at all disturbed by the turbulence of the water.

"Where are the Merriwetters?" Pedro asked.

"I don't think Pearl was feeling well. She left," Mrs. Bernbaum said. Obviously she wasn't bothered by the movement of the ship.

"Actually, I'm not feeling well, myself." Richard did look pale. "I wonder if you can excuse me." He stood up, paused a moment as if trying to get a feel for which way the ship was moving and lurched off towards the door.

"Oh, dear, I hope he takes some of the medicine he gave Anita." Mrs. Bernbaum gazed after him with a concerned expression on her face. Then turning towards Claire, she said, "Not that it seemed to help Anita any." She nodded her thanks to Pedro, who just set down her plate of roasted chicken.

"Mrs. Bernbaum, was your nephew able to contact Anita today?" Claire spoke in a low voice so her words wouldn't reach the others at the table.

"No, no one answered the phone. I'm still very worried. Did you hear from your friend?"

"Yes, I did. He said no one answered the door and the neighbors reported that Anita went on a cruise to Alaska and they didn't expect her back until Wednesday. My friend suggested we contact the Juneau police and have them check the hospitals and," she hesitated a fraction of a second, then finished, "the morgue. He says it appears she didn't return to San Francisco, so something might have happened to her in Juneau to prevent her returning to the ship."

"Oh, dear, now I'm really worried. I hope she didn't have an accident. The poor thing. What if she's in the hospital, waiting for me to find her? I didn't think Anita would just desert me. I should have insisted they look for her right away."

"I don't think you could have done much, Mrs. Bernbaum. I believe there is a waiting period before the police take any action on a missing person. But maybe if you talk to the cruise line's security people, they can start the steps to look for her in Juneau?"

"Yes, you're right. After dinner I'll ask Dickie to contact the security people." Then she remembered. "Oh, dear, I forgot Dickie left." Then she straightened her spine. "Well, no matter, I think I can use the phone. I'll just call them."

Claire nodded. "Don't worry, I'll walk you back to your cabin and even stay with you while you call, if you like."

"Oh, thank you dear. That will help." She took a bite of chicken before continuing. "You know, my dear, I'm a little disappointed at Dickie's attitude. He refuses to consider that Anita missing the ship could be a serious matter.

"He didn't like Anita, you know. Well, it was mutual. She didn't like him either. I admit she was very suspicious of Dickie, but really, Anita wouldn't do any thing to harm me. As disapproving as she was of this trip, she did come rather than have me be on my own, so I find it very strange she would become so annoyed she would leave, and without even telling me. No, I'm sure something happened."

"You know this lurching and rolling is getting to me. I'm going to skip dessert and head down to the cabin for an early night. Please excuse me." Ruth was the next casualty. She put down her napkin and got to her feet, holding firmly to the table. Then seeing Millie's worried expression, she reassured her. "Don't worry about me, Millie. I'm fine. I'm just tired and not inclined to continue fighting this roll. I'm going to bed and let it rock me to sleep. See you all tomorrow."

Claire noticed, as she watched Ruth weave an unsteady path through the tables, how many of the diners had left. Tonight was not a good night for dinner.

"Is she not feeling well?" Pedro asked, picking up Ruth's almost full plate.

"No, she's passing on dessert. How about you, Pedro? Does it ever bother you?"

He gave an exaggerated shrug, rolled his eyes. "Not much. I am a sailor you see. We walk like this." He lurched around the table gathering their finished plates while they laughed at his antics. "Problem is, we try to walk that way on land and then they think we're drunk."

"We've really been lucky on this trip, don't you think?" Lucy asked him. "This is the first rough weather we've had."

"Yes, we're very lucky this trip. This is our last trip to Alaska this season and some years the winter moves in too quickly and we get storms on our last trip. But this year is good. You are very fortunate."

"So where do you go next?" Lucy persisted.

"We will go through the Panama Canal and then up and down the East Coast between South America and Miami. The weather will be lovely. You should come with us. South America is very exciting."

"Ah, Pedro, you are tempting me. But my publisher is expecting another book, and he can be very demanding."

"Forget about writing books, come work on the ship. Then you can travel and enjoy while you're earning a living. That's what we do." He used his hand to gesture to the other waiters and servers in the near vicinity. "It's a great life."

Pedro handed out the menus with the dessert choices and announced, "Our maitre d' visited the kitchen today. He has prepared a special dessert for this table. He calls it Melting Glacier. It is a warm chocolate cake with hot fudge sauce on vanilla ice cream. Very delicious. It is not on the menu, only for you, but if you'd like to try it, he will be pleased."

"He cooks? Lucy, this is a man of many talents," Ian said with one raised eyebrow. "Pedro, I will have the special. How could I resist."

Everyone agreed to try the special dessert. Lucy sparkled, flattered at the attention. "Those Italian men, they certainly know how to woo a woman," she murmured, smiling.

"Apparently so," Mrs. Bernbaum said dryly. "Be careful, my dear, you may end up with your one true love after all."

"Not a chance, but it is fun. And he's a great dancer."

"And he comes in and out of San Francisco half of the year," Millie commented.

"That too, we'll see what the future brings."

The plates of dessert were beautiful, the rich fragrant chocolate oozed over the peaks of vanilla ice cream and it did look like an iceberg.

"Ooh," they breathed in unison as they spooned the dessert into their mouths. It was delicious. "How do you suppose he got permission to work in the kitchen? I thought they had all these rules in place because of that stomach virus plaguing the ships? I know, that's what they told me when I asked for a kitchen tour," Millie said between bites.

"Oh, Antonio is also a chef. He graduated from Cordon Bleu. He worked first in the kitchens on the ship before becoming maitre d'. And of course, he is good friends with the chef here. He told me he helps out sometimes, when he has time or inspiration. I guess he was inspired."

"Well, Lucy, this dessert is inspiring me. It's wonderful. I wonder if he would consider sharing this recipe?" Millie was always interested in adding to her immense collection of recipes.

"I'll ask him for you, Millie. But if he does share it, you have to promise to make it for me some night." Lucy finished the last bite reluctantly. "I would like to have this again. Actually, I'd like more now."

"Ah, you'd like more?" Pedro was at her elbow. "I can get another serving if anyone would like." He looked around the table, pausing with his eyes on Ian.

"No, no. I'm sure we'd like more, but it's too late, and it's too rich. But my compliments to the chef. Will he be dropping by the table?" Ian laid down his spoon.

"No, regretfully, he has been called elsewhere, but instructed me to tell you," Pedro bowed to Lucy, "he would be seeing you on the dance floor later." Pedro gestured to Juan to pour the coffee as he collected the dessert plates.

"Dancing tonight? That should be fun with the ship rolling like this. Are you going, Claire?"

Claire shook her head. "I'm going to help Mrs. Bernbaum back to her cabin."

"Let me help. I have pretty good sea legs," Ian offered.

Claire and Mrs. Bernbaum both nodded, accepting his suggestion. Ian put down his napkin and came around the table to help her up.

"I'll see you at breakfast, Mom. I hope Ruth will be all right." Claire stood up, glad that Ian was going to help as she wasn't sure how steady she was.

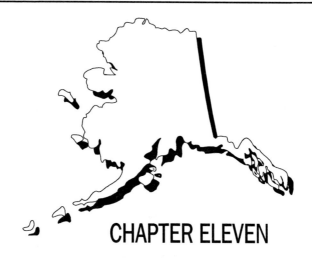

CHAPTER ELEVEN

"Now I know why they have this railing installed in the halls all over the ship." Claire held on to the one stretching down the corridor leading to Mrs. Bernbaum's cabin, while Mrs. Bernbaum clung to her arm. Ian held Mrs. Bernbaum's other arm and braced his other hand on the opposite wall of the corridor. Carefully they made their way along with a minimum of lurching and hardly any stumbling.

Finally they reached the cabin door and Ian gallantly took Mrs. Bernbaum's key card, inserted it in the lock, opening the door for them. They were all relieved when they reached the chairs in the sitting area and sitting, immediately felt more grounded.

"It's kind of amazing how a ship of this size can be bounced around so by the waves, isn't it?"

"It gives you a real appreciation of what a power Mother Nature really is," Ian said. "I can just imagine what it would be like in a real storm like a hurricane." He shuddered.

"I wouldn't want to be on the seas then, no matter how big the ship," Claire agreed. So far she was not seasick, but she wouldn't want to test it further with a real storm instead of what the Captain had announced on the speaker system as "rough seas".

"Now, Mrs. Bernbaum, did you want to call security or do you want me to do it for you."

"I'll do it, dear. Just help me over to the desk where the phone is, please."

"Is there a problem?" Ian looked alarmed.

Claire nodded. "Mrs. Bernbaum's caregiver, Anita, didn't return from shore in Juneau. Anita had been sea sick and very cross since they left San Francisco, so Mrs. Bernbaum thought she just went home."

"We had a bit of a tiff, you see," Mrs. Bernbaum added, in a way of explaining Anita's behavior. "I thought she got mad and left so I would worry. But now I am worried. We checked and she hasn't arrived home in San Francisco and I just don't know what happened to her."

While Mrs. Bernbaum dialed the phone Ian whispered to Claire, "What does she think happened?"

Claire shrugged. "That's the problem. She has no idea what happened to her. She thinks the Juneau police need to search for her."

"Well, the security officers are on their way up here," Mrs. Bernbaum reported as she hung up the phone.

Ian stood up. "I'll be getting out of your way." He paused a moment before adding, "Unless there is something you need me to do?"

"No. Thank you so much for escorting me back from dinner, Ian. You were a big help."

Claire walked to the door with him. "I'll just stay with Mrs. Bernbaum, but I'm sure security will take care of everything. Thanks again, Ian. We'll see you tomorrow." Claire closed the door gently, trapping the security chain between the door and the sill to prevent it from closing completely.

"He's a very nice man, isn't he? But I sense that your mother prefers his brother. What do you think?"

Claire looked at Mrs. Bernbaum with surprise. Then thinking a moment, "You may be right. She does seem to be spending some time with him. He is very nice too, perhaps not quite as sexy as Ian, but very comfortable to be around. I think I'll just have to keep my eyes open. Wouldn't that be a surprise, if after all these years she finally took a beau?"

The knock at the door chased those thoughts from her head as she called out, "Please come in. The door is unlocked."

The first man, very professional looking in his dark blazer with the discreet security patch, went right to Mrs. Bernbaum and shook her hand. "Larry Smithston, madam. I was here the other night."

"Yes, yes I remember you. Please sit down." And she looked inquiringly at the second man.

"Mark Belossa, madam."

"Please, both of you sit down. This is Claire Gulliver. She is a friend of mine and was good enough to help me back to my cabin after dinner."

The men nodded politely at Claire.

"I am now very worried about my caregiver, Anita Fernandez, who did not return from shore in Juneau. At the time I assumed she decided to fly home to San Francisco because of a little disagreement we had that morning. However, since then my nephew, Dr. Walmer, tried to call her in San Francisco, but couldn't reach her.

"In addition, Claire contacted a friend in the San Francisco Police Department and they sent an officer out to Anita's house and interviewed some of her neighbors. No one has seen Anita and they don't expect her home until Wednesday.

"I'm afraid something has happened to her." Mrs. Bernbaum sat back, waiting for the security officers to respond.

Claire thought the men were very professional as they questioned Mrs. Bernbaum, recording her answers and offering suggestions. They took her concerns seriously and agreed something could have happened to Anita. They said their agent in Juneau had already done a search of the hospitals and morgue, but they would now instruct him to contact the police and report Anita as "missing."

And by the time they left, Claire was certain these men would be following the search for Anita carefully.

"Well, do you think they'll find her?"

"They seem very competent, don't they? My guess is they'll find her. I found it very reassuring that they had already had their agent check the hospitals and morgue." Claire nodded her head, feeling optimistic about the meeting.

"Yes, that's a load off my mind. I hated to think she might have been hurt, or worse, and waiting for me to find her."

Claire stood up cautiously, bracing against the next roll of the ship. "Mrs. Bernbaum, is there anything I can help you with before I leave? Do you need help getting ready for bed?"

"No, dear. You've been very sweet. I'll just take my time. And hold on to things. I've got a big day tomorrow and I have lots to think about."

"Mom said you were going to have a ceremony for Nate tomorrow. She wants to attend. Is that all right?"

"I would appreciate it. It will be in the afternoon. The Mulligan Mortuary is arranging it. You can check with them about where it will be."

"Okay, we'll see you then. But if you need anything, just call me." She went to the little desk and wrote her cabin number down. "There, I'm in cabin number twenty-five, twenty-three." Then she launched herself at the door and, hanging on to the rail, she quickly made her way down the corridor to the elevator.

* * *

Sometime in the wee hours of the morning the seas calmed to a gentle roll and by the time the ship sidled up to the dock at Skagway the passengers hardly noticed the ship was now stationary. Claire emerged from the second deck door and walked down the gangway in the crisp bright sunshine to find their ship docked right behind a huge Princess cruise ship. The two ships in a row took up the entire dock, which must have stretched about a quarter mile below the bluff.

The dark gray stone side of the bluff towered over the ships and was adorned with the logos and names of the countless ships which had docked at Skagway. Tradition was when a ship first docked there members of the crew were dispatched to add the ship's name to the history recorded on the bluff. Judging by the height of the cliff it couldn't have been an easy chore, yet it was obvious there was some rivalry involved, because many of the names were ornately recorded and some of the logos were artistically rendered. Many were recorded in difficult to access areas, taxing the viewer's imagination as to how they had been achieved. And they all stood the test of time and weather, a permanent record of ships docking at the tiny historic town.

The four ladies stood a moment on the dock studying the bluff, then remembering the time, they walked briskly down the dock toward the end where the tours were assembling and where, they had been told, they could catch a bus into town.

This morning all four had scheduled a trolley bus tour of Skagway. This afternoon they would split up. Lucy and Ruth had elected to take the afternoon train to Chilkoot Pass, the famous route the gold miners took to the Yukon Gold Fields, while Claire and Millie had opted for a bus to the top of the pass on the new highway. Both options were certainly faster and more comfortable routes than the miners had available. During the height of the gold rush each would-be miner had to carry one thousand pounds of supplies up the steep icy steps over the Chilkoot Pass in order to be allowed to enter the Gold Fields. It was hard to fathom the determination of those miners, which drove them burdened like animals to the top, where they stockpiled their goods and returned to the bottom only to find a place in line again with another load. Horses and mules died en route, but the men pressed on in pursuit of their quest for gold.

"Oh, look at those cute buses." Millie led the way holding out her ticket to the young woman dressed in a flowered, full skirted dress of the 1920's and who was clutching her straw, flower bedecked hat on her head with her other hand to keep the brisk icy wind from snatching it.

"Ladies, find a seat we'll be ready to leave in a moment or two." She gestured to the door of the brightly painted, very old, yellow bus.

They found a pair of empty benches halfway down the aisle.

"Oh, there's Heidi." Millie waved and smiled. Then nodded to another couple across the way she knew from the ship. "Move over a smidgeon, Ruth, or the first time we turn a corner I'll be on the floor."

"I can't move over. These are really small seats. Just hold on."

It didn't take long for the bus to fill completely and the charming young lady did a count just to make sure she had everyone. Then she jauntily slid into the drivers' seat and with much ceremony she started the engine, shifting the stick beside her as she announced, "Welcome aboard. We are so lucky to have such a beautiful day to see Skagway. Think back to that time in the 1920's when this bus was made and how the town looked then. Actually, it's not much different today as you'll see when we drive through it. Skagway is a year-round town, but from September to June we have less than a thousand residents and not much happens here during the winter months. But come June, the sun, the summer workers and the tourists arrive.

"Skagway was born out of the Gold Rush and at one time was the largest city in Alaska. In the begining, Dyea was the most important town. Dyea is not far from here and while it was a booming Gold Rush town then, now you can barely see the ruins that mark where it existed. But Skagway is still here. Skagway survived because of the railroad and its port."

"Are you a year-round resident?" Someone asked her.

She headed out of the parking lot, shaking her head. "Nope, I spend half of the year in Portland and the other half here. My family owns this tour line and we all work here during the season. My older brother is the manager and he does live here all year. But when winter comes it takes a special kind of person to make it through to spring." She laughed. "Not me. I'd go batty."

She continued with her spiel. "So when this trolley was made, the town was here and had about the same number of year-round residents, but from the beginning many of the residents wintered outside. Citizens from the whole area would arrive in Skagway before the last ship left for the outside and return in late May or early June when the ice broke."

Millie leaned forward and whispered to Claire seated in front of her, "That's the story Mrs. Bernbaum told us about Nate's family. Remember, they left from here on the Princess Sophia, the last ship. Just remembering the story sends chills up my spine."

Claire turned around and looked at her mother and shivered. Suddenly that story seemed more real. She followed the driver's lively chatter closely, trying to imagine life here in the early part of the last century; thinking how tragic that loss would have been to this isolated area.

Skagway was only four blocks wide between the railroad tracks and the river, but stretched twenty-three blocks long from the Ferry Terminal to the end of town. The business section was only a few blocks, but they could see in passing that it was crowded with interesting shops, a saloon, ice cream and candy shops and some museums. Claire knew they would take the time to explore this area some time later in the day. Meanwhile, she was letting Daisy, their driver's, entertaining spiel lull her into a dream of yesteryear, and of life on the frontier. Daisy told them of the horrors of living under the thumb of Soapy Smith, the notorious scoundrel who controlled the town until Frank Reid called him out in a duel. The heroic Frank Reid shot and killed Soapy, freeing the town from his grasp, only to die a few days later from wounds he received courtesy of Soapy.

Daisy drove them to their theatre for a slide show of the town. It was especially interesting to see the pictures tracing several local families through the generations they lived in Skagway. Then she drove through town and up the hills on the Dyea Road to a lookout where they could see the entire town and the two mammoth ships docked near the Railroad terminal. The wind buffeted them, making it hard to take their pictures. This was only a sample breeze, Daisy told them, as compared to the wind which would thunder through this pass in winter dropping the temperatures to fifty below zero. In fact, she said, the name Skagway meant "Land of the North Wind" in the language of the local tribes. They were glad to board the trolley again for their ride back to town, this time stopping at the Gold Rush Cemetery to visit the graves of Soapy Smith and the town hero, Frank Reid.

Daisy told them about Martin Itjen, Skagway's original tour director. He converted an old truck into a tour bus to accommodate the Presidential tour of Skagway. He subsequently drove his bus to Hollywood and somehow became a favorite date of Mae West, all the while drumming up tourist business for Skagway. It seemed that this little town had a colorful past.

"Skagway, even today is an exciting place. People are close. They rely on each other to survive the winter. Several years ago a McDonald's finally opened in Juneau. The town sent the Medivac plane to Juneau to bring back their order of hamburgers and fries, and then met in the school gym for a feast. The McDonald's opened at two in the morning to fill the order. It was quite the occasion around here."

The passengers laughed, appreciating that picture of the little town. One of the men near the front of the bus asked Daisy about the time the sun went down.

"I thought we were going to have daylight most of the day, but it's nearly the same as it is at home."

Another added, "And I thought we would see the aurora borealis, but so far no luck."

"Well, you're here at the wrong time for long days of sunshine. The longest day of the year was June 22. If you had been here then, you would see the sun set about eleven at night and rise again about two in the morning. Would that be a long enough day for you? But now we're halfway toward the shortest day of the year, December 22, and so sunrise and sunset adjust accordingly. But if you were further north in June the sunrise would come very shortly after sunset and it wouldn't even get dark. And if you are looking for the Northern lights you need the dark skies to see them. Come back in December, or better yet, stay through the winter. You'll see plenty."

The tour was over and Daisy offered to drop them off in town or take them back to the ship. They opted for town. They wanted to check out the shops, Millie wanted to check with the mortuary about when the service for Nate would be, and they all agreed a visit to the Red Onion Saloon was in order.

* * *

It was very quiet in the cemetery. This was not the picturesque old cemetery they had visited earlier on the tour of Skagway. This one was newer, located across the river from the Gold Rush Cemetery and not swarming with tourists all day. Here, tree limbs swayed in the breeze. The birds sang and the bees buzzed about their business. Here the peace and tranquility was only broken by the arrival of new tenants. Here, in this sheltered spot, it seemed possible that loved ones could really rest in peace.

Richard nodded at Claire, so she turned toward the gates and the car provided by the mortuary. Mrs. Bernbaum was still sitting close to the site where Nate's ashes had been buried with his parents and sister. Since she couldn't bring herself to leave just yet, Millie had told them to go on. She would wait until Mrs. Bernbaum was ready to leave and bring her back then. Mr. Mulligan from the mortuary was very understanding, assuring them he would send the car back to wait for them. So now Richard and Claire were headed back to the ship.

"Auntie told me you had someone in the police department check out Anita's house. That was very kind of you," Richard said in a low voice.

"It was no trouble, and it established she wasn't there."

"This flare-up between Auntie and Anita was destined to happen." His expression conveyed clearly his frustration with the problem. "Auntie is a pretty feisty woman. She has been very independent, doing just what she wanted. At least she did until Anita came to work for her. As far as I can figure out, Auntie had apparently become very despondent about that time. Perhaps it was coping with her advancing age and a failing body. She had no family around and I think she just didn't care any more.

"So, Anita took charge of Auntie's life. Anita did everything the way she wanted and Auntie just let her. It must have been an easy job for Anita, not much to do. They watched the television programs Anita wanted to watch. I think it suited her that Auntie was housebound, dependent on her.

"Then I came along and disrupted everything. Because then Auntie perked up and started taking an interest in life once more.

"I've seen that happen so many times in my practice when someone, who has lost all hope, finds out they can still do things. Maybe not the same things they did when they were young, but certainly some form of the activities which interest them. After all, contrary to all the excitement about longevity, no one wants a long life if every day is an endless bore.

"So my arrival annoyed Anita, because suddenly my aunt didn't want to sit around all day. Auntie wanted to go out. She liked it when I dropped over for dinner. And when I began treating Auntie with my vitamin therapy she had even more energy. Suddenly she realized it was possible to do some of those things she always meant to do, but hadn't. She started making a list of life quests to be completed before her time ended.

"And her most important life quest was to come to Alaska and bury Nate's ashes with his family here in Skagway. We talked about it at length before we decided a cruise would be the best, as it would be the most comfortable mode of travel for Auntie.

"Anita was vehemently opposed to the whole idea. Perhaps she saw it as the final break in her eroding control over Auntie and the life they had been living. In spite of the countless reasons Anita came up with to cancel the trip, Auntie was determined. I've suspected Anita insisted on coming with us to prove she was right about how foolish the trip was. In fact, I think Anita's seasickness really was a manifestation of her anxiety over losing control of Auntie.

"But my aunt is really a gutsy woman. Apparently, all those months, actually years, of doing nothing provided her too much time to think. And one of the things she thought about was her inability to part with Nate's ashes. She realized when she was gone no one would see that his ashes were buried with his family. She wanted to make sure he's safely settled here in Skagway before she passes on."

Richard shook his head, pausing while he gathered his thoughts. "So my arrival in her life meant it was possible for her to honor her promise to Nate.

"And I'm happy I could help her. I believe, whenever possible, a person should be encouraged to complete those tasks which drive them. I'm pleased to say I think I was instrumental in helping her do this."

Claire nodded, surprised that Richard, who normally was rather aloof, was taking the time to explain all this to her.

"Anyway, Anita is at cross purposes with Auntie. She doesn't know the independent, self-sufficient woman, Auntie really is. She wants their relationship to be back the way it was. I think she could see Auntie was enjoying this cruise. That it wasn't going to fail like she predicted. So she just took off and is holed up somewhere in Juneau, thinking Auntie is worrying about her disappearance, thinking Auntie is struggling to get along without her. Then Anita will appear to save the day and take care of her again."

Claire's eyes widened in surprise. "But that's so childish."

Richard nodded. "Precisely. But still, I think that's where Anita is. She's determined to return to that time before I appeared when she could rule the household. She catered to Auntie's little demands then, because she didn't let her do anything else. Auntie lived a shut-in life with only television and naps interspersed with meals. So Anita wasn't bothered by other people and she didn't have to expend herself except on those rare occasions Auntie went to the doctors. The hairdresser even came into the building once a week. Auntie never went shopping or to social events. She didn't entertain. Anita seemed to like that life. But those days of boredom were suffocating my aunt."

Claire looked at him thoughtfully. "How do you know so much about your Aunt? I thought you only met her a few months ago."

Richard laughed. "Right. Yes, you're right. But how could I not know her after listening to her stories. After all, you've talked to her. Do you think she's a shy, retiring little old lady? Can you imagine her as a docile, agreeable patient?"

Claire smiled at that and shook her head.

"No, it's obvious she's a strong minded, determined woman. Anita has been all wrong. And she's wrong now if she thinks she can come back and all will be forgiven. No, when she shows up she will find herself without a job. Auntie needs to find someone else, someone who understands what the job requirements are and will do what Auntie wants her to do. And that will not be Anita."

"Mrs. Bernbaum told me you work with elderly people. How lucky is that for her?"

Richard nodded somberly. "We don't treat our elderly citizens well. As a nation, I think we tend to dismiss them. Once a person retires, their opinion is no longer valued. People humor them, but mostly ignore them. Yet these are the people who have the experience, and the understanding, and the wealth to help us solve our problems. We should appreciate the richness they can bring to our lives. We should revere them as the Chinese do their elders. Think what a difference that would make in our society."

Claire blushed as she remembered her reaction to Mrs. Bernbaum when she first found herself sitting next to her at the dinner table. It didn't take long to learn Mrs. Bernbaum was an interesting person. But it bothered her how quickly she had assumed she was going to be a bore. "You're right, Richard. You make a wonderful advocate for the senior generation. You should write a book or something. I can just see you on Oprah."

"Sorry, I guess I was on my soap box again."

"No, no I was serious. You are doing important work. I can imagine you make quite a difference in the lives of your patients. And it's really very noble of you because inevitably these patients are going to run out of time. It must be very hard on you when that happens."

"Sometimes," he admitted. "But I try to remember we're all going to die sometime. My patients are the lucky ones. They've lived a long life and hopefully, I've helped them remain active so they enjoy their time. And when they go, it's a natural ending, not the tragedy of someone taken in their prime before they have accomplished their goals. No, my patients can go anytime. They know it and I know it. We try not to be surprised when it happens."

Their driver pulled up to the dock and Richard got out, holding the door for Claire. Then he thanked the driver and they headed down the long dock to the boarding ramp.

"Mrs. Bernbaum seemed quite worried about Anita's disappearance when we talked about it last night," she said tentatively.

"Yes, she is worried, but eventually she'll think it through. You wait, when Anita shows up, Auntie will be relieved, but then she'll be mad, really mad. That will be the end of Anita's job. You'll see."

Claire saw from his look of satisfaction that he was certain he was right. But she was distracted with the flurry of getting her card out to run through the machine at the entrance to the ship. Inside she waved good-by to Richard and headed for her cabin to get rid of her heavy jacket.

* * *

When the call came she expected it to be Nate's lawyer telling her he had managed to have the charges dropped because they had raised enough money to reimburse the investors for their losses. Instead he told her gently Nate had been taken to the hospital. They thought it was a heart attack. The doctors weren't optimistic. He said he would meet her at San Francisco General. She should hurry.

Her footsteps echoed loudly as she hurried down the dim hall. She nodded at the policeman sitting on the chair outside Nate's room, but didn't wait for his permission before she pushed open the door and entered the dim hospital room. Her heart was pounding so hard she felt faint. She was afraid of what she would find.

There were two beds in the room, but only one was occupied. It would be hard to mistake Nate's large form, even shrouded as it was by the sheets and attached by tubes to mysterious equipment around the bed. She crept *forward, hardly daring to breathe, praying he was going to be all right.*

But she didn't need a medical degree to see that wasn't likely. His face was a strange shade of gray, and his breathing was very shallow in spite of the oxygen mask strapped to his face. His eyes were open and he was watching her mutely.

She pulled the chair close to the side of the bed and sat down heavily, her legs wouldn't support her any longer.

Gingerly she picked up Nate's hand, squeezing it, as tears flowed down her cheeks.

"Flo, Flo, I need you to promise me something." She could barely understand his words, garbled as they were by the mask on his face. She leaned closer to reassure him.

"Promise me, Flo, will you?"

"Anything Nate, you know that." It was hard for her to speak without breaking down completely.

"Give it back."

"Pardon, I don't understand. Give what back?"

"Give it back. The Heart of Persia. It's cursed. Evil! Give it back and make it all right again."

"Nate, what are you saying? Give it back to whom? Why?" She wondered if he really knew what he was saying.

Now his voice came stronger, clearer. "I cheated. God forgive me for it. Remember that card game I told you about, the one where I won the jewel? It happened; it was all true, but what I didn't tell you was I cheated. During all those winters in Skagway as a boy I didn't just learn to play poker, no, I mastered a deck of cards. My fingers are like a magician's. I can stack a deck while I'm shuffling. The guys in Skagway never allowed me to deal when we played cards. They didn't trust me. They wouldn't give me a chance to cheat them even though I never did cheat them. But, I did cheat that one time, that one game."

"Nate, I don't believe it. You wouldn't. Tell me you didn't." Florence leaned close to her husband, willing him to change his story.

He shook his head only slightly, but she could see in his eyes he was telling the truth. He gave a pathetic smile. "You know what they say about 'deathbed confessions', love. It's the truth and I need your help to make it right."

She couldn't contain the sob, struggling to calm herself so as to not upset Nate further. "What can I do?"

"Find him, apologize to him and give it back to him. He'll be mad, I know." His voice was getting weaker again. The words were slow coming, but she didn't try to hush him, she could see he was determined to tell her.

"I remember it all so clearly," Nate said and she leaned closer to hear him.

"It was a long game, lots of money on the table. We were waiting for our orders to go home, you see? Most everyone else was gone and there was nothing to do but play cards and wait our turn. I set him up. I didn't know about the Heart of Persia, but I could see the amount of money he had already won. So I waited for my turn to deal and chose to play Seven Cards Stud. I was very clever. I didn't just deal him a full house; I dealt another guy a flush and one guy a set of aces. Three of them were each sure they had the winning hand. None of them suspected the pair of threes in front of me matched a pair of threes I had in my hole cards. The betting kept accelerating. Then Rourke, the Irishman from Chicago, pulled the Heart of Persia out of his pocket and asked who could match its value. That's when I offered the deed to my dad's gold mine. I had it, you see, because when he died they sent the deed to me while I was stationed in England.

"The set of aces folded; he didn't have the money or the hand to stay in despite the Heart of Persia and a genuine gold mine in the pot, but the flush stayed in. And of course I won it all.

"I was proud of myself. The Heart of Persia was gorgeous. I knew you'd love it. I knew my luck had turned when I met you. Only good things were going to happen to me from that point on. I thought taking that pot was one more example of what my life was going to be. I thought it was my right to take what I could. But I was wrong.

"These past weeks in jail have given me a lot of time to think about this. My decision to cheat to win that game was the equivalent of my dad's determination to send my mom and sister outside for the winter, when she didn't want to go. It was a disaster in the making. When I made that decision to cheat I sealed my fate.

"My dad was so sure he was right. He didn't listen to my mother's protests. He dismissed her dreams of disaster. He was certain he knew best. Later he was destroyed by that decision. It was as if he killed them himself. I grew up seeing what that did to him. You'd think I would have learned. I should have been more careful to protect what we found together.

"You were the one good thing that happened to me. Your love kept me safe on all those bombing missions. It was the need to come back to you that kept me going, no matter how dangerous those times were. And I jeopardized our future with that cheap trick of cheating. Why?

"For the money? Not really, more because I could. It was the fun of fooling them all and getting away with it. I thought the world was mine. I thought I could do whatever I wanted.

"I could have sold the mine for enough money to start a small business. I could have worked it myself to get enough to invest in something else. But no, I choose to go into business with that scum, Smithy. I believed him when he said we were going to be rich. What a joke."

He managed a wobbly little smile. "Only it wasn't so funny, was it?"

"Nate, honey, it's not too late. Our lawyer settled with all the investors. They agree to drop their complaints. And you can get better and give the Heart of Persia back yourself. You know I don't care about the money or the jewelry. I just want you." She pleaded with him in a broken whisper. "Please, you have to get better. It can all be fixed."

"No Florence. I'm sorry. It's not going to happen. You can't know how sorry I am to leave you, but I'm not going to survive this. And I don't have time to fix it."

Florence nodded. She knew he was telling her the truth, already his skin was taking on a slightly green tinge and she could see how much effort it was for him to talk to her.

"His name was Sean Rourke. He was from Chicago. I'm sure you can track him through the Army records. He's going to be mad, but he won't be mad at you.

"He said he got it from a Russian refugee he met in France. Rourke was shot down over France and somehow he made his way to the coast. Somewhere along the way he met up with this refugee and his daughter, who had been trapped in France when the Germans invaded. They were also trying to reach the coast, so he took them with him. The man was so grateful when they reached England he gave Rourke the jewel. The refugee told him it had been in his family for generations, but swore it was a small price to pay for his daughter's safety. Rourke had been dumbfounded by the man's insistence that he take it."

Nate was quiet. The noise of the heart monitor seemed even louder in the silent room. "I guess the refugee understood the real value of the jewel."

Florence put her face down on his hand resting on the bed and quietly wept. She wanted to scream and rail at all the tubes that were connected to him, keeping her from cradling him in her arms.

"Florence? Promise me you'll return the jewel? It belongs to Rourke, he should have it."

She nodded, not even attempting to lift her head. She didn't bother to tell him she no longer had the Heart of Persia. It didn't seem important just now.

"And Flo, love, take me back to Skagway. Bury me with my family, will you? That's where I belong. My whole family was marked by tragedy. We need to be together again as a part of the Alaskan soil.

"You're still young; you can have a good life, for both of us. I'll be watching out for you. You know I love you more than I can ever tell you."

He was so quiet that at first she thought he had died. But when she raised her head she could see he only slept. He didn't die until later that night, but he didn't speak again. There was nothing for Florence to do but hold his hand and pray. But God didn't save Nate.

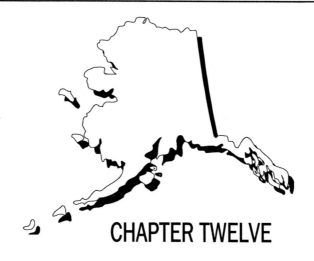

CHAPTER TWELVE

"Oh, there you are dear. I thought I'd find you around here." Millie dropped into a chair sitting next to the cocktail table in the nearly empty lounge. "Have you seen Lucy or Ruth? I wondered if they were back yet."

Claire shook her head, carefully inserting her bookmark in her book before slipping it into her tote bag. "I haven't seen either of them, but I expect they'll show up soon.

"How is Mrs. Bernbaum?" Claire inquired with concern.

"The poor dear. It's not easy, you know. It doesn't really matter that he died more than fifty years ago, a burial somehow brings it all up again. I took her to her cabin. She said she was going to take a little nap and frankly, I thought she looked like she could use one.

"She told me the story of when Nate died." Millie proceeded to recount the story Mrs. Bernbaum had told her. "It's so sad. She had already sold the *Heart of Persia*, along with everything else she owned, in order to obtain enough money to reimburse the investors. So, of course, she couldn't give the jewel back. And then Nate died and she said she was in a fog of depression for months. She said she always intended to bury Nate's ashes, but she could never bear to part with him.

"And after she married Bernie and several years later when he surprised her by repurchasing the jewelry she sold, she didn't have the heart to tell him about the *Heart of Persia*. She just kept it and wore it. It made Bernie happy and so it made her happy.

"But she said she had promised Nate, and she always intended to keep those promises. Then one day she realized she still hadn't followed through on either promise to Nate. And she thought she was too old then. She didn't think she could make the trip to Skagway. That really depressed her. But then Richard arrived on her doorstep. He was full of optimism; he refused to believe 'old' was a good enough reason to give up. He encouraged her to make a list of things she still wanted to accomplish in her lifetime. He said he would help her fulfill her life quests. So while she was sad about leaving Nate in Skagway, she said she was relieved she finally delivered on her promise to him."

"What about the *Heart of Persia*?" Claire asked. "She still wears it, so obviously she didn't give it back."

"You know, she didn't mention it." Millie thought a minute before saying, "I'm sure she is planning to do something about that, too. She seemed very determined to honor her promises to Nate. I felt so sorry for her. It was such a sad story and I could see how distressed she was even after all these years.

"Really Claire, I don't care how valuable that jewel is. I think it's really ugly. I just can't understand why she would even want to wear it after all the grief it brought her."

Claire nodded thoughtfully then changed the subject. "Well, I had an interesting discussion too, with Richard. Perhaps it wasn't as interesting as yours with Mrs. Bernbaum, but it certainly gave me a different perspective. In fact, I think I may have misjudged the man."

Millie's eyebrows rose with surprise.

Claire nodded. "He's always so aloof and remote. He never acts like he's enjoying himself and, except for his aunt, he doesn't seem to be interested in anyone at the dinner table. I just thought he was so full of himself he was bored with us. But after talking to him today, I don't think that's true."

"Well for goodness sakes, what did he say?"

"For one thing, he has a whole different slant on Anita's disappearance." She proceeded to explain Richard's theory about Anita's disappearance.

Millie nodded. "Well, it's possible. It's easy to see Mrs. Bernbaum wouldn't take to being patronized for long." She shook her head. "And he's right, you only have to listen to her a short time to understand what she's like. But I find it hard to believe she was so docile and willing to let Anita take control to begin with." She thought a moment. "Well, of course if she had given up, if she didn't really care anymore, then I guess I could see how she would just allow Anita to take charge."

She gave Claire one of those looks she used when Claire was a child and she wanted a truthful answer to an important question. "You met Anita a couple of times. What did you think of her?"

Claire inwardly squirmed, careful to choose the right words. That look always unhinged her. "I thought she was a very strange person. I knew she wasn't feeling well, so I tried to give her the benefit of that excuse even though she muttered what I thought were inappropriate comments under her breath so Mrs. Bernbaum wouldn't hear her, but I could. Of course, that's when I thought Mrs. Bernbaum was overlooking her negative attitude because of all the years of faithful service Anita had given her. But then Mrs. Bernbaum said she had only worked for her a few years. That surprised me, and I couldn't think why she put up with Anita's grumpiness."

"So Richard might be right. What a mean, childish thing to do." Millie was indignant.

Claire nodded. "That's what I thought. And frankly, I'm inclined to believe Richard on this. I'd rather think it was a cruel childish prank than something more sinister."

Millie nodded her agreement.

"But Richard also talked about his work with the elderly. He's very passionate about it. I would have never guessed. He has some very definite ideas about the need to help the elderly complete their life quests, about tapping their experience and wisdom for the good of society, and about treating them with the respect they deserve. I must say, it gave me an entirely new view of him as a person."

"Good afternoon to you, ladies. Did you have a good day?" Ian smiled down at them, effectively ending their conversation about Richard and his aunt.

"Ian, we did. Did you? Sit down and have a drink with us, why don't you? Tell us what you've been doing. Where's your brother?" Millie looked around and, then seeing Sean entering the lounge, waved to him.

Ian pulled out one of the empty chairs at the same time signaling to the waiter for service.

When the drinks had been ordered, they turned their attention to finding out what everyone had done with their day.

Millie told them about attending the interment of Nate's ashes, concluding with, "It was very sad, but I think she was relieved to have it done. I think it was haunting her."

"What did you do, Sean?" Claire asked.

"This morning we went on a tour of the town and out to Dyea, at least where Dyea used to be. This afternoon I took the train. In fact, I joined your friends. It was a lovely trip. We saw mountain goats, a moose and several eagles as well as stunning scenery." He looked around. "Where are they? I expected to see them here."

"Don't worry, they'll show up. It's cocktail time," Millie said with a smile.

Claire looked at Ian. "Didn't you go on the train?"

He shook his head. "No, too tame. I felt I needed something a little more strenuous. I went out with a group of rock climbers. It was only a short trip, but fun. And it got some of the kinks out." He flexed his shoulders.

Millie shook her head in wonderment. "You're so energetic, Ian."

"Now that I'm retired, I have the time to pursue all those activities I used to hear about and wish I could try. Now I feel I need to try them all."

Lucy and Ruth joined them with a burst of chatter. "Millie, come on, we need to move into the theatre for the show. Don't you remember?"

Millie started. "Oh, that's right." She glanced at her watch. "My church friends took this cruise in the spring and told us not to miss this show. This guy lives here in Skagway, year round, and he does these shows about the Klondike times for some of the cruise lines. He will do two and then get off before the ship sails. We need to go if we're going to get a good seat." Then correctly interpreting the dismayed looks on the brothers faces, "Don't worry, you can order cocktails in the show."

"You know who this is, don't you?" Ruth asked. Then seeing the blank faces she told them, "Daisy's brother. Remember, she said he manages the tour company and lives here year-around? Well, he is also the director of the show and the theatre they have in town. I saw his picture when we stopped there. Judging by the spiel Daisy gave, I expect this to be good." They moved into the vast theatre to find choice seats.

* * *

Claire was shocked at Mrs. Bernbaum's appearance when she sat down next to her at dinner. She realized that although she had originally thought Mrs. Bernbaum was ancient, as she got to know her, she had ceased noticing her age. But tonight Mrs. Bernbaum's eyes were dull instead of snapping with interest, her smile gone, her lips were compressed in a narrow grim line, and her crepe paper skin was now very grayish in color. The total effect was alarming.

"Mrs. Bernbaum, how are you doing?" She reached over and gently laid her hand on Mrs. Bernbaum's where it rested on the table.

"I'm fine, dear. Really!" Mrs. Bernbaum sighed. Then tried to answer Claire's obvious concern. "Just tired. It's the memories you see. All those memories just fill your head and exhaust you. I truly appreciated you and Millie coming to the cemetery. It was very kind of you and somehow it made the task a little easier." Her attempted smile was pitiful.

"Good evening ladies and gentlemen." Antonio stood near Lucy, beaming at the entire table. "I invite you to join me for a champagne toast this evening. It's a wonderful way to start your dinner." He gestured grandly and Pedro and Juan set out graceful tulip shaped champagne flutes and one of the sommelier's assistants brought three bottles of champagne. Antonio popped the cork on the first bottle and filled Lucy's glass, then each of the ladies' glasses while Pedro popped the cork on the second bottle and filled the men's glasses. Then Antonio, with a flourish, lifted a glass of his own. "Here's to another delightful dinner with congenial friends. Thank you all for joining our cruise." And everyone responded with, "Hear, Hear" and sipped their wine.

Antonio smiled happily at everyone, bent over and whispered something in Lucy's ear and then left them to enjoy their champagne, shrugging off their thanks for his generosity.

"I love the way the bubbles tickle my nose, don't you?" Mrs. Bernbaum whispered to Claire. "I know it sounds kind of strange, but I think this is just what I needed to finalize today's ceremony." She took a generous swallow. "Somehow it makes me feel better."

Claire took another sip and nodded. It was a nice way to start the meal. And she noticed how merry the others seemed.

Richard chatted with his aunt in a relaxed manner. Harold and her mother were discussing something, while Pearl laughed with Ian and Sean. Ruth whispered to Lucy and, even though Claire couldn't hear what they said, she was positive it was something about Antonio. She could tell from Lucy's pink face. It was a congenial group, almost as if they had become family. Everyday they were all off doing a variety of activities, but every night they gathered together and shared their adventures, enjoying each others experiences, enriching their own experiences. No wonder people raved about cruising. It was truly a wonderful way to travel.

Ruth tried to explain to Pearl and Harold about the show they had seen before dinner.

"It reminded me of a show I've seen in Wales," Lucy added, then leaning forward she called down the table to Claire. "Claire, didn't the show tonight remind you of that variety show you saw in Wales?"

Claire nodded, smiling. "Yes, now that I think of it. Of course, that one had a variety of skits, one after another; still this one was as much fun, certainly. The man is very talented and fun, don't you agree?"

The others nodded and tried to explain to those who had missed it why it was so good. "You should have heard this man, Richard. He played the guitar and sang ditties and somehow managed to play the harmonica at the same time." Sean laughed. The noise level at the table increased exponentially with their enthusiasm, or perhaps it was with their sips of champagne.

The meal proceeded in a leisurely fashion. Sometimes the conversation was global including all ten of them, sometimes it split up, multiple concurrent conversations going on at once. But Claire watched Richard keep an eye on his aunt. Obviously he, too, was concerned about her energy tonight.

When the sommelier poured the last of the champagne, Ian ordered two more bottles. "Can't let the table go dry, now can we? Lucy, I hope you let Antonio know how much we appreciate his attentions. We realize who he is trying to impress, but truly he has impressed us all with his cooking and his generosity, heh?" He looked around the table for agreement.

Lucy smiled, taking the ribbing good-naturedly.

"We were talking to a couple on the shore excursion today," Harold added. "They said Antonio hasn't even stopped by their table."

Pearl giggled. "You should have seen the look on their face when we told them about the special starter he had served us."

"Yes, I think we can thank our lucky stars that we were seated at Lucy's table. And I don't mean just because my wife is a fan of hers." Harold's droll comment made everyone laugh.

"I'm stuffed. Everyday I promise myself to skip desert, but I never do." Pearl put down her napkin and got ready to get up from the table. Her husband hurried to stand and hold her chair for her. "I think we need to go and get our exercise. Anyone want to join us?"

She laughed at the surprised expressions turned her way. "I get my exercise feeding coins to the slot machines. It helps me work off dinner." She giggled as she left.

Everyone took that as the signal to disband and Claire asked Mrs. Bernbaum if she needed an escort back to her cabin.

"No, dear, thank you. Dickie will take me." Richard helped his aunt stand up and then, holding her arm, he guided her through the jumble of empty tables and chairs.

"She looks awful," Claire couldn't help saying.

Millie nodded. "It's like she aged twenty years."

"Yeah, and that would make her well over a hundred and ten. Isn't she feeling well? Did you ask her, Claire?" Ruth was concerned.

Claire nodded as she moved towards the exit. "She said she was fine, just tired."

"It was probably harder than she expected to bury Nate," was Millie's opinion.

"Oh, that's what she said. She told me the memories were very tiring. I hope she's okay."

"Well, fortunately she has her physician with her," Lucy reminded them. "Let's check out the casino for a while. I'm feeling lucky tonight."

"I thought you'd want to go dancing." Ruth's sly reference was ignored by Lucy.

"Later. Are you coming, Ian?"

"Yes, I think I might play a little blackjack."

"What about you Claire? I think I hear that Slotto machine calling to you again?" Ruth was excited. She loved the casino almost as much as she loved playing cards.

"No, I'll come, but I think I'll just watch, or maybe I'll play one of those nickel machines."

"Millie, I'll show you the machine I told you about." Sean bent toward Millie as they walked. "I think you'll like it."

* * *

The pianist was finishing his last set in the dim cozy piano bar. The few patrons still up clapped politely as if it was too late to get up much enthusiasm.

"Where have you been? I've been waiting for hours," Kim hissed, annoyed. "Sorry, it's hard to get away." He ordered a drink. She shook her head at the waiter's inquiry.

"Is everything okay?" she whispered. With the music gone the lounge seemed too quiet.

He grinned. "Everything is great. I think tomorrow is the day. After we leave Ketchikan..." He fell silent as the waiter placed his drink in front of him and gave him his card and receipt back. Then he raised his glass to her. "Thanks to you, it's working perfectly." He took a sip of the drink and sighed, relaxing.

The piano lounge was very clubby in appearance. It was tucked away on the far side of the casino. The walls were paneled in dark wood, the fireplace was always lit, and the air conditioning guaranteed the right temperature was maintained. Leather club chairs and big sofas were scattered in conversation groups. It was a cozy comfortable haven and it was a favorite spot for them to meet late in the evening.

Kim drained her drink. She felt edgy, nervous, and she was feeling deprived, which she blamed on him. "Well, it can't be over too soon for me. I'm sick and tired of skulking around. I'm tired of watching other people have fun. I want to dress up in my pretty clothes and join the party. I want to show off my dance skills the way I see that couple does. You know, the woman who wears all the hats to match her outfits. They're at all the dances taking up more than their share of the dance floor with their elaborate dance routines."

Her voice was sour, her jealousy obvious. "After this trip you're going to owe me plenty." She glared at him, truly angry. This had not been an enjoyable cruise for her, maybe because she couldn't really take advantage of the amenities, nor mingle with the other passengers. She needed to be invisible, so she spent her time on the outside, observing the fun others were having, while she waited for her time with him. She had suggested she leave the ship after completing her role in the scheme, but he wouldn't hear of it. He said it might direct attention towards her and their whole plan was to divert attention and suspicion.

So she tried to fill her hours, but only in activities where she didn't need to participate with other passengers, and therefore, become known to them. She couldn't play trivia, which she was especially good at, because she would be part of a team. She couldn't play card games as each table of players developed an intimacy between them. She could and did play Bingo as there she was just another face in the huge audience. She could swim and workout at the gym, which she did every day, careful not to nod or make eye contact with any of the others who might make a friendly overture. She saw most of the movies and went to all the theatre productions. She ate in the buffet set up every night for those who didn't want a formal dinner so the people assigned to her table never even saw her. She went to many of the lectures, but two she attended she found to be too intimate, so she didn't stay. The whole environment of the cruise seemed to foster involvement and lean toward creating friendships; she had to do the opposite without anyone noticing. That was the only way she could remain anonymous.

He looked at her appraisingly. He didn't want her to be upset. He appreciated her willingness to take care of Anita when it became apparent that Anita's presence would interfere with their success. And he was truly amazed at how skillfully she dispatched her. He had never imagined she would be good at it. He remembered how excited she had been afterwards. That disturbed him a little, but he shrugged it off deciding to think about that later. Now he needed to reassure her. He needed to keep her happy for a few more days until they arrived back in San Francisco.

"Kim, you're the best. I appreciate everything you've done. I know it's been hard, but wait, you'll see, it will have been worth it. I promise you that. And maybe after everything is settled, we'll go off on a cruise of our own. Maybe to the Caribbean? You'd like that. Sun and fun with lots of partying, with a younger group of passengers and no one will care who we are. And we won't care if they notice us or not." He smiled, coaxing an answering smile from her. He put his empty glass on the little side table and got up. Holding out his hand to her, he escorted her back to her cabin for some physical reassurance.

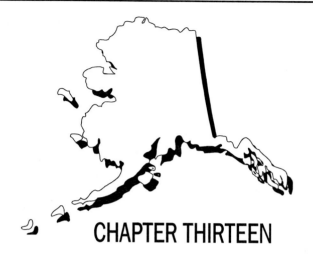

CHAPTER THIRTEEN

"About time you got back." Lucy was ready. "I almost decided to come up and find you, but I thought I'd probably miss you. You are either very slow on the computer or they're missing you at the book shop."

"Both, I am a little slow this morning. I think I stayed up way too late last night. And I know you did, although I didn't even hear you come in."

"I was pretty quiet," Lucy said with a grin. "When you come in that late you don't like to call attention to it by making noise."

Claire laughed. "True. And I appreciate your stealth. How do you suppose Antonio keeps up with the pace? He has to work every day."

"Practice, I imagine," was Lucy's droll response. "Are you ready to go out? Did you notice the weather?"

"I'm ready." Claire pulled out her scarf and jacket. "It's cold and cloudy. Dress warmly. How about we find a cup of coffee first thing? I'm feeling the need for more caffeine. And don't forget your ticket for the DUCK Tour."

"Yes, mother. I've got it right here. Let's go, coffee sounds good to me."

The friends made their way down the corridor to the door on their deck where the disembarkation was going on today. Millie and Ruth had left very early to join the Gallagher Brothers on shore today. They planned to hire a local to take them on their own special tour after deciding that none of the offered excursions were quite what they wanted. Ian had complained they wanted to do everything, see everything at this last port in Alaska and the tours offered were too restrictive. They decided to pool their money and hire a local so they could do just the things they wanted to do and stay as long as they wanted at each place. They figured it still would be cheaper than the excursions the cruise line offered.

Claire, on the other hand, wanted a lazy day. She needed to spend some time catching up on her emails. After all, she still had a business to attend to. Besides, after Sitka and Skagway, she wasn't ready to spend another busy day on shore. Lucy, battling sleep deprivation from her late nights with Antonio, was in agreement with her. They decided to explore the town at leisure late in the morning, signing up for the DUCK tour to make sure they saw something of the town with minimal effort on their part.

After their coffee and a pastry in lieu of breakfast for Lucy, they wandered the town ending up in the picturesque area of Creek Street. There Ketchikan's former infamous red light district clung precariously over the creek. The old wooden buildings now housed shops catering to tourists. It was hard to imagine now, how it had been then, in spite of the one house which had been turned into a museum of that time. The intent of the museum was to maintain the house as if it was still in use. The docents agreeably dressing the part in feathers, ruffles and heavy make-up didn't fool the visitors for a minute. Still they enjoyed their visit even though they dawdled too long and had to hurry back to the dock to catch their DUCK.

"Oh, look at that. Some of my customers told me about taking one of these in Boston, but somehow I didn't imagine it so big, and awkward."

The big amphibious vehicle was painted a bright, garish yellow. It looked like a barge, on wheels, sitting in the middle of the street. The driver had let down a ladder like contraption that people were already struggling up to gain access. Claire and Lucy waited their turn and then held on to the rope guide while they ascended. Inside was like a big bus with a canvas top. All the windows were closed against the weather today, but it still wasn't really cozy inside.

They selected seats and Lucy generously waved Claire into the window seat. After all, she had a camera and would be trying to get pictures of everything. The driver's seat was separated from the passengers. It looked like he would be sitting in a little hole. Beside him was a place for his assistant. Soon the passengers were in place and counted, the driver settled in his niche and the assistant pulled up and secured the ladder. They were ready to go.

"Boy, I'm glad I'm not driving this thing. It would be like driving a Hummer in those little lanes in Cornwall. What a behemoth!"

Claire agreed, holding her breath as the driver somehow got them through the streets around the Creek Street area. It wasn't a long tour. After all, Ketchikan was a rather small town, and the DUCK quickly made it seem smaller. Since much of the town was built up the side of the mountain, many of the streets were too steep or too narrow to allow the DUCK access. Then after going through the warehouse district near the waterfront, the driver paused and with a great grinding sound coming from the front, he drove into the water and they were floating. It was a very strange sensation. Soon however, it was apparent that the DUCK was much more comfortable in its role of a water-going vehicle. There it seemed to be more graceful, more responsive. They made their way cautiously through the harbor while the tour director told them about the huge canning capacity the town had, and of the colorful fishing history of the town.

When the first huge bird blotted out the view by diving into the water right outside one of the windows the passengers drew back frightened. They didn't know what was happening and the birds were way too big and ferocious to be seagulls. It was incredible. Suddenly, they were in the midst of a flock of eagles, diving into the water all around them. There must have been over a hundred. It was fantastic and frightening.

"See them sitting on the roof? They have learned how easy it is to get a meal when the cannery is operating. What you're not seeing is the offal of the fish, which the cannery is pumping out through a long pipe, and dumps right about where we are."

More birds dived while some settled back on the roof of the cannery waiting for another turn. "The eagles know when the cannery is operating. They're intelligent enough to know this is an easier way to get a meal then their usual hunting. You won't see any seagulls around when the eagles are here. I suppose the eagles wouldn't mind eating the seagulls if they were stupid enough to try to compete for the fish entrails."

"Did you get any of those on film?" Lucy asked.

"Don't know. It's kind of hard with all the swooping and diving. I tried to get the ones on the roof, but I'm afraid they'll only look like little dots from this distance. I don't think anyone will believe it when we tell them."

Their driver guided the DUCK out of the harbor and there was the same grinding and shaking as before. Then they were off down the streets, dripping sea water, heading back to the cruise line dock.

"Well, that was fun," Lucy admitted when they were safely on the ground again. "But now I'm starved. Let's have lunch at that restaurant we saw down the way. It looked good."

Claire agreed. Their ride on the waves had apparently activated her appetite too. But after a pleasant lunch, Lucy was ready to go back on board. She wanted a massage.

Claire wasn't quite ready. "I'm going down to check out the Discovery Center we passed on our tour. It looked interesting."

And it was. The Southeast Alaska Discovery Center was crammed with interesting displays including an entire rain forest ecosystem. She spent over an hour there before she happened on the book store tucked in the back corner of the center. Here was an entire shop dedicated to books about Alaska. Here was everything anyone thought or experienced about Alaska. They carried no fiction on these shelves. Nevertheless, they had plenty of adventure stories. Claire took off her jacket as the cheery fireplace kept the store too warm to last long in her outerwear. She made a list of titles and publishers she thought would be appropriate to add to her own stock for customers planning a visit to Alaska, and she couldn't help purchasing a couple books to read on the voyage. One was *The Sinking of the Princess Sophia* by Coates and Morrison, and another, *I Married the Klondike*, by Laura Beatrice Berton. She intended to share the first with Mrs. Bernbaum and her mother. Knowing that Nate's mother and sister died on the ill-fated vessel made the book even more intriguing.

* * *

Claire found an empty table with several chairs along the front window on the non-smoking side of the Starlight Lounge. All during the voyage this seemed to be the place they all congregated, so she was certain her friends would be showing up before the ship cast off. It was still early, but it was a pleasant place to read while she waited for the others to arrive. She turned her chair toward the window, laid her binoculars and camera on the little table, having learned her lesson to keep them ready at all times, and settled down with her book.

"Look who has her nose in a book. Why am I not surprised?" Ruth, with Ian in tow, found her first.

Claire smiled. "Must be cocktail time."

"You bet. And we're just in time to help the captain navigate."

"What's the drink of the day, today?" Millie, right behind Ruth and Ian looked pretty tonight, perhaps the cold weather was making her cheeks pink and her eyes sparkle.

"Do we need more chairs?" Sean, trailing slightly behind, wrestled a chair from a table behind them that wasn't yet occupied. "How many?"

"Better get a couple more," Ruth instructed. "There's one." She pointed at a table not far away and the occupants graciously admitted they didn't need the chair.

"Where's Lucy?" Millie asked.

"Don't know, but she'll show up shortly," Claire assured her, then said to the waiter, "I think I'll try the drink of the day, the Mango Daiquiri, please."

"I'm buying today," Sean insisted handing his card to the waiter. "Please let me as it's so much cheaper than buying champagne for the table as others have done."

They laughed at Sean's attempt to portray himself as a cheapskate. They already knew from the past few days what a generous person he was.

"Well, how was your day?" Claire's questions started a deluge as they all tried to describe their day at the same time. What she got from their onslaught was it was a very successful venture and it was too bad they hadn't thought to do it earlier, as it was a very satisfactory way to see a port.

Lucy, as Claire predicted, arrived when the waiter brought their drinks. After she ordered she offered with a guilty smile, "I had a wonderful massage and then went back to the cabin and fell asleep. What a great afternoon."

"Well, as long as you didn't miss cocktails..." Ruth said.

"Not a chance, I have an internal clock that lets me know the proper time. I can be in my office, immersed in my writing and when cocktail time arrives it's like an alarm goes off in my head. I have to wrap it up for the day. I'm very disciplined that way."

Just then the horn blasted and the ship eased back from the dock. Claire looked at her watch. The ship was leaving right on time.

"Oh, look at that view of Ketchikan. What a pretty little town it is, even on a gloomy day." Millie pointed. "Claire did you get a picture of it from here?"

Claire nodded, pointing to her camera sitting on the table. "First thing I did when I sat down. I'm afraid I snapped several. You know how it is, if one is good, ten are better."

The lounge had filled with others who liked to have their pre-dinner cocktails in the front of the ship. The band was playing and some brave couples were on the dance floor, apparently not concerned about the ship movement landing them on the floor in front of everyone.

"Look, there's Maude and John." Millie nodded toward the dancers, who were doing an intricate tango with some panache. Today they were wearing cream and pink, and Maude's cream colored crocheted hat was covered with large pink sequins which sparkled with her every move.

"Kind of hard for a man to wear pink," Ian observed. "But I have to say they look good."

"Oh, they look like they're having so much fun. I talked to Maude and she told me they cruise everywhere. She says she likes *Call of the Seas* cruises because they have the best music and the most dancing. She was a dancer on the New York stage for many years, and I have to say she looks like she's been."

Trust Millie to have talked to the couple and learned their entire life's story, Claire thought.

"There's Miss Smiley." Lucy nodded at another couple. The woman was a well-stacked blond and with a huge smile which previously Lucy had said unkindly, was to show off her newly whitened teeth. She was with her partner, a very large, prosperous looking older man who may or may not have been her husband. They too, loved to dance.

They watched an elderly couple, both very tall, walk carefully, with creaky, uncertain steps to the edge of the dance floor and then, while the watchers all held their breath, they saw them glide out on the floor as smoothly as if they were young again.

"Well, I guess I can do that too. Millie, would you care to dance?" Sean held out his hand gallantly and Millie followed him to the dance floor.

One of the dance hosts approached the table and asked Lucy to dance, so she left. Ian eyed Ruth and Claire. "Do either of you feel inclined?"

Claire shook her head. "It's more fun to watch."

"I agree, unless you feel the need, Ian. Otherwise, let's just sit and critique."

So they enjoyed their drinks, the music, and watching the dancers as the ship moved steadily out into deep water.

* * *

"Oh, where's your aunt tonight, Richard?" Millie asked, concern ringing in her voice.

"She decided to have soup in her cabin and watch a movie. She said she was resting up for the formal night tomorrow," Richard said, sitting down in one of the two remaining available chairs. "I think yesterday's events were a little much for her. She needs some quiet time. But she's fine, really."

"I noticed she didn't act her usual self last night," Millie agreed.

"And she looked very tired. I was worried about her, too," Claire added. "Is there anything we can do?"

"No, rest and quiet time is what she needs and she's getting those. You'll see tomorrow that she will be all right." He then turned his attention to the menu Pedro had handed him.

Claire decided on the grilled salmon and sat quietly while Pedro took the rest of the orders. Then Lucy launched into a description of their DUCK tour. She had the entire table spellbound listening to her telling about the eagles over the bay. That's the writer in her, Claire thought. She definitely has a way with words. She could see everyone felt as if they were there, experiencing it themselves.

"Oh, how thrilling. I must say we haven't seen nearly enough wildlife on this cruise. I was hoping for a lot more."

"Well, Pearl, it's because they're wild, you know. They usually avoid humans. We have a reputation for killing them, on purpose or just out of ignorance," Ian reminded her.

"Did you see the naturalist's presentation on otters the other day? He's so funny; he makes you feel like he is one. He was lying on his back on the stage with his feet in swimming flippers and his head out of the water and I swear he looked like an otter." Pearl bubbled with enthusiasm.

"I didn't see that one, but I saw the one he did on whales. Did you know he kayaked from Seattle to Juneau three separate times? He says it takes him three months each trip. Can you imagine doing that?" Millie was wide-eyed just thinking about it. "I'm sorry I missed his presentation on otters. I don't know what I was doing then. Claire and I saw a couple of colonies of otters when we took that wildlife trip out of Sitka. They were so interesting."

"I think you can catch a video of his presentation on the ship's channel. It's twenty-three, I believe. I noticed they usually repeat videos of the lectures for people who miss them," Harold offered.

"I'll look for it. We should have more time in the next couple of days."

"For sure. I'm looking forward to some days at sea. I think all this touring in ports and all these tempting excursions are too wearing. This is supposed to be a vacation, isn't it?" Lucy complained.

"Lucy, none of us are feeling sorry for you. I suspect you're wearing yourself out with the hours you're keeping. And you're old enough to know better." Ruth was smug. She was still being true to her new love in San Francisco. She wasn't wearing herself out with a shipboard romance.

"Ruth, don't discourage her. We're all enjoying the benefits of Lucy's romance," Ian protested.

Lucy stuck her tongue out at Ruth and turned her attention to her appetizer while Millie, Ian and Sean explained to Pearl and Harold the advantages of doing their own tour.

It wasn't until desert was served that Sean mentioned the comedian who was appearing in the theatre later. "Who wants to join me? I think a few laughs will just cap a perfect day for me. Ruth? Millie? What about you, Claire?

Millie and Lucy decided to join him. Ruth declined having agreed to meet some of her new friends for bridge after dinner. Claire was undecided, torn between joining them and heading back to her cabin for a quiet evening with her book. Pearl and Harold were going; they had seen the comedian earlier in the cruise and said he was very good. Ian and Richard were noncommittal; neither really said what their plans for the rest of the evening were.

When they left the dining room and headed up to the theatre, Claire trailed along. She didn't decide to leave until about fifteen minutes into the comedian's routine. By then she found while everyone else was laughing uproariously she just wasn't getting his brand of humor. She leaned over and whispered good night to her mother and quietly worked her way out of the room. It wasn't until the doors closed on the elevator that she thought of Mrs. Bernbaum. She quickly jabbed the button marked eight, deciding to stop by and see how the old lady was feeling.

The corridor on eight was very quiet. She turned around the bend where the corridor changed directions just in time to see Ian's back disappearing into Mrs. Bernbaum's cabin.

How nice of him, she thought. He hadn't said anything, but obviously he was concerned about her, too. She hurried, smiling, pleased to catch him doing a good deed.

She was going to knock, but she noticed the door, while closed, was not latched. The safety chain had been laid between the door and the door jam preventing the door from closing tightly. So Claire pushed the door open, entered and said brightly, "Caught you..."

Ian's head swiveled toward her. His expression was one of shock. His face paled visibly in the dimmed lights of the cabin. His outstretched hand gleamed with the brilliant red of the *Heart of Persia*.

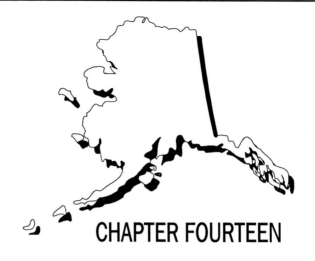

CHAPTER FOURTEEN

Claire froze. She didn't know what to think. In fact, she could barely think. This was not at all what she expected. She whispered hoarsely, "Ian, what are you doing?"

They both stood motionless. Then Ian brazenly challenged her with, "Not what you're thinking, for sure! I just stopped down to see if I could do anything for Mrs. Bernbaum and found the door open. I tiptoed in to check on her, but saw this on the table. I just wanted a closer look."

Claire thought about his very plausible answer a moment before responding drolly. "And you just happen to be wearing latex gloves because why?"

Ian didn't have a ready answer for that. He looked at his hands as if surprised to find them attached to his body. His glove covered hand was still holding the blood red jewel. It was obvious he had been caught.

"I can't believe this! You were going to steal her jewel? What are you, some kind of cat burglar?" she hissed at him as her brain started functioning again. "How did you get in here anyway? I don't believe for a minute the door was unlocked." She glared at him, all her protective genes gathering force to protect Mrs. Bernbaum.

He started to answer her and then shrugged, giving it up. "I have my ways. The locks aren't very good you know. Any professional could get in without much effort. The cruise lines don't consider it's cost effective to spend a lot of money on a better door locking system."

"Professional? You're a professional? I can't believe it." She leaned against the wall for additional support, afraid the trembling in her knees would cause her to collapse. "And your brother? Is he a thief too?" She thought with alarm about her mother, wondering if Millie was finally interested in someone, only to find he was a scoundrel.

"No, he's just a nice guy, retired, widower, just as he claims. Unfortunately for him, he's related to me."

Claire just stood there, trying to absorb this shocking information.

"Look Claire, why don't I just put it back? No harm done. I promise to leave it alone, if you'll just forget this whole thing happened." His winsome smile infuriated her.

"No harm done? Because I walked in and caught you, that's the only reason no harm was done." Claire's voice was increasing in volume as she spoke. She found herself becoming more indignant with every word.

"She's an old lady, Ian. She is very attached to that piece of jewelry. To you it might mean money, to her it represents the love of two men. I don't think we can just forget this."

"Shhh," he cautioned her.

They looked at each other, realizing at the same time how strange it was that Mrs. Bernbaum had not heard them. She might be old and decrepit, but she had demonstrated several times how keen her hearing still was.

"Where is she?" Claire murmured.

Ian shook his head. "I assumed she was sleeping. I didn't look."

They stared at each other, each willing the other to look in the bedroom, but neither moved.

"You check on her. I'm keeping my eyes on you so you can't disappear with the jewel."

"Look, I've put it down. See, I put it right where I found it." He lay it down on the table beside a watch and some earrings. "I'm not going to run away. We're at sea, for God's sake, where would I go?"

She nodded. It was true. She could always find him or the security people could.

"You check on her. What if she's in bed? She'd be frightened if she woke up and found me in her bedroom," Ian whispered pleadingly.

"Oh, all right. But don't you dare move an inch." She crept into the bedroom, while her mind churned with terrible thoughts. What if Ian was worse than a thief? What if he was also a murderer? Her heart started beating at a furious rate and suddenly she was afraid of what she would find.

She told herself to calm down. Commonsense told her if he was a murderer, surely she would already be dead after catching him red-handed. So Mrs. Bernbaum was probably just sleeping deeply. She was just tired like Richard had said.

The bedroom was dark with only a little light from the living room reaching through the open doorway. Claire skirted the first bed. The one Anita had used, and moved toward the mound she assumed was Mrs. Bernbaum, in the second bed. "Mrs. Bernbaum," she whispered. "Mrs. Bernbaum, wake up."

The old lady didn't stir. That seemed alarming. She said in a louder voice, "Mrs. Bernbaum. It's Claire. Wake up. Please wake up."

She jumped back startled at the glare of the lights. Ian had switched them on when he came in the room. But it didn't matter. It was obvious the light wouldn't disturb

Mrs. Bernbaum. Nothing would. She lay under the covers; her eyes open. Dead!

"Oh, poor Mrs. Bernbaum." Claire was so upset her voice shook. "She buried Nate yesterday and now she's gone. It was just too much for her."

Ian took Claire's arm and pulled her back to the living room, switching the light off as they went.

"I suggest we just leave and let someone else find her."

Claire looked at him, horrified.

He looked sheepish. "I didn't think you'd go for that. Well, I could disappear and you could call security?"

She shook her head. There was no way he was leaving her here to handle this by herself.

"Well then, I think we need to get our stories straight before we call security."

Claire looked at him numbly. Then she realized what he was saying. "Of course, how are you going to explain your presence here?"

"Right! Actually, this changes things somewhat, doesn't it? Now, it won't harm Mrs. Bernbaum if I take the brooch. It's perfect. We both can have what we want."

She glared at him.

"It's worth a fortune. You could have a cut, after I sell it of course."

"Forget it. The jewel stays, along with all the rest of her jewelry. In fact, I think it would be smart if we just put it all in the safe for her. You can do that, can't you?"

He nodded reluctantly.

"Well, do it." Claire was irritated and upset. And her anger was directed at Ian. She knew it was because of Mrs. Bernbaum's death and she knew Ian wasn't to blame for that. But she didn't try to temper her feelings now. She blamed him for trying to steal from Mrs. Bernbaum, and she blamed him for wanting to take advantage of the old lady's death. She watched as he quickly worked the dial. It didn't take long for him to identify the code programmed into the safe and open it. She handed him the jewelry from the table and watched him put it in before closing the safe again.

"Now, I would suggest you get rid of your gloves before we call."

He ripped them off his hands and stuffed them in his pocket as she went to the phone. After she completed her call she turned and said, "I think we should just say what happened. We stopped by to see if she needed anything and found the door closed, but not latched. We came in and found her."

He nodded his agreement, his gratitude obvious in his eyes.

The door, which still hadn't been closed completely, burst open and people filled the cabin. Claire indicated the next room and the woman, who was apparently the doctor, disappeared. The two attendants followed, one still pushing the wheelchair he had arrived with. Then the security personnel arrived. The last one through the door shut it firmly behind them. They were conscious of the need to keep any passengers, innocently passing, unaware of what was going on.

The doctor returned, shaking her head. The attendant pushed the wheelchair back out to the corridor. There was no use for it now. "Steve is going for the gurney," the doctor told the security officer, who seemed to be in charge. Then she turned to Ian and Claire. "I'm sorry. There is nothing I can do. Did she have a medical condition which may have caused this?"

Claire shook her head. "I don't know."

"Are you the closest relative?"

"No, no, we're just friends. We're seated at the same dinner table. We stopped by to see if she needed anything, but..." Her voice trailed off as the enormity of the situation struck her. She sat down heavily. Luckily there was a chair behind her. "Her nephew would know. He was her doctor as well as her closest kin." She realized in horror how quickly she had referred to Mrs. Bernbaum in the past tense. It made her feel callous, unfeeling.

The lead security man introduced himself as Kramer and indicated the doctor. "This is Dr. Carolton. She will take care of everything. I'm afraid we will have to move the body to the mortuary until we reach San Francisco. I see from our records that no one else is occupying this cabin as Mrs. Bernbaum's companion left the ship in Juneau?"

Claire nodded. "She didn't come back from shore. We're not quite sure what happened to her. Mrs. Bernbaum talked to your department about doing a search for her and reporting her missing to the Juneau Police Department. Do you have a record of that? I think she spoke to...," she hesitated a moment and then remembered, "Larry Smithston. Yes, that's who she spoke to."

"Yes, I have that information. So far we haven't heard anything from Juneau, but we'll continue to pursue it. Meanwhile, we will be securing this cabin. Who is the nephew she's traveling with? Can you give me his name and his cabin number?"

"He's Dr. Richard Walmer, but I'm afraid I don't know his cabin number. Do you Ian?" All eyes turned to Ian.

He shook his head. "Afraid not. It's on one of the lower levels, I remember him saying, but frankly I have enough problems remembering where my own cabin is."

"You seemed to find this one," the security officer said with a touch of sarcasm.

Ian started, then recovered. "Well, yes, but I've been here a couple of times. We all came to a party to view the glacier, and one night I helped Claire escort Mrs. Bernbaum back to her cabin when the sea was rough. And, of course, tonight I came with Claire. She's been here many times."

"And just why have you been here so many times?" The cold stare was leveled at Claire now and she felt uncomfortable.

"I told you, we became friends. She invited me to tea. I've stopped by to visit. I sometimes walk her back to her cabin after dinner, certainly not for any sinister reason." She found herself getting annoyed at the way he made her feel, as if she needed to defend her actions.

"Of course, I didn't mean to imply anything else." He made a note in the book he carried.

There was a knock at the door and when the other security officer opened it the attendant wheeled in a gurney like affair, followed by Jorges, Mrs. Bernbaum's cabin steward. He wasn't ringing his hands, but almost. He was visibly upset.

"Ah, I'm so sorry," he said to Claire, immediately recognizing her from her visits with Mrs. Bernbaum. "I was here earlier tonight, about six I think, to make sure her dinner was satisfactory. Her nephew said she would be all right until morning when I should bring her usual breakfast tray. She was fine then." Then he paused. "Well, maybe not. She looked very tired. A little gray. Was it her heart?"

Claire shrugged, looking at the doctor.

"I don't know. We will investigate, but it looks like natural causes. How old was the victim?" the doctor asked.

"I think ninety-two."

The doctor nodded. "Well, she could have died from any number of causes, but probably it was just old age. Body parts wear out eventually. I'm truly sorry." She turned away and re-entered the bedroom.

"Well, I have your names and cabin numbers, so I don't think there is anything else you can do. I'm sorry this incident happened on your cruise. We have these occurrences regularly so we're used to it, but I know it is upsetting, especially when you know the person. I hope you won't let it mar your vacation."

And then they were out in the hall. Claire looked at Ian. "They didn't ask many questions."

"No, why would they? It all seemed like a normal situation. Thanks, Claire, it could have been really bad for me."

Claire shook her head. She didn't want to talk about Ian's role. She didn't even want to think about it right now. "I think I'd better go find my mother. She would want to know. She will be upset about Mrs. Bernbaum."

* * *

"Darn, almost got it that time."

"Almost doesn't count on slot machines, Kim. You either hit, or you don't." He watched the reels spin as Kim hit the button once more.

"I need some more money." She held out her hand with a little pout on her mouth. "Please?" she begged prettily.

Grudgingly he dug out his wallet and extracted a couple of bills. "Christ, can't you play a quarter machine? Or what about those nickel machines? They look like fun."

"Now don't get all stingy on me. I like the old fashion kind of slots with the reels 'cause I love the clinking of the coins coming out when they hit. Those nickel machines are tricky. They're all electronic. How do I know what they've programmed them to do?"

He looked at her with amazement wondering how she could possibly think the electronic ones were more likely to cheat her. But she didn't notice as she was feeding his money blithely into the bill slot on the machine.

The machine provided five pay lines to maximize the opportunities to win. Unfortunately, as Kim explained to him, the player needed to play all five lines each time to make sure of a win. On this machine, five lines was the equivalent of five dollars. It made him cringe to watch how fast his money disappeared. But he realized she was happy, and she wasn't complaining about how bored she was hiding out below decks as she had every night previously. And there were only two more days until they docked in San Francisco and this trip would be over.

He ducked back behind Kim as he spied some of his dinner table mates at the other end of the casino, then he reminded himself that there was no harm in them seeing him. What could be more natural than a bachelor, who was hanging around a pretty blonde? In fact, he told himself, it probably would make him seem more normal, less suspicious.

"Did it happen?" Kim said in a low voice.

"Huh?" Then he realized what she was asking. "Yeah, very simple. Just like we planned."

"Did it make you feel powerful? You know, as if you were in control?" She paused and looked at him. "It did me. I actually liked it. I mean, of course I'm not looking for an opportunity to do it again, but I wouldn't hesitate if I had a reason. It's not nearly as scary as I was expecting."

He almost shuddered at the look in her eyes. He didn't want her to do it again. God, he hoped he hadn't unleashed a monster. "No, it didn't make me feel like that. It was just something that had to be done, so I did it. Simple." Of course it wasn't as simple as he said. He suppressed a shudder as the horror of what he had done washed over him once more. He had actually found himself liking the feisty old woman, who was his last living relative.

"Just like that? No evidence; no one will suspect anything?" She couldn't seem to let it go.

"No evidence. Everything is perfect."

She hit a small jackpot and squealed with excitement. The payoff only reinforced her belief the big one was coming.

He sat there watching her play the machine, investing all his money and her winnings in more attempts to hit the big one, while thinking about her question of evidence. What bothered him was he realized there was evidence if anyone was looking for it.

But who would look for it, he asked himself?

No one!

But what if they did?

He felt sweat rolling down his back as he realized that his precipitous exit from her cabin earlier had been foolish. Even with all his careful planning, with all his intention to avoid any suspicion, he had been so rattled that all he could do was hurry away from her cabin as soon as he finished. What he should have done was take the time to toss the evidence off her balcony. He went icy cold as he touched the breast pocket of his jacket and felt the bag right where he had shoved it. The sweat now pooled under his arms and his eyelid began to twitch. He realized he needed to get rid of that bag now, right now.

"Look, Kim, I have to go do something." He fished his wallet out and handed her several bills. "You play a while longer and I'll be back in a minute. Okay?"

She nodded, satisfied with the money, hardly caring that he was leaving.

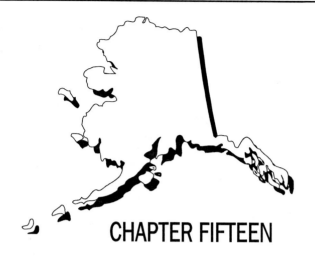

CHAPTER FIFTEEN

"Claire, what are you doing still here? I thought you went off to bed and your book a while ago."

"I did, but I stopped by to see how Mrs. Bernbaum was." Claire's throat started to constrict.

"Oh, that was sweet of you, dear. How is she?" her mother asked, concern on her face.

Claire just shook her head. The words were choking her and tears sprang to her eyes. Finally she managed, "Not good." She gulped and then said, "Mom, she's gone. We found her alone in her cabin, dead." She gestured vaguely toward Ian, who was right behind her.

Her mother was on her feet, her arms around her daughter in a comforting hug.

"Oh, the poor soul." She held her daughter tightly. "It's like she mustered all her energy to bury Nate and then she just gave up the struggle. I'm so sorry. And I'm sorry you found her." She patted Claire comfortingly.

"How's Richard taking it?" Millie asked softly.

Claire pulled her head off her mother's shoulder and looked at her, admitting with chagrin, "I don't know. He wasn't there. The security officer said they would notify him."

"Oh, that's not right. We can't just let some stranger tell him. He's going to be devastated. I know he told you he was used to that sort of thing, but believe me, Claire, this is going to be different. We need to break it to him gently. We need to tell him ourselves."

Millie looked around at her friends, their concern obvious on their faces as they clustered around the table in the cocktail lounge between the casino and the theatre. "I saw him a bit ago in the casino," she said thoughtfully.

Ruth nodded. "Yes, he was playing one of the slot machines with a young blonde."

"Well, I just passed him a moment ago when I returned from the *Gents*. I think he was headed out on deck." Sean gestured toward the set of doors between the lounge and the casino which allowed deck access.

"Okay, I'll try to find him. Coming, Claire?"

Claire nodded. She knew when her mother had made up her mind it was best to just go along with her. But she wasn't looking forward to breaking this news to Richard. However, she agreed with her mother; knowing how fond he was of his aunt, she was sure he was going to be very upset.

It was cold outside and the pool of light from the door didn't quite reach the light attached to the side of the ship. The women paused, peering through the darkness.

"Over there. I see him." Millie headed off, striding quickly down the deck with Claire hurrying behind her.

Richard was standing at the rail near one of the beams supporting the deck above him. He was leaning over the side slightly, as if looking at something in the water. Suddenly Millie darted forward and snatched a white object from his hand just as his hand opened to let it drop into the water.

"Richard! What are you doing? Don't you know plastic bags kill porpoises?" Millie's voice was full of horror as she backed away from him clutching the plastic bag protectively against her breast.

Richard actually jumped when Millie's hand snaked out and grabbed the bag in midair, right before his eyes. He turned his head and his surprised expression turned to fury. Then he lunged, both arms outstretched to grab Millie. Claire acted without thinking, stepping instinctively between her mother and Richard.

Richard's strength, fueled by his anger, was more than she expected. They danced awkwardly together as Claire tried valiantly to hold him back, but was soon flung unceremoniously onto the deck chairs lined up along deck opposite the railing.

"Give me that!" Richard snarled, lunging again, but this time it was Ian who stopped him.

"Easy, man. Let's not kill the messenger." Ian held Richard tightly, not bothered at all by his desperate struggles. "Get a hold of yourself, man. Millie and Claire just wanted to tell you themselves rather than have you hear the news from strangers. And now look what you've done. I hope you haven't hurt Claire."

Millie rushed to her daughter, as Claire struggled to her feet, gingerly extracting her limbs from the tangle of deck chairs. She was shocked and embarrassed at how ineffectual her effort was in protecting her mother, and she was confused by Richard's fury.

"Claire, are you hurt?"

"No, I don't think so, Mom. Maybe a few bruises, but nothing serious." Already she was on her feet and more interested in what was happening between Richard and Ian.

Richard started to calm down as Ian's words seemed to penetrate his brain. "What are you talking about?" he finally asked.

"Your aunt. They came to tell you that your aunt passed away this evening."

Richard shook his head as if to clear his hearing. "What are you talking about?" he repeated.

"Richard," Millie said gently from where she stood near Claire, "your aunt died this evening. Claire and Ian found her when they stopped by to see if she needed anything."

Richard's head swiveled from Ian to Claire. "My God, Auntie is dead? I've got to go...," he headed for the door. Then he stopped, half turned back. "My garbage..." he said looking at the bag which now lay on the deck where Millie had dropped it before going to Claire's aid.

Millie waved him on. "Go. Don't worry. I'll find a trash can and dispose of it where it won't endanger any porpoises."

He looked at her a moment, clearly undecided, then making up his mind, he nodded and left.

"Whew, thank goodness you followed us out here, Ian. I don't know what he was thinking. Surely he couldn't have forgotten all the warnings from the wildlife experts about how dangerous plastic bags are to porpoises. And he got so mad when I grabbed it, like a boy who lost his favorite toy." Millie went over and picked up the bag, looking around for a trash can.

Claire, picking up the contents of her tote bag, which had spilled out in the melee, said over her shoulder. "Here, Mom, give it to me. I'll throw it away for you." She took the plastic bag and shoved it in her tote to deal with later.

"Ladies, shall we get out of the cold?" Ian said gallantly as he ushered them towards the door.

Claire realized how chilled she was. She couldn't stop shivering. Her mother noticed. "Claire, we need to get you warmed up. It's the shock from getting pushed over, I imagine. You could use a cup of tea, or hot chocolate."

"Chocolate? Funny you should mention that." Ruth caught the last word of Millie's sentence as they joined the group again. "The Chocolate Decadence Midnight Buffet just opened. I think we should take a look before bedtime, don't you?"

Claire had heard about the nightly buffets, but had yet to see one. They never finished dinner until ten and then she was too full to even think of more food. But the thought of hot chocolate was very tempting. She agreed tonight might be just the night to check it out.

Ian and Sean were happy to escort the three ladies to the dining room where the chocolate extravaganza was laid out. They found a table and sat tasting plates of chocolate goodies while Claire sipped her hot chocolate, and they all discussed the irony of Mrs. Bernbaum's passing. They were shocked and grieved, but philosophical. Everyone but Claire was of an age where they were experiencing an increasing number of deaths among their friends and colleagues. It had to be accepted. There was no alternative.

Sean said it best. "I'm sorry it happened so suddenly and that Claire and Ian had the shock of finding her. But I'm so glad it was after she had the satisfaction of completing her life quest. She was quite a gal and a great addition to our table."

The others nodded solemnly and Ian said quietly, "That she was."

The hot chocolate was working. Claire no longer felt cold. Now she just felt very sleepy. She caught Ian's surreptitious glance her way as if he was checking on her. She noticed how he was sticking close to her. Perhaps he was worried about what she might say if he wasn't close enough to keep tabs on her. Actually, it was lucky he had been following her, because his arrival on deck when Richard was being so irrational proved to be provident. She hadn't thought of Richard as a violent man, but she didn't want to let him get his hands on her mother. He had been way too angry for some reason she didn't understand.

"Dear, maybe you should go down to bed."

"Yes, mother." Always the obedient little girl, Claire now was happy to follow her mother's suggestion and quickly headed for the elevator. This time she noticed that Ian didn't follow her.

* * *

The knock was muffled so as to not disturb the neighboring cabins, but the quick rat-a-tat-tat conveyed his urgency. He had to repeat it several times and just when he decided to go to his cabin and call her, the door opened.

"It's the middle of the night, are you crazy?" She didn't sound very welcoming, but he entered her cabin and trudged over and sat on the edge of her bed, his shoulders slumped with depression.

She turned on the light, then seemed to notice how he looked.

"What's wrong? Why are you here so late?" she queried, acting a little warmer.

"Shit, everything's wrong. And I'm here so late because I just got through with all the paperwork."

"What happened?" Her concern was mounting; he was always confident, in charge. She didn't know him acting like this.

"First I decided I'd better get rid of the syringe and bottle. You kept talking about evidence and I started to worry about what would happen if someone found it. You know, in case someone searched; in case someone became suspicious. So I decided to just dump it overboard. I thought that would be the safest way to get rid of it. Well, it wasn't. I went out on deck and found a secluded place. I had it over the side. I let it go." He looked at her with disbelief. "And Millie Gulliver just appeared out of nowhere and snatched it out of midair. I was so shocked I just stood there while she went on and on about how plastic kills the porpoises, or some such drivel.

"Then I just lost it. I got so mad, I swear, I would have dumped the sanctimonious old biddy over the side with the bag she was holding if her prissy daughter hadn't gotten in my way."

Kim was bending toward him, breathlessly waiting to hear what happened next.

"She's stronger than she looks and it was hard to shove her out of my way. But then before I could even get to Millie, Ian showed up. Do you remember, I pointed him out to you? He's one of the guys at our table, and he's big, and man, he's strong, even if he is old. He just held on to me and I was really struggling. I was so mad, you see. Anyway, I finally calmed down enough to hear what he was saying. It seems that he and Claire had stopped by to see my aunt and found her dead. Of all the rotten luck!

"I had to pretend I was shocked. Actually, I was shocked because I expected Jorges, Auntie's steward, to find her in the morning when he delivered her breakfast.

"And of course that's what would have happened if that nosy Claire hadn't interfered." He took a deep breath, then another in an attempt to calm himself.

"Well anyway, I had to play the part of the grieving nephew and go down to security and then the morgue. The doctor had a million questions for me, but I don't think she has any suspicions."

"What happened to the stuff you were throwing overboard?" Kim really was a sharp woman. She kept her mind on the issues that were important.

He shrugged. "I had to leave it there. Millie said she would throw it in a trash receptacle where it wouldn't hurt the porpoises." He said the last words in a prissy tone, as if imitating Millie. "I just hope she did," he said grimly. "And I hope she didn't poke her nose into the bag to check what was in it before throwing it away."

"So it's still here, on board the ship?"

He nodded. "They hold all the trash until they reach port and then off-load it. If anyone wanted to search, they could find it."

"Hell. That meddling old bitch. You should have pitched her overboard," Kim told him, and she acted as if she meant it.

"What are you going to do now?"

"Somehow I need to get that bag back, or at least find out if she saw what was in it before she dumped it."

"And if she did see what it was?"

"Then, I think, Kim, we'll just have to see that Millie has a tragic accident and disappears."

* * *

After breakfast, Claire, Millie and Ruth all went by the library to pick up the little news sheet, a brief recap of world events and the *New York Times* crossword puzzle. They sat for a while working the puzzle before Claire decided to give up on hers. "I'm going down to do my emails and I'll meet you both later at Bingo. Save me a seat." The ladies nodded distractedly. Both were intent on the last few clues.

The computer room was empty this morning, so Claire selected a computer near the back, overlooking the water. It amused her that the room was situated on the side of the ship along a great expanse of windows. It was as if the cruise line didn't want anyone to forget for one minute they were at sea.

She sat down carefully on the little chair, remembering painfully, the bruise she had discovered in the shower this morning thanks to her collision with the deck chairs last night. She didn't bother to mention it to her mother, thinking it was best just to forget the whole incident. She was surprised at the number of accumulated messages she had in spite of the fact she had responded to all she had pending only yesterday. It seemed that her promptness only spurred more messages. She finally arrived at the one she was waiting for from Mrs. B, her assistant manager at the shop. There had been a question about a big order that came in and she had asked Mrs. B to check some figures for her. And here they were. She looked around the work station for a pen with no success. She picked up her tote bag from the floor near her feet to get the one she carried with her and found the bag of trash Richard had tried to dump overboard. She had completely forgotten about it. She pulled it out of her tote bag meaning to toss it in the trash as she had promised. But she couldn't help wondering what it was he so urgently had to discard that he selected the ocean rather than search for a trash barrel.

Naturally she opened the bag to look inside. She put her hand in to move some paper out of the way. "Ouch. Damn." She withdrew her hand quickly and after close examination of her finger concluded the skin hadn't been broken. She shook the bag a bit, so now she could see it contained a syringe and a small bottle. No wonder he didn't want to throw it in a trash can, someone could jab themselves with the syringe. She studied the bottle's label intently, wondering if it was the vitamin cocktail he used on Mrs. Bernbaum. Since she was sitting in front of a computer she clicked on a search engine and simply typed in the name on the label. She studied the choices and selected one which offered an encyclopedia of medical information.

"*Potassium Chloride, Uses,*" she read. "*Potassium chloride* is used for making fertilizer by stimulating growth. It is used as a chemical feedstock for the manufacture of potassium hydroxide and potassium metal. It is also used in medicine, scientific applications, food processing and in judicial execution through lethal injection."

Judicial execution! She felt the hairs on the back of her neck stiffen. Lethal injection? She held her finger up and looked at it again. She was assured once again that the skin had not been broken. It seemed likely the syringe and the bottle were together in the bag because the syringe had contained the contents of the bottle and she certainly didn't want something used for lethal injections inadvertently poked in her finger. Her heart began to race as that last thought, *something used for lethal injections,* replayed itself loudly in her mind. Could that be the reason why Richard was trying to dump these items overboard?

Suddenly it was hard to catch her breath. She forced herself to remain seated, to be calm and think about this. She told herself she was jumping to conclusions. She was acting as if life was like a *CSI* episode on television. She breathed deeply in and out, forcing herself to calm down.

She reminded herself how much Mrs. Bernbaum loved Richard. And it was obvious to all of them that he doted on his aunt. So why did she immediately think the worse when she saw those words on the computer? That's when she remembered Mrs. Bernbaum only met Richard about six months ago, when he came from Florida to search for his lost relatives. What did Mrs. Bernbaum really know about her nephew? So she typed Dr. Richard Walmer in quotation marks and Googled him.

Her eyes widened in surprise at the long list of hits appearing on the screen in front of her. She clicked on one from the *Miami Herald.*

Longevity Physician Released, authorities drop criminal charges. Dr. Richard Walmer went free this morning after authorities admitted they did not have enough evidence to charge him. Dr. Walmer, senior associate of Life of Joy, Medical Association, was arrested Thursday on suspicion of second degree murder when his patient, Alma Myerson, died of unknown causes. Mrs. Myerson's children reported their mother had been a patient of Dr. Walmer's for about six months. They said Dr. Walmer was treating their mother with vitamin therapy designed to counteract the ravages of age. They had pleaded with their mother to stop what they thought was dangerous therapy to no avail. They charged Dr. Walmer with wantonly endangering their mother's life with unproven and untested methods of vitamin injections. Theodore Myerson, Alma Myerson's eldest child, reported he and his siblings will now seek damages against Dr. Walmer in civil courts, saying, "He must be stopped before he kills more old people."

Dr. Walmer says his vitamin cocktails are safe and healthy. They have been used extensively on members of the elderly community to heighten seniors' abilities to live to their full potential in the latter years of their lives. He said Mrs. Myerson's unfortunate demise was not due to the vitamin therapy, rather to the natural progression of life and its ending.

"Oh, my God!" Claire muttered softly. "I can't believe this." She remembered Richard, or was it Mrs. Bernbaum, said he had left his practice in Florida and was seeking a new practice in the San Francisco area. Now she knew why.

She signed off the computer and gathered up her things and went to find a phone. She needed to report this to the security department. But when she called them they were very reluctant to tell her where they were located. Seemingly they considered security and secrecy to be synonymous. Finally she convinced them she had to talk to them privately and did not want to meet in her cabin or in any other of the public places on board, only then was she given directions to their office.

* * *

"So, basically, you're not going to do anything?" She was incredulous.

"Well, not exactly. We'll keep our eye on him. And when we dock in San Francisco we'll turn this and all our notes over to the San Francisco Police. We've already notified them we have a suspicious death, although our own physician, Dr. Carolton, thinks it's most likely natural causes due to her advanced age," Larry Smithston, the Director of Security on board, assured Claire. She felt, however, he wasn't taking her concerns seriously. The look in his eyes told her all too clearly he thought she was a nuisance. That hurt. She wasn't used to treatment like this. She had enjoyed the privilege of having her opinions valued, first by her family friend, Captain Sean Dixon, in the San Francisco Police Department and later by Jack Rallins and his associates in various law enforcement agencies. And truthfully, her opinions and theories had proven to be valuable, several times. Now here she was being humored.

She tried once more to convince him, but clearly exasperated he told her, "Ms. Gulliver, I understand your concern, but truly, we act on evidence. And that is somewhat sketchy in this situation. I will hand these items over to the investigating body, which is the SFPD, and we will watch Dr. Walmer carefully during the remaining days of the cruise. But frankly, there doesn't seem to be any reason to incarcerate him. I don't see any immediate danger from him. And we know he won't be going any where in the next two days. Therefore, he will be available when and if we need to talk to him. So I'm asking you to forget about this and enjoy the rest of your cruise. Trust me, we, and the SFPD, will take care of this situation." He forced a smile, then standing up he indicated the interview was over.

But in the elevator going up to the main decks Claire's anger got the better of her. She pushed the button for the deck where the computer room was located. She wasn't going to just let this go. Richard was out of control last night when he pushed her. How did she know he wouldn't get that way again? She had her own resources and she intended to use them.

After she sent a long email to Sean Dixon at the SFPD with the whole story and including links to the websites with the description of the potassium chloride and the article in the Miami Herald, she glanced at her watch and realized she had totally missed Bingo. She decided she had better go find her mother and see if anyone won. And she was going to quietly alert her mother to Richard's past. It would be prudent to stay away from the man.

"Hey Ruth, did you win?" Then looking around, "Where's Mom?"

"No I didn't win, nor did anyone we know. I didn't even come close to the big one." During every session of Bingo they played one game to fill all the squares in a certain number of pulls; if someone won, they would receive the huge jackpot which had been accumulating since the beginning of the cruise. The last Bingo game would pay out the jackpot, no matter how many balls were pulled.

"And your mother went down to Mrs. Bernbaum's cabin to help Richard pick out an outfit for her to be buried in."

Claire felt the blood drain from her head at that news. "Mom..., Mom went to help Richard?"

"Yes, he came to apologize for his behavior last night. Then he looked so sad, and he was so totally at a loss to know what to get for the funeral. You know your mother, she insisted she go help him select an outfit for the wake."

Claire's brain was spinning frantically. Her first impulse was to call security for help. But then she realized that wouldn't work. They didn't think Richard was a danger.

"How long ago did she leave?"

"Just a while ago, maybe ten minutes at the most. Why? Do you need something?"

She shook her head, realizing it wouldn't do any good to get Ruth all concerned.

"You haven't seen Ian anywhere around have you?" she asked, perhaps a shade too urgently, because now Ruth was watching her carefully.

"Why, yes. I saw him in the casino a while ago."

"Ruth, can you find Ian and tell him I need him in Mrs. Bernbaum's cabin, right away. And tell him to hurry."

Ruth had already risen. "What is it Claire? What's wrong?"

"I'll tell you later. Just find Ian. Fast. Okay?" And she hurried to the elevator. Then not wanting to wait for it to arrive she took the stairs down the two flights to the eighth deck.

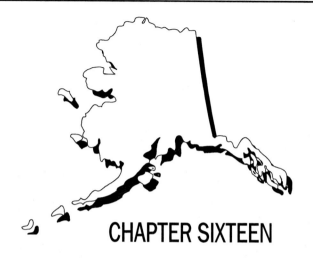

CHAPTER SIXTEEN

Millie knocked on the door, thinking how easy it was to believe Mrs. Bernbaum was still here. But Richard's sober expression when he opened the door and gestured her into the cabin didn't allow her to continue that pretense.

She tried to be positive. "Well, Richard, it looks like you're making progress here." She nodded toward the two suitcases sitting near the door.

"Mostly thanks to my friend, Kim."

Millie turned to see the beautiful blonde emerge from the bedroom. She smiled at her in answer to Richard's introduction. "How nice of you to help, Kim. I'm sure Richard appreciates it. This is a painful task. Believe me, I know."

Kim nodded and then went to a tray of coffee things sitting on the table, saying, "Would you like a cup? It's time for us to take a break and this was just delivered, so it's fresh."

Millie didn't really want any more coffee, but saw they wanted a break, so she nodded, accepted a cup and sat on the sofa while Kim poured for Richard and herself.

"Millie, I just wanted to apologize once more for my boorish behavior last night. It was so very kind of you and

Claire to come to tell me about Auntie Flo, and then I don't know what happened to me. I just lost it."

"Richard, don't you worry even a minute more. We all have times like that. Actually, I shouldn't have startled you like that, but I was just so horrified you might drop that bag overboard after all we've heard about how destructive plastic bags are. I'm afraid I just reacted without thinking. But, the incident is over. I apologize for startling you and I accept your apology for pushing Claire, as I'm sure she'll tell you herself the next time she sees you." She sat back and sipped the coffee which did taste good even though she didn't really want it.

"Well, the funny thing is, I've now realized the throat lozenges I bought at the drugstore in Ketchikan were probably still in that bag I threw away. I've had a severe sore throat for several days and needed something to ease it. You don't remember where you dumped it, do you?"

Millie looked startled and then shook her head. "Well, no. I didn't actually throw it away after all." She felt a little guilty about that as she tried to explain. "There wasn't any trash can near there as you probably know. I imagine that's why you were going to toss it overboard. So Claire took the bag from me. She said she'd throw it away some place."

Richard actually winced. Then he looked at Kim.

Kim shrugged. "I say do them both," she said with a grim look on her face.

"Kim! You're a little over the edge here. How do you think you could cover up multiple disappearances? Think about it. It's way too risky."

"It's too risky to just ignore," Kim said in a hard tone talking to Richard as if Millie wasn't even in the room.

Millie looked from one to the other not understanding what exactly they meant, but feeling decidedly uncomfortable about the way they were watching her as they talked. She set her coffee cup on the table and got to her feet, saying briskly, "Well, Richard, let's check the closet. I was thinking that mauve dress your aunt wore to one of the formal dinners might be just the thing. It was very flattering..."

They both stared at her as if she had just committed some horrible social gaff, and her words just faded away.

She tried again. "Look, with Kim here to help you, you don't really need me. I'll just be going. Thanks for the coffee." She nervously edged toward the door.

Richard and Kim both sprang to their feet. "No, wait," Richard protested. Then they all froze at the loud pounding on the door.

*   *   *

Claire knocked again. Actually she pounded on the door with her fist, looking up and down the corridor hoping to see one of the stewards. The door opened revealing Richard, who filled the partially opened door, blocking her view into the cabin.

"I'm looking for my mother, Richard. Ruth said she was coming here," she said brightly as she stretched her neck trying to see around him. He stepped back and gestured for her to come in. She shook her head. Now that she suspected him of such a heinous deed she didn't want to be near him, certainly not in the same room with him. However, she didn't want him to know how she felt. She could see her mother behind him and said in a loud voice, using a tone she knew her mother would respond to, "Mom, could I see you out here in the corridor a minute?"

Richard didn't wait for Millie's response. He grabbed Claire's arm, pulling her quickly into the cabin. He then shut the door firmly behind her. "Come in, Claire. We were just talking about you."

Claire, a very reluctant guest, moved toward her mother. "Mom, I need you for a minute, could you come...?" Her voice trailed off as she turned to find Richard and a blonde woman now standing right behind her. They blocked the path to the door, and neither looked inclined to move out of her way.

"Your mother said you took the trash bag last night to throw away, and," he smiled self-deprecatorily, "I now find I left something I need in the bag. I wondered what you did with it. Maybe I can find it."

"Oh, I'm sorry, Richard, but I threw it in the trash container near the casino last night. I would imagine they've emptied it by now," she lied, trying to keep her face immobile in order to hide what she knew about that bag.

"She knows," the blonde woman hissed. "See, look at her eyes. She knows, Richard!"

Richard ignored her, looking at Claire with a hard expression. "That's too bad. I really wanted to find that bag. You know, I think you and your mother are interfering, nosy bitches?"

"Richard! That's not nice," Millie protested indignantly.

"Mom, Mom, forget it. Let's get out of here." Claire grabbed her mother's hand and tried to push past Richard and the blonde to get to the door.

Her mother was angry and dug her heels in, refusing to budge. "Wait Claire, why is he being so rude? What would Mrs. Bernbaum think of him behaving like this?"

"Mom, I'm sure Mrs. Bernbaum now understands just what Richard's all about, doesn't she, Dickie?" She couldn't help herself, her loathing just oozed out.

Richard only sneered at her. The blonde woman said, "See, I told you, she knows. It's the only way out now."

Millie's eyes widened, looking from her daughter to Kim and Richard as Claire continued, not able to disguise the disgust in her voice. "Why'd you do it? I thought you were such a great advocate of the aged. Hah, some advocate. You couldn't even let your own aunt live out her allotted years? You had to help her along? Or wasn't she even your aunt? Is that it? Was it all just a scam of a little old lady?"

"What do you know about it? Who are you to judge me? Of course she was my aunt, by marriage, but still we were related. And I was glad to find her. She was happy about that too. I helped free her from her depression. I made her last days meaningful. I made it possible for her to fulfill her life quests, didn't I?"

Millie's mouth fell open with growing horror at what she was hearing, at what she now realized had happened to Mrs. Bernbaum. She couldn't help saying, "But she loved you. And..., and you killed her?"

"Well, let's just say I gave her a little shove in the right direction. Hell, she was a crusty old girl. She might have lived for another five years...maybe more. I didn't want to wait that long. I have plans for my own life. She had lived hers. It was time for her to go. Trust me, she died happy. She didn't know what happened."

"Oh, well I certainly feel better knowing that." Claire's voice dripped with sarcasm. Not waiting for more, she pulled on her mother's hand and again tried to push her way toward the door.

Kim grabbed Millie, but Claire barreled through, hoping to get the door open so she could yell her head off in the corridor. No such luck. Richard wrapped an arm around her waist, pulling her roughly back before she could reach the door.

"No, you don't. Kim, open the door to the balcony," he ordered, tightening his hold on Claire while capturing her arms and pinning them to her body with his other arm. Claire twisted and squirmed, trying to break free, but Richard dragged her backwards toward the balcony.

234 • Cruisin' for a Bruisin'

Meanwhile, she could see bits of her mother's struggle with the woman called Kim. Kim held Millie's arm, alternating between shoving her and dragging her out on the balcony toward the railing. But Millie wasn't going quietly. Kim finally managed to press Millie back again the rail, with her head and shoulders hanging out in space. Still she couldn't lift her captive high enough to push her over the top of the rail. She panted from her efforts as she hit and pushed Millie. Millie flailed and kicked and yelled at Kim, giving, almost as good as she got.

"Help me," Kim hollered at Richard in desperation.

"Hit her with something," Richard muttered, his hands full of the writhing Claire.

Kim let go of Millie to run into the cabin in search of something to use as a weapon. As soon as Millie was free of Kim, she attacked Richard, who now had a choke hold on Claire and was squeezing her neck, cutting off her air supply.

Millie was a tiger. She raked Richard's face with her nails as she attempted to reach his eyes. Richard turned away from Millie, trying to avoid her attack by keeping the fading Claire between them. He yelled at Kim to get Millie away from him. And while he didn't let go of Claire, he did relax his hold on her neck enough for her to get her lungs full of air and revive enough to score a couple of good kicks on his shins and one painful stomp on his instep.

Kim returned holding the heavy brass lamp from the desk. She swung viciously at Millie, missing her head, but thumping her painfully across her back. Millie had to back away from Richard to protect herself. Kim brandished the lamp as if it was a club, but Millie didn't intend to let Kim get her, even as she was being backed once more against the railing. The four of them, desperate and determined, twisted and turned, while executing their intricate dance between death and survival on the balcony.

Richard tightened his hold on Claire's neck in order to choke the life out of her. He needed her unconscious and helpless so he could help Kim dispose of Millie. Then he and Kim could easily lift Claire over the side. But Claire fought to remain conscious even though she started to fade out, blackness sweeping over her.

Then suddenly the pressure was gone and with her arms suddenly free she managed to grab the rail to keep from falling to the ground. Not yet fully conscious, Claire couldn't quite understand what happened. It seemed that suddenly the balcony was really crowded.

Millie now held one of her arms, half supporting her. Someone, a man she didn't know, held her up on the other side. Together they moved her into the cabin and guided her onto a chair. Millie, eyes still flashing her anger, leaned close to her daughter. "Claire, dear, can you talk? Are you all right?"

Claire nodded, massaging her throat as she tried to speak. "Where are they? What happened?" she croaked as she looked around with alarm. She tried to clear her throat, then coughed a few times. She saw lots of people, some standing in clumps in the living room. Richard and Kim were now standing quietly, perhaps because they were each held tightly by men wearing the security blazers. Then Ian came barreling through the door followed closely by Ruth.

"Hey, Claire, you wanted me...?"

"Millie, what happened? You're bleeding. Are you all right?" Ruth's voice was high with alarm.

Larry Smithston separated himself from the group around Richard and approached Claire and Millie. "Perhaps you can tell us what's going on here?"

"I'll tell you what happened." Millie was still mad. "I came down to help Richard select an outfit for his aunt to be buried in, just as he asked me to." Millie turned and glared at Richard, then turned back to Larry. "They,

Richard and Kim, started talking strangely about people disappearing. I got quite nervous, actually. Then Claire came by and wanted to see me. I was ready to leave, let me tell you! But instead they pulled her into the cabin.

"Richard killed his aunt, you know. He told us that and then started dragging us outside. They were going to throw us overboard!" she said with outrage as she looked at Richard. "What on earth were you thinking?"

"Oh, would that be harmful to the porpoises too?" he sneered. His face marred with bloody scratches radiated his hate, while Kim, her hair in wild disarray, her expression sullen, glared at Millie.

Millie backed up a pace, shivering.

"Ms. Gulliver?" Larry asked Claire. "I thought you were going to just enjoy the rest of your cruise."

"Well, I would have liked to, but it just didn't work out that way. I know you didn't think Richard was dangerous, but I didn't agree with you. Not after I saw the way he tried to grab my mother last night. I was the one he pushed out of the way. He didn't seem harmless then. So when Ruth told me my mother was down here helping him I immediately became alarmed and decided I would have to rescue her. But..." She shrugged before continuing.

"He wanted to know where I threw that bag of trash, so I just made up something. No way, was I going to tell him what I found in that bag, or that I gave it to you. But she," she dipped her head toward Kim, "didn't believe me. They wouldn't let us leave. They said they were going to dump us over, and I believed them. They certainly tried their best to do that."

"Well, apparently, I was wrong about him not being a danger. And who is this lady?"

Claire shrugged. "One of the passengers. I've seen her with him a couple of times."

"Her name is Kim," Millie said.

Larry nodded at his men, and they all watched as Richard and Kim were led away so discretely no one would even guess they were being escorted to the ship's jail.

When the cabin door closed behind them the room was silent, everyone thinking about what had happened.

"How did you know we were in trouble? How did you get here in time to save us?" a puzzled Claire asked Larry. "Did Ian call you?"

Ian, who hadn't said a word after his initial question when he arrived, shook his head in denial. She looked at Ruth, who shrugged helplessly, shaking her head.

The Head of Security smiled broadly. "It was the porpoises." He pointed out at the balcony. They all went to the window where they could see the large school of porpoises swimming along side, playing and leaping and twisting while they escorted the ship.

"Everyone on this side of the ship is apparently hanging over the rails of all the balconies and decks watching the porpoises. We had five calls about the disturbance on this balcony and I immediately radioed my men to get down here. The phones were still ringing when I left my office. Kim and Richard would have never gotten away with it. There were way too many witnesses. And if he had dumped one of you over, we would have gotten a rescue boat in the water pretty darn fast."

Claire looked at him, wondering if he thought that was any comfort to them, and shuddered, returning to her safe chair before her knees gave way.

"You know, I may have been a little reluctant to believe Richard engineered his Aunt's death, but I certainly couldn't ignore those calls.

"And I admit, Ms. Gulliver, I was having second thoughts about Dr. Walmer after you left. Of course, that email I got from Captain Dixon of the SFPD would have given me second thoughts anyway."

She was a little embarrassed. "He didn't take long to respond."

"No, he seemed rather concerned. I gather he thinks you and your mother are very special people, and he said if you suspected foul play I had better have a good reason to ignore you. I take it you have worked with him in the past?"

Both Millie and Ruth nodded vehemently. "Oh, yes," they chorused.

"It was because I asked her to stop by and take care of my cat. I didn't know what would happen." Ruth started to explain, but Millie cut her off.

"It was so scary. The cat got out and she tried to coax it back from the back porch. How was she to know the men sitting on the next balcony were drug lords? It wasn't her fault."

Ruth wouldn't keep quiet. "I didn't know. Josie, the woman who lived there was in Guatemala visiting her family and her cousin's son was house sitting. They didn't want to be seen and they knew I was gone, so they thought it was a perfect setting for their meeting. Then Claire surprised them by coming out on the deck of the kitchen. They thought they had to get rid of her. You know, because she had seen them."

"Well, they almost did," Millie broke in continuing the story. "First they knocked her out and left her in an abandoned warehouse rigged to ignite. Fortunately she came to and managed to get out before the warehouse burst into flames. Sean got involved of course. He was my husband's partner before my husband was killed all those years ago, and he's been watching out for us since.

"But the police couldn't figure out what happened to Claire, why she was in the warehouse. No one connected it to the people on the deck next door to Ruth's house. But later, after that car tried to run her down and lost control, killing the driver, Claire thought he looked familiar. She finally realized where she had seen him. So then Sean's people set up a sting operation."

"Oh, it was very exciting. They used my house." Ruth tried to interrupt again, but Millie wasn't giving up the floor. After all, it was her daughter; she wanted to tell the story.

"Anyway, it turned out those men on the balcony were part of a drug cartel that had been plaguing the police for a long time. They were able to catch them, and convict the leader. Claire was a hero to the SFPD. I guess maybe she still is." She looked at Claire proudly.

"I see." Larry looked at Claire. "Well, I've sent for the doctor to come up and check you both. She'll take care of that cut on your mother's forehead. And while we're waiting, is there anything else you want to tell me about this whole episode?"

Claire looked directly at Ian and then nodded. "Well, there is one thing."

"Yes?" Larry was very interested this time, as were Millie, Ruth and Ian, whose face was visibly paling.

"Well, Mrs. Bernbaum was carrying her jewelry with her. She had a very valuable collection and I know for a fact it is stored in the wall safe there." She pointed to the cupboard holding the wall safe. "I would suggest you remove it, inventory it and keep it in a more substantial safe until you turn it over to the authorities in San Francisco."

"Good idea." He shook his head. "We tell people not to bring their valuables on these cruises, but they never listen to us. I'll get someone here immediately." Just then one of his men admitted the doctor carrying a bag followed by her nurse pushing a wheelchair. Everyone forgot about the jewelry except Ian, whose pale face was now suffused with red as he glared angrily at Claire.

* * *

The four of them moved down the corridor toward the elevator, glad to be free and safe.

"I need a drink," Ian announced.

"Me too," Ruth agreed. "And a bite to eat. It's a long time until dinner."

Millie glanced at her watch. "I think they're serving hors d'oeuvres in the Starlight Lounge. We could have a drink and a bite before going down to get ready for dinner."

"That's right, formal night." Ruth grimaced.

The elevator arrived and Ian pushed the button for the top deck. When they arrived in the corridor outside the lounge, Millie and Ruth excused themselves to use the facilities and Claire found herself alone with Ian. He ushered her gallantly into the lounge, pointing to a table near the front windows.

"That was very mean of you," he said in a low voice.

She didn't even question his meaning, she knew. "I didn't think you needed the temptation. And frankly I wouldn't sleep worrying about it. It seemed the most sensible solution." She selected one of the chairs, slipped her tote bag off her shoulder and sat it down by her feet.

"What are you, a grown up Nancy Drew? Just my luck you found me with my hand in the cookie jar," he complained.

"Hardly a cookie jar. I'd say you were really lucky it was me and other things distracted me so I didn't report you. I still can't believe it. What do you do? Make your living taking cruises so you can steal from little old ladies?"

"Now you're just being cruel. I told you I retired. I just had some unfinished business to attend to."

"Sure, sounds like monkey business to me." She settled back into her chair and looked carefully at him. "Well Ian, now we know each other a little better. You know

I have connections with the San Francisco Police and I'm inclined to use those if necessary. And I know you're not just a mildly flirtatious retired businessman. You're a jewel thief on a mission. I think it is best if I don't have any reason to suspect your involvement in any crimes in my immediate vicinity and then I won't have any reason to meddle in your business, will I?"

She thought for a moment. "And we'd better both pray that your brother and my mother aren't developing a serious relationship, so we have to stay connected when this cruise ends."

He nodded. "Amen." Then rose to his feet as Ruth and Millie arrived, holding plates in each hand piled high with the assortment of appetizers laid out for the passengers.

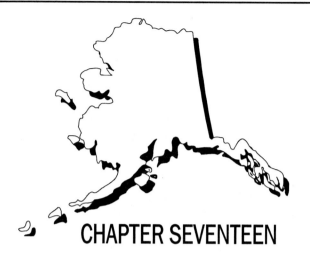

CHAPTER SEVENTEEN

Ian emerged from a cloud of steam in the tiny bathroom to find his brother lounging on the bed watching the replay of a lecture on porpoises given by the wildlife expert earlier in the cruise.

Sean smiled. "Hey Bro, where you been? I looked for you earlier, but it's amazing how many places there are to look on this ship."

Ian nodded, getting a fresh shirt out of his drawer. "So, tonight's the last formal night. Can you stand getting gussied up once more?"

"Sure, actually, it's been kind of fun. Where I live I only need my tux for weddings. I kind of enjoy dressing fancy for a change. And of course the food they serve helps." He rolled off the bed. "I guess I'd better shower and shave. I have to keep up with the standard you set."

When he emerged his brother was fixing his tie. He hesitated just a moment then asked, "Listen, Ian. Did you get it?"

Ian paused, looking at his brother. "I don't think you really want to know, do you?"

"Probably not, but I keep thinking about it so you may as well tell me."

Ian shook his head.

"Does that mean you didn't do it or you're not telling me?"

"I changed my mind. I thought about what you said about Pap letting his quest for retrieving the *Heart* ruin his life, and I decided I was smart enough to learn from his mistakes."

Sean's jaw actually dropped. He paused, watching his brother, then said, "Well that's about the biggest load of shit you've ever tried to lay on me. And I don't believe it! You're just going to let it go? Now when the old lady is gone? When no one else knows those jewels as she does? Hell, her heirs may not even miss it. Now you're telling me you're going to let it go?"

Ian nodded sober-faced and then grinned sheepishly, admitting, "Claire caught me in Mrs. Bernbaum's cabin with the *Heart* in my hand. Another two minutes I would have been gone." He paused, his look of disgust all too real. "So she knows. I tried to talk my way out of it, but that didn't work. I was wearing my gloves, you see. I couldn't explain why. So, as of now I don't dare go near it."

His brother nodded. This explanation made more sense to him.

"It was just unfortunate that Mrs. Bernbaum died and we found her. Or maybe not, because Claire got so distracted by that she didn't turn me in. That was a real break for me because she seems to be totally on the side of law and order."

"Wow, I'd say you were lucky. So this trip has cost you a bundle, for nothing. Except, I've had a great time. So any time you want to do it again and need me to help cover for you, I'll be happy to oblige."

Just before they left the cabin Sean asked, "So what are you going to do?"

Ian shrugged. "I'm going to retire with what I've managed to put away and live the good life down on the

Gulf near New Orleans. I have plenty of money to travel. I'll spend some time in Mexico, summers in the mountains and I'm going to keep my ears open. Somewhere, sometime there will be another opportunity. For sure the *Heart of Persia* is going to come back to our family. It belongs to us. Pap got it for saving those peoples' lives. He did a heroic service for them. He deserved it. He should still have it. It should have been his legacy to us."

* * *

The dining room glittered with the finery of the guests. A small orchestra nestled again at the top, where the grand staircase connected to the balcony. The soft notes of the music floated over the room. It was the last formal night and everyone on the cruise seemed to be of the mind to celebrate a great trip. Their table, number seventeen, was now short two persons. But those remaining spread along each side leaving the two end seats vacant so the table appeared comfortably full. Everyone expressed their sorrow over Mrs. Bernbaum, but seemed to accept it as an event which was sure to happen. No one asked about Richard. Four of them knew where he was. The other four just assumed he was avoiding the festivities because of his aunt's death. It seemed only natural to them.

Everyone was dressed in their finest tonight. Claire had a moment of panic when she saw the dark marks on her neck, which she knew would initiate far too many questions. She solved that problem by wrapping a filmy colorful scarf around her neck twice and letting it flow down her back. It added color to her simple long black gown and hid her bruises.

Harold bought the first champagne saying, "I guess I can't expect Lucy's friend to buy every night."

Claire surprised everyone by ordering the next two bottles. When all the glasses had been filled again she stood and said, "I would like to propose a toast to Mrs. Bernbaum." She looked around the table as everyone picked up their glasses and said somberly, "I didn't know her long, but she made an impact on me. I will never again dismiss someone because they are old, because she showed me how interesting old people can be. I will never let myself vegetate because I think I have become too old, because she showed me you can pursue your interests to the end. I salute Mrs. Bernbaum, wherever she is." She raised her glass and then took a sip. The others followed suit and soon those bottles were gone and Ian ordered the next.

Thus dinner progressed gaily. The chef exceeded his previous menu offerings with Beef Wellington, lobster thermidor, roast duck in cherry sauce, pork tenderloins a la Oscar and roasted portabella mushrooms on fettuccini. It was difficult to choose, so Harold didn't. He ordered two entrees.

Antonio stopped by their table to salute them, smile at Lucy and remind them of the dance to be held after dinner tonight.

"Don't worry, we'll be there," Sean said, sweeping his hand around to include the entire table. "We're going to enjoy every minute we have left, right ladies and gentlemen?"

Everyone nodded and Antonio moved off rather reluctantly. He obviously would have liked to stay and join their party. The seat next to Lucy was temptingly empty.

"Lucy, this cruise is ending day after tomorrow. Aren't you going to miss Antonio?" Ruth asked sympathetically.

Lucy nodded. "A little, but neither of us want it to be more than a shipboard romance. It's been fun, he's been fun, but already my mind is working out the beginning of my next book. This has been a delightful vacation. Still, I'm anxious to get back to real life. What about you?"

Ruth nodded. "I admit while I've enjoyed every minute, I still miss George." Her face turned slightly pink. "I know that sounds rather juvenile, but I guess that's because he makes me feel young again."

Sean sitting next to Ruth raised his eyebrows. "So, Ruth you have a beau you left behind. Why didn't he come with you?"

"Well, this was kind of a *girls'* thing. You know, like you and your guy friends going on a fishing trip."

He nodded, getting the idea. "That's why Ian and I took this trip. It was a chance to bond again. We were very close as boys, even as young men. Then our lives went off in different directions. We still stayed in touch. We were still brothers, but we weren't close any more. You know?"

"What a good idea. And we're certainly glad you decided to cruise. You both have added immensely to the bonhomie of our table to say nothing about handy on the dance floor," Millie told him, patting his hand fondly.

Pearl, who had been following the conversation from across the table wanted to tell them about her and Harold. "You know, I've wanted to cruise for years. I suppose since the *Love Boat* was on television, but Harold just wasn't interested. Until, I suggested this trip to Alaska. I finally found a destination which interested him. And we have both loved this trip. It has been like a booster shot for us. Getting dressed up for dinner, dancing, meeting people, all the activities they have for us and then seeing all these quaint Gold Rush towns has really been wonderful. And while we might have done some of them at home, here it's all compressed into a short time frame. How anyone could not love cruising, I just don't know."

"It has been great. I was just being a sourpuss, I admit. Well, we're going to do it again. Maybe the Mediterranean, you know romantic moonlit nights, little Greek Islands, Roman ruins? It will make me seem romantic when I'm not." He smiled at Pearl. "Gotta keep her happy, heh?"

Suddenly the lights dimmed further, the music swelled with the notes of *Funiculi Funicula*. They looked up to see a procession of waiters, each holding a platter of flaming Baked Alaska high above their heads, stream down the central staircase. Behind them came the assistants, and the busboys, and the wine stewards and even some of the kitchen staff in their distinctive chefs' hats. Everyone who was not carrying a flaming platter held a white napkin over their head, waving it in a circle in time to the music. The passengers oohed and aahed; standing at their places they spontaneously waved their napkins over their heads to join the fun. The parade was so well received it went around the dining room once more. Finally the orchestra's resounding conclusion of the song brought the parade to an end before the Baked Alaskas melted.

After the dessert was finished and the last drop of coffee drained, Sean suggested more champagne. "My treat this time, upstairs where I intend to dance until I drop."

"What a great idea." Ruth stood up, ready to continue the festivities of dinner.

Everyone seemed of like mind, heading once more for the Starlight Lounge.

* * *

Claire dashed across the tiny cabin to grab the phone. It was only eight and Lucy had her head buried under her pillow while Claire dressed. She had been out until some ungodly hour and wouldn't get up for hours yet. Claire usually crept around quietly in the morning so as not to disturb her.

"Good morning," she whispered tentatively into the phone.

"Ms. Gulliver, this is the Security Office. We wanted to alert you to an appointment we scheduled for you to meet with the representatives from the San Francisco Police Department today in the conference room on the second deck near the disembarkation station. Can you please present yourself there at 9:30 a.m.?"

She murmured her agreement even as she wondered how representatives of the San Francisco Police Department had appeared magically on board. That question was answered when she joined her mother at breakfast. Millie and Ruth had saved her a seat at a table they shared with Heidi and Bob and another couple.

"Good morning, dear. Is Lucy still sleeping?"

"Of course." She smiled her greeting at Heidi and Bob and cordially exchanged names with the other couple.

"Did you all see the helicopter this morning?" Heidi asked. "It was so exciting. It landed right out front on that space marked with a big circle. Bob and I were doing our walk early and there it was, just coming in to land. I thought it was here to pick up someone who was sick, but Bob thought it was that entertainer we had the other night leaving. Anyway, we were both wrong. People got out, but no one got back on before it took off again."

Claire glanced at Millie and could see from her startled look that she probably had an appointment scheduled this morning too. But she just let the others discuss possible purposes of the helicopter's visit. Finally, they exhausted that topic and moved on to the activities scheduled for the day. Claire arranged to meet her mother and Ruth for the final bingo session. She was feeling lucky and knew someone was going to win the big jackpot today. It was certainly worth the cost of the bingo cards. She was also interested in the last wildlife session and agreed to go to that too. But other than those two activities she said she intended to finish her book, *I Married the Klondike*, which she purchased in Ketchikan, and watch for porpoises and whales while she lazed away the day.

Ruth had scheduled a busy day. She was doing bingo, bridge, the horse races, the lecture and trivia before her massage scheduled later in the afternoon. She was thinking she might have time for a swim if she skipped lunch.

"Skip lunch? Are you sure, Ruth? It's a long time until dinner," Millie questioned her friend knowing how she liked her meals, especially since they weren't charged for them.

Ruth shrugged. "Maybe I should have lunch. Let's meet at the buffet at one, if I don't see you before then. I'm sure I could manage a little bite then."

After people started leaving the breakfast table, Claire and Millie were left to finish their coffee.

"How are you this morning, dear? Could you sleep after all that excitement yesterday?"

Claire grimaced. "Barely, but I was so tired the waves finally rocked me to sleep. I have some terrible bruising on my neck. I've had to search through my clothes to find a few things with high necks. It's worse than having a hickey."

Her mother's look of alarm caused her to quickly change the subject. "Mom, are you meeting with the police this morning?'

Millie nodded. "Yes, I'm scheduled for nine. You?"

"Nine-thirty. Look do you want to meet for coffee later, say before the lecture? Then we can compare notes."

Millie nodded. "I'm a little nervous. But I'm just going to tell them what happened."

Claire patted her hand. "Don't worry, you'll do fine. They just want to gather all the evidence. I guess, since Heidi said the helicopter took off without anyone getting on board, that Richard and Kim are still here."

"I guess so. The security man, Larry, said they had a jail on board. Imagine that? This ship is like a whole city. They have a morgue and a jail and that doctor we saw last night said they have a hospital and even operating facilities. I guess they're ready for anything." The ladies left the dining room. Today was their last day and they didn't intend to waste a moment of it.

* * *

"Ms. Claire Gulliver?" The man waved her into the small conference room. "Please have a seat. I'm Lieutenant Phil Washington." He displayed an open wallet with his police identification in a window compartment opposite his gold badge. "This is Sergeant Nancy Keely." He nodded at the attractive black woman seated at the table."

She stood up and offered her hand to shake while holding out her badge and identification with the other.

"Coffee?" he offered, then seeing Claire's head shake, proceeded. "Ordinarily, we would board when the ship docks, but because of what transpired here yesterday Captain Dixon thought we'd need a bit more time to process the crime scene. Six of us arrived this morning by helicopter. We have a forensics team checking out all three cabins. We have two teams interviewing the witnesses."

"Now, Nancy, can you show Ms. Gulliver the information we have on her to make sure it is correct?"

"Call me Claire," she murmured as she looked at the paper with her name, address and other vital information which Nancy held out to her.

"Yes, this all looks correct."

"Now we'd like to record this conversation. Is that acceptable to you?" The lieutenant was very polite."

"Fine, no problem."

So Claire told them about meeting Mrs. Bernbaum, the visits to her cabin, the friendship that developed between them. She spoke about the strangeness of Anita's disappearance, her request of Sean Dixon to check Anita's house in San Francisco and her concern about Mrs. Bernbaum's well-being when she didn't come to dinner the night they left Ketchikan.

She told them absolutely everything except about finding Ian with the *Heart of Persia* in his hand when she walked in on him in Mrs. Bernbaum's cabin that night. Nor did she mention they locked up Mrs. Bernbaum's jewelry before calling security to report her death. She told herself neither of those events effected the case against Richard and Kim and would, in fact, probably only muddy the waters.

"Now, Ms. Gulliver, um, Claire, had you seen or met this woman, Kim, before yesterday?" Nancy asked.

"No. Well, I had seen her. I saw Richard with her a couple times. Once he was in the casino with her. Once I saw him with her in the piano bar late, but I didn't have any reason to think she was connected to him or Mrs. Bernbaum in any way. I have no idea if Mrs. Bernbaum knew her or not. I just assumed it was someone Richard met on board and was attracted to."

"Did you ever see her with Anita?"

Claire was startled by that idea and then thought about it. Finally she shook her head. "No, I don't remember ever seeing them together. Actually, I don't think I ever saw Anita except in Mrs. Bernbaum's cabin the first couple of times I was there." Then she asked, "Why? Do you think Kim was involved with Anita?"

Then she said thoughtfully, "You know Richard was certain Anita had gotten off the ship to teach Mrs. Bernbaum a lesson about how important she was to her. But now, considering what Richard did to Mrs. Bernbaum I'm not sure I can give any credence to his theory."

"We found some personal items in Kim's cabin which we believe belonged to Anita. A small bag with a hairbrush, toothbrush, make up and a few clothes, and more importantly, we found Anita's ship identification card in the bag," the woman told her gravely.

"Oh, my god! You think they did something to Anita, don't you? Oh, my god! This was all planned!" Her voice quaked with horror as she sat back from the table. She felt chilled and at the same time she felt perspiration running down her back. "And he was so caring, so attentive. That poor woman. He was just conning her, and all the time he was planning to kill her." She couldn't stop the shudder that ran through her.

The lieutenant and sergeant just looked at her, keeping their expressions neutral, however their eyes were sympathetic. They had not yet become so inured to evil that they couldn't be appalled by what people were willing to do to get what they wanted.

"It appears so. Kim came out from Florida with him. We think they intended to see what they could get from his only relative. Luckily for him she was wealthy and alone. She must have appeared to be an easy mark except for her caregiver, who was apparently too protective. That was unfortunate for both Mrs. Bernbaum and for her caregiver. We got lots of information from Miami. The Captain appreciated your sending the link to that newspaper story. Dr. Richard Walmer has quite a history in Florida, no wonder he was thinking of moving his practice to California."

When they finally finished with Claire, she staggered out of the conference room in time to slip into a seat in the darkened theatre, part way into the lecture, happy for the time to help put her thoughts back in order. She didn't know why she was so shocked and horrified when she heard how Richard had planned this whole trip so he could kill his aunt. She knew it was true. It had all become clear to her when she found the syringe. But thinking it and hearing it stated as fact by the police were two different things. She still felt chilled by the cold brutality of it. She still wanted to scream at him; to claw at him; to somehow hurt him for his gall in sitting there at the table with all of them, night after night, pretending. And all the time he was planning, calculating how to rid himself of his aunt.

And what about Richard's blonde friend, Kim? She looked normal. Pretty, youngish, vivacious, yet she was a vicious monster. She not only was willing to push them overboard, but she seemed to be an advocate of that action. And now it appeared she might have played a role in Anita's disappearance. It all seemed too wicked, too vile, to accept.

When the lecture was over she found Millie. Her mother didn't even mention that Claire didn't show up for their tentative coffee date, which led Claire to think that Millie's own interview was probably as stressful as hers had been. They agreed to meet Ruth for lunch at the buffet and went their separate ways. Millie went to a cooking demonstration, and Claire to find a quiet corner to read her book or just to stare out at the passing nothingness of the ocean.

* * *

The ship had slipped under the Golden Gate Bridge before the sun had even risen and was secured to Pier Thirty-three by six o'clock. When Ruth, Millie, Claire and Lucy met in the dining room for their last breakfast the entire ship was in an uproar as everyone prepared to leave. They had all been issued color coded luggage tags the night before, which dictated the order of the disembarkation. The luggage had to be packed and placed outside their doors before midnight last night, each passenger keeping only the essentials for the morning.

Their luggage, sporting lavender luggage tags indicating they would not be processed until ten o'clock, was long gone, the last of their essentials were packed in their carry-on bags, so now the ladies were going to have a leisurely last breakfast.

Last night had been bittersweet. Everyone at the table had exchanged addresses, and Claire, Pearl and Ian had taken so many pictures it was as if the paparazzi were on board. And as this was the last night, it was also time to distribute their little envelopes with gratuities to the dining room personnel. This was done with many thanks and hugs and promises to remember. Then people dispersed to their cabins to get their packing done. Later Lucy and Claire had gone up to the Starlight Lounge and found Millie and Ruth, Sean and Ian. Later Antonio arrived and had a drink with them before he and Lucy disappeared.

Claire had watched them go, wondering if Lucy was really as unconcerned with this parting as she said she was. But now today, Lucy appeared in fine spirits, anxious as they all were to get home and back to her life.

That's what Ruth said to them. "Isn't it funny that no matter how much fun you have on vacation you're still so happy to get home?"

Lucy nodded in complete agreement. Millie looked surprised. "Do you feel that way too? I thought it was just that I don't travel much, so naturally I am anxious to be home."

And Claire thought, but didn't say, that every time she took a trip she was just thankful to get home alive. What was it about travel that seemed to put her in danger? But Lucy, who knew about Claire's other trips muttered so only Claire could hear, "And for once you had a trip that was just normal, Claire. This is how traveling is supposed to be. The excitement of travel comes from seeing new things and having new experiences, not from avoiding death and destruction."

Claire looked at her smiling friend with amazement. Just then she realized that Lucy was entirely clueless about Richard's perfidy and Mrs. Bernbaum's death. But this was neither the time nor place to tell her about what had really happened. Oh, well, she thought, let her have this time to enjoy, the newspapers will apprise her of the real excitement of this cruise soon enough.

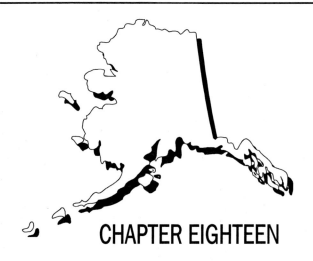

CHAPTER EIGHTEEN

"Hey Mom, where are you?"

"In the kitchen, dear. Come on back." Millie looked up and smiled at her daughter. "How nice, you're early. I hope you're not too hungry to wait for Ruth. She won't be here until about 5:30."

"No, I'm early because I talked to Sean Dixon this morning, and he said he would come by and give us an update. He'll be here in a few minutes, okay?"

"Of course, I'll be glad to see him, you know that. And I confess I'll appreciate hearing what is really going on. I swear between the television reports and the newspapers, I'm not even sure I know what happened, and I was in the middle of it."

Claire nodded. She felt the same frustration. The newspapers were full of the story. It was just what they loved to exploit, a local woman, intrigue and treachery, and a romantic setting on board the ship. But even though she had been there, it was hard to reconcile what she knew happened to what the papers said happened.

She smiled at the memory of the phone call she had gotten early one morning when the story first appeared in the newspaper. Lucy couldn't believe she had been so involved in her shipboard romance she missed the entire drama unfolding around her, including, and this really rocked her to her toes, Richard's attempt to rid himself of Millie and Claire by dumping them overboard. "But why didn't you tell me? We were rooming together for god's sake," she protested.

Claire finally calmed her down by reminding her that it happened near the end of the cruise and the few times they were together they were also surrounded by other people. It wasn't appropriate to tell her then. She wasn't keeping it from Lucy, she assured her. After all, Lucy was privy to details of some of Claire's other adventures which no other person knew; it was more that she just hadn't had the opportunity to tell her.

So Lucy had been mollified, as well as stupefied, but finally satisfied. Now she was in England on another research trip for her current book, so she would miss their first halibut dinner. Ruth caught the fish, Millie was cooking it and Claire agreed she would help eat it.

Claire helped herself to a bite of the tomato her mother was cutting up for the salad when the door bell rang. "That's Sean. I'll let him in."

After all the hugs and inquires about Sean's wife, Maureen, and the newest antics of his grandchildren, they settled around the kitchen table to talk. Claire and Millie had wine, but Sean declined, saying Maureen had him on a tight regime to control his escalating blood pressure.

"Well, ladies, Richard's fingerprints were all over the syringe and empty bottle of potassium chloride. The coroner found the needle mark on Mrs. Bernbaum's arm. But if you hadn't grabbed the bag before it dropped into the ocean, Millie, we would never have had proof that Mrs. Bernbaum hadn't died a natural death. Apparently potassium chloride is hard to detect in the body, so if you hadn't alerted us to the possibility the coroner says he most likely wouldn't have detected its presence. Richard was being very clever. If he had held onto that bag of stuff and hidden it in his luggage he would have, most likely, gotten away with murder."

Millie put her hand over her heart, her eyes wide as she shook her head in disbelief. "I still can't believe it. I wasn't thinking about what he was throwing away. It's just that when I saw that plastic bag, I grabbed it. I felt I had to save the porpoises."

"Lucky for us you happened to catch him as he let go of it. Apparently he became very nervous about someone checking for evidence, and he felt he had to get it off the ship. It was just his bad luck that you were looking for him to tell him about his aunt at the same time he was trying to dump it."

They all looked at each other a minute thinking how one small thing could destroy a carefully wrought plan. Except for Richard's determination to get rid of the evidence, he might have been sucessful.

"We discovered Kim rented a car in Juneau and we have a few of Anita's fingerprints on the inside and the passenger's door handle of that car. So there is a connection, somehow, between Kim and Anita, but we don't have a body. The Juneau police are using tracker and cadaver dogs to search in areas that match the mileage recorded on the odometer during the rental, but winter has moved in there and the weather has hampered them. They say now they will have to give up the search until spring. But, I think we can safely assume that Anita was murdered even if we never find a body," he told them gravely. "The D.A. thinks he has a strong case against the two of them. And who knows, come spring, they might find a body. And, of course, your testimonies will be important in getting a conviction."

"That wicked, wicked man." Millie was enraged all over again. "I hope he won't be getting any of Mrs. Bernbaum's money." She looked at Sean questioning. "He won't, will he? Isn't there a law about that?"

Sean nodded. "Mrs. Bernbaum wrote a codicil to her will before she left on the cruise leaving the bulk of her estate, which is substantial, to Richard. However, if he's found guilty of either her murder or complicity in her murder he will not inherit and it will go to the charities, which were originally named."

"So it was all about her money? I hope he rots in jail."

"He might get the death penalty. Premeditated murder can carry the death penalty in California," Sean said grimly.

Millie paled. "Death? I don't know about death," she stammered. Then her anger flared again. "Well, I won't be on the jury so I won't make that decision, but I have to admit that while we were struggling on that balcony I could have easily killed him to stop him from choking Claire. I guess it was lucky for all of us I didn't have a weapon available."

Claire nodded. She knew there was nothing like fighting for your life to stir your adrenalin. Then it was pretty hard to make moral decisions about whether or not you believed in the death penalty.

"There was another item of interest in her will though." He continued, "It was about that brooch you told us about, the *Heart of Persia*?"

Millie and Claire nodded, their expressions expectant.

"Well, it turns out it's paste."

"Paste? What do you mean paste?" Millie didn't understand.

"Paste, not quite worthless my experts tell me. After all, there is some skill in producing the piece, but still of no serious value. The rest of her jewelry was genuine and quite valuable. And we've done our research, so we know there is a *Heart of Persia*. The last time we were able to trace it was in a robbery attempt in the late fifties. It was returned to its owner then and no one has seen it since."

"But that can't be. Mrs. Bernbaum said it was real. She loved that piece. Her last husband, Bernie, was a jeweler, so surely he would have known if he had a paste copy when he returned it to Mrs. Bernbaum." Millie looked at Claire, seriously confused. "I just can't believe she had a fake and didn't know it."

"Mom, maybe she did know. Maybe she had a copy made and gave the original back as Nate asked her to do?" Claire liked that option because there were other explanations she didn't like at all.

"Maybe she did. That would make sense."

"Well, if that was the case, why was the *Heart of Persia* listed in her will? She willed it to Sean Rourke, of Chicago Illinois, actually Sean Gallagher Rourke, or to his heirs. The attorney is searching for him now."

Claire and Millie looked at each other. "Sean Gallagher? There was a Sean Gallagher on the cruise. Mom, did Sean or Ian say anything about Rourke being a family name?" Claire asked.

Millie shook her head. "No, Claire, I don't believe that. It's too far-fetched. Sean, Rourke, and Gallagher are all common names. And we even have a Sean right here. We don't suppose he has anything to do with it, do we? Why would we think Ian and Sean were connected in some way to Mrs. Bernbaum's brooch?"

But Claire wasn't convinced. She didn't say anything more. How could she when she had never told anyone about Ian's interest in the *Heart of Persia?* But she was sure there was some connection.

Now she wondered if Ian had somehow switched the real *Heart* with a fake, and so they had put the paste copy in the safe.

Or maybe Bernie Bernbaum had given his wife a paste copy of the original to make her happy? Surely, as a jeweler, he would have known the difference between real and paste.

Or had Mrs. Bernbaum replaced the *Heart* with a copy and sold or given the original away? And if she had, why had she left the bequest in her will?

Or perhaps someone had stolen the *Heart* from her sometime during all those years Mrs. Bernbaum had kept it in her house, replacing it with paste so she never knew the difference?

Or had the brooch won in that card game so many years ago only been a paste copy? Had any jeweler ever appraised it?

This puzzle made Claire's head hurt and the worse part was she suspected she would probably never know the answer to this riddle. Even if she asked Ian she knew she wouldn't believe his answer.

"Sean, thank you so much for stopping by and sharing this information with us. I admit I was getting very confused from all the stories I read in the papers." Millie hugged Sean when he stood up to leave.

"Well, it's the least I can do. I swear I don't know how Claire gets involved in these situations, and this time you were put at risk too. But, I do appreciate her attention to details. It would be a shame to let these people get away with their crime." He smiled at them both and turned to head for the door.

"Here, Sean, I'll see you out." Claire hurried after him.

At the door she said, "Sean, do you think it's something I do? Could I avoid these situations, do you think? Did I put my mother in jeopardy somehow?"

He patted her on the shoulder in a fatherly manner. "Claire, you can't look the other way when a crime or an injustice happens right before your eyes. I wouldn't want you to, and your mother wouldn't either. I don't know why. Maybe you have too much of your father in you. He was a great police officer, you know. I do worry about you, and so does your mother, but you can only live your life as it comes. And thanks to you, Richard Walmer is not getting away with his scheme."

She shut the door behind him thinking about his words. She was satisfied that Richard wouldn't be living "happily ever after" on Mrs. Bernbaum's money.

She'd keep in mind that Mrs. Bernbaum died painlessly. She led a long and active life and in the end she had successfully completed her life quest. It was the best spin she could put on the whole affair and, even if she never knew what happened to the real *Heart of Persia,* she would remember, after all, much of life was a mystery.

THE END

If you enjoyed this book, or any other book from Koenisha Publications, let us know. Visit our website or drop a line at:

Koenisha Publications
3196 – 53rd Street
Hamilton, MI 49419
Phone or Fax: 269-751-4100
Email: koenisha@macatawa.org
Web site: www.koenisha.com

Koenisha Publications authors are available for speaking engagements and book signings. Send for arrangements and schedule or visit our website.

Purchase additional copies of this book from your local bookstore or visit our web site.

Send for a free catalog of titles from
KOENISHA PUBLICATIONS
Founder of the Jacketed SoftCover™
Books You Can Sink Your Mind Into